INTIMAT

Also available from Headline Liaison

Intimate Strangers by Cheryl Mildenhall
Fortune's Tide by Cheryl Mildenhall
A Family Affair by Cheryl Mildenhall
Dance of Desire by Cheryl Mildenhall
Flights of Fancy by Cheryl Mildenhall
Second Chance by Cheryl Mildenhall
Private Lessons by Cheryl Mildenhall
The Paradise Garden by Aurelia Clifford
The Golden Cage by Aurelia Clifford
The Journal by James Allen
Sleepless Nights by Tom Crewe & Amber Wells
Hearts on Fire by Tom Crewe & Amber Wells
Aphrodisia by Rebecca Ambrose
Dangerous Desires by J J Duke
Love Letters by James Allen
Voluptuous Voyage by Lacey Carlyle

Intimate Disclosures

Cheryl Mildenhall

Copyright © 1997 Cheryl Mildenhall

The right of Cheryl Mildenhall to be identified as the
Author of the Work has been asserted by her in accordance
with the Copyright, Designs and Patents Act 1988.

First published in 1997
by HEADLINE BOOK PUBLISHING

A HEADLINE LIAISON paperback

10 9 8 7 6 5 4 3 2 1

All rights reserved. No part of this publication may be
reproduced, stored in a retrieval system, or transmitted,
in any form or by any means without the prior written
permission of the publisher, nor be otherwise circulated
in any form of binding or cover other than that in which
it is published and without a similar condition being
imposed on the subsequent purchaser.

All characters in this publication are fictitious and any
resemblance to real persons, living or dead, is purely
coincidental. Similarly, all businesses described in this book
are fictitious and any resemblance to companies that may
exist now, or in the future, is entirely coincidental.

ISBN 0 7472 5589 X

Typeset by Palimpsest Book Production Limited,
Polmont, Stirlingshire
Printed and bound in Great Britain by
Cox & Wyman Ltd, Reading, Berkshire

HEADLINE BOOK PUBLISHING
A division of Hodder Headline PLC
338 Euston Road
London NW1 3BH

Intimate Disclosures

Chapter One

The pale meringue buttocks belonging to Kurt the postman filled the TV screen. Like floating islands they drifted across the room, the resulting wide-angle shot showing a narrow back, heavily blemished and with a scattering of acne. His objective was the Scandinavian beauty laying, legs akimbo, on the double bed. Her pale blonde hair, lacquered to resemble a haystack, kept her head slightly raised from the pillow and her wide pink lips were poised in a permanent pout.

'Why is it all the women in these films are gorgeous, while the men are so yukky?' Nina asked Tom as she rolled over to face him. 'Yukky or gay,' she amended, popping a couple of green grapes in her mouth and chewing thoughtfully.

'You don't know they're gay,' Tom admonished gently, flashing her a fond glance over his bare shoulder.

'Mm, I do,' Nina insisted, popping more grapes. 'Everyone knows that. The men they use in these films are totally homo. That way there's no chance of them offending the censor by getting an erection.'

Nina grinned confidently and offered to share a grape with him. Holding it between small, slightly crooked teeth, she smiled invitingly with her eyes. Hazel with flecks of amber and green, they sparkled in her heart shaped face. Her dark blonde hair, shot through with natural golden highlights, was tucked behind her ears. She was pink from the shower and slightly more flushed around the throat and on her cheeks.

Although she had been keen to watch the video when she

brought it home with her from work, now she felt slightly embarrassed. Well, more than embarrassed actually, she admitted to herself. She and Tom had only watched about ten minutes of it so far and already she felt horribly demoralised by the pneumatic breasts of the actress, her perfect hair and neat figure.

'Do you think *she's* beautiful?' Nina asked, changing the subject.

Tom considered the actress for a moment then turned to look at Nina again. 'She's attractive,' he said hesitantly.

Nina rolled onto her back and gazed up at the ceiling before looking back at him. 'Not beautiful then?'

'Well, I wouldn't exactly kick her out of bed.'

Tom saw the frown cross Nina's face and instantly regretted his remark. In all honesty, he thought the actress was pretty off-putting. She reminded him too much of a Barbie doll when he preferred real women, with real curves and lumps and bumps. Women like Nina. Somehow though, he thought, he wouldn't be doing himself any favours right now if he voiced his thoughts, no matter how well intentioned they might be.

Naked and looking achingly lovely as always, Nina also looked as though she could cheerfully smash in his face, or the TV screen, or both. She had now folded her arms across her generous breasts – in self-defence he presumed – and had wriggled the lower half of her body under the duvet. Stay away from me until you can make up for that last remark, her body language warned him. And so, not knowing what else to do, Tom turned back to continue watching the video.

Eventually, Nina gave up sulking and rolled over on to her stomach again. She propped her chin in her hands and moments later, kicked off the duvet. The moment of tension dissolved and it was as if their brief conversation had never happened.

Quite a lot had gone on in the unremarkable Stockholm bedroom, since they had last looked at the screen. Kurt the

INTIMATE DISCLOSURES

postman and the actress, who hadn't bothered to introduce herself when she dragged Kurt into the house and stripped him in three seconds flat, were hard at it, humping away like crazy.

I suppose, Nina mused, being the postman he already knew the woman's name.

And in the meantime they had been joined by another man. In contrast to skinny, mousy-haired Kurt, he was stockily built and swarthy. Someone who looked, to Nina at any rate, like a Mafia hit man and whose chest, back and shoulders were covered by a thick mat of black hair.

'Who's the gorilla?' she asked, giving Tom one of her special smiles for which he felt absurdly grateful.

'Mario the telephone repair man,' Tom said without taking his eyes from the screen, adding, 'she's a girl this one.'

Nina's cheeks dimpled. 'How clever of you to notice.'

After ten minutes of watching Mario taking the nymphomaniac Swedish housewife from behind and then being treated to the sight of her pouting lips going down on Kurt, Nina pressed the OFF button on the remote control.

'I can't stand any more,' she said, 'do you mind?'

Tom shook his head and grinned. 'What's the alternative?'

'Me.' Nina gave him a coquettish smirk and lunged at him, forcing him over on to his back.

Kneeling at Tom's side she gazed fondly down at him. He was a truly lovely guy, she thought. Not too tall for a girl who barely reached five feet four in stilettos. Naturally olive-skinned. With lovely thick dark hair. Not to mention twinkling blue eyes and lashes to die for.

At twenty-six she considered herself lucky to have already found her perfect man. It had taken her quite a while to realise it though, she remembered as she lay a trail of damp kisses across his chest. They had been the original boy- and girl-next-door – childhood sweethearts for about three months, which at fourteen, she remembered, was the equivalent of a long-term relationship.

Then had come the inevitable split. He had admitted to fancying sullen but randy-natured Dawn, whose father ran the garden centre where he worked on Saturdays. And Nina had become tired of regularly turning down the school heart throb, Glen, who had floppy blond hair and a moped.

The intervening years had passed with barely any contact between Nina and Tom. Then, nine months ago, at a local nightclub where Nina had been celebrating her twenty sixth birthday with a group of girlfriends, she and Tom had bumped into each other again. Older, wiser and still – they quickly discovered – very much in lust with each other, they decided to give togetherness another go. This time, without the pressure of homework and curfews and nosey parents, they found their relationship worked. It worked so well, in fact, that within six weeks Tom had moved into her Putney flat.

That was then and this is now, Nina reminded herself, abruptly returning to the present. Her mouth had reached Tom's navel and his cock was prodding insistently at the base of her throat. Moving further down his body she pressed her face into his belly for a moment, pausing to breathe in the special musky scent of him. Then she continued her journey, her tongue trailing the fine path of hair that arrowed delightfully from his navel to his groin.

Glancing up she saw that he had his eyes closed. And a secretive, pleasurable smile drifted across his finely hewn features. She loved his face, it was so beautiful. His cheekbones were high, dipping into shadowy hollows. His mouth was broad and full lipped, a sulky, petulant mouth which felt so good when pressed against her lips, or sucking at her greedy sex.

Quivering at the recollection, she hastened to stroke his cock and cover it with her lips. She always felt so anxious for him, so desperate to feel his mouth on her most sensitive parts and his beautiful cock deep inside her. Above average length and breadth and perfectly formed, it was circumcised and much to Nina's liking.

Tom's cock, she mused as she drew her head away momentarily to consider it, was lovely, with every tiny millimetre eminently visible. She could see every ridge and vein and the little scars that his circumcision had left behind. At the moment its bulbous glans was a deep burgundy in hue and glistened under a film of her own saliva.

She licked her lips, enjoying the prospect of taking it in her mouth again. The tips of her breasts, generous in size and with a slight droop, brushed his inner thighs. His feet were turned outwards, leaving his genital area looking exposed and vulnerable, completely at her mercy.

'Prepare to die of ecstasy,' she said to Tom in a deliberately provocative voice. Then she lowered her head, relaxed her throat and swallowed the entire length of him.

Inside his head, Tom sighed with pleasure. He couldn't resist Nina's oral skills. It seemed she knew just how to tease him, to tantalise and draw him right to the point of climax before changing tack completely. Experiencing the same thing now, he found it enticed him to a permanent and ever increasing state of arousal.

His cock felt so hard he was worried it might burst. He could feel the tightness in his balls, and the blood pumping up the stem and engorging his glans. He didn't want to come yet, he wanted to wait and come inside Nina. Please God, he prayed silently, let me hold on until she gives into the demands of her own body first.

Although a sensualist, who loved to take her time stroking and caressing, Nina was also greedy and found it difficult to restrain herself. She loved receiving pleasure and often begged him to go down on her, or caress her in the most unlikely public places and at blatantly unsuitable times. It made him suspect that much of her sexuality still lay dormant. He was no Casanova by any means but he'd sown enough wild oats and read enough copies of *GQ* and *Maxim* in his time to know that women were capable of being far more adventurous sexually than they often liked to admit.

Reaching forward as far as he could, he combed his fingers through her hair and caressed the smooth sweep of her naked shoulders. Drawing her up his body, away from his cock, he pulled her close enough for a deep, probing kiss. She tasted fruity and slightly alcoholic. In any case, he mused, her kisses were intoxicating enough. Like the most expensive champagne, she went straight to his head.

Her breasts thrust enticingly as she arched her back and he slid his hands up her torso to cup them. A couple of sunbed sessions, as a preliminary to the gradually warming sun of early summer, lent her silky skin a sun-kissed hue. The generous 36Cs were tipped by delicate bud-like nipples and encircled by areolae the colour of toasted almonds.

Tom knew Nina's bra size because he had made it his business to find out. He enjoyed buying underwear for her. Flimsy, filmy little items just made for ripping off. Or tarty, satiny things with froths of lace that pushed up and together, or featured lewd little slits. Peephole. Crotchless. Strapless. Underwired. Basques. Corsets. G-strings. Bras. Panties. Knickers. Suspender belts. He loved all the words involved and the permutations of lingerie design. So much so that he happily whiled away many a lunchtime making his selections and embarrassing the sales girls into the bargain.

Whatever he chose, Nina was always thrilled with his purchases. She enjoyed putting on his gifts and modelling them for him, striking pose after saucy pose. Sometimes she even let him take photographs of her before they both succumbed to the erotic provocation and allowed themselves to revel in the inevitable results.

Nina's mind was far removed from her lingerie. She was more intent on the lack of it at that moment and how wonderful it felt for her and Tom to be touching flesh on flesh.

INTIMATE DISCLOSURES

A sizzle of pure lust shot through her as Tom captured one breast in his hand. He fed the nipple between greedy lips and clutched at her buttocks with his other hand.

She slid her lower body further up him, moving her legs so that she could straddle him. His hard cock pressed into the blossoming length of her slit, his hairy balls tantalising her vaginal lips. Trickles of moisture oozed from her, soaking his silky pubic hair as he drew her nipple deeper into his mouth and tantalised it with the tip of his tongue.

The rounded nails that tipped his fingers dug with passion inspired cruelty into her breast, marking the soft flesh – she imagined – with pale crescents. Meanwhile the fingers of his other hand lewdly explored the cleft between her buttocks.

This was one of the many things she loved about Tom. The way his personality changed from charming and affable one moment, to passionate and ever so slightly sadistic the next. Moment by moment, she never knew what to expect from him and that, she felt, was one of the main things that kept their relationship alive.

They shared a strong sense of oneness and yet each day she spent with him was like the first day and with every night came something different. The spiritual beauty of knowing each other, their likes and dislikes, what turned each other on, and the special intimacy of relaxed sensuality, was heightened night after night by the erotic frisson of unexplored sex.

The best of all worlds, she told herself as she ground her throbbing vulva against his cock and thrust breast and buttock alike more wantonly into his hands. I am such a lucky girl.

Slivers of dawn slunk through the gap in the curtains, the pinkish yellow light touching Nina's face and waking her from a dream in which Tom had been fucking her in a room full of people. Barely five hours before she had slipped into the blissful arms of thoroughly satiated sleep but now she felt overwhelmed by sensual desire all over again.

Clasped spoon-like around her, his early morning erection nudging her acquiescent buttocks, Tom still slept. Nina couldn't see him but could imagine how he looked in slumber. Soft faced and tousled like a young boy, his long lashes feathering over his cheeks, fluttering slightly as he dreamed.

Wickedness gripped her and she rubbed her buttocks provocatively against his delicious rod. Picking up his hands, limp with sleep, she drew them up to her breasts and cupped his fingers around them. She pinched his fingertips together, trapping her nipples between them. Rubbing. Teasing. Presently, she felt the moist caress of his lips as he softly kissed her shoulder.

'Horny little bitch,' he murmured, caressing her nipples of his own accord, 'don't you ever get enough?'

As she shook her head and mumbled something into the pillow, he moved one hand down, sliding it over her hip and buttocks. His exploring fingertips encountered the moist warmth of her vulva. She was already fully aroused and he couldn't help wondering if wet dreams were just the prerogative of men, or whether women actually enjoyed them too. His fingers probed her gently, widening her vaginal lips and then sliding right inside her on the warm tide of her own juices. When he thought she was well and truly ready for him, he replaced his fingers with his cock.

In his dreams, the Swedish housewife in the video film had become muddled up with Nina. And he had watched the Swede-Nina composite woman being fucked by a succession of swarthy, hairy guys in BT overalls. Abandoned to the untamable caprices of dreamtime, he had found the whole thing believable and incredibly erotic. And now, as he thrust inside the grasping willingness of Nina's body, he found his pleasure heightened by the vague fantasy of watching Nina being fucked by a complete stranger.

INTIMATE DISCLOSURES

They came tumultuously and almost together, Tom's fingers seeking out the swollen nub of Nina's clitoris and bringing her to a climax that precipitated his own. Afterwards they lay, still joined, for several blissful minutes until the shrill burst of the alarm clock forced them into their respective days.

For Nina, this meant a quick shower and small bowl of cereal before dashing to the top of the road and hailing a taxi. Tom, an architect, could enjoy a more leisurely start. He worked partly on his own computer system at the flat, partly from the company that paid his salary and spent the rest of the time on the road in his red Porsche 968 convertible – Nina's only rival for his affections – visiting various clients who were dotted around London and its environs.

Fulham was Nina's destination. It was too far away from her flat in Putney to walk but close enough for her to enjoy the luxury of travelling there and back by taxi every day. She loved her job, undervalued though it was. As a researcher for a television production company it was lively, varied work. And it brought her into contact with a bewildering variety of people. The social side, which Nina loved the most, made up for all the hours she spent at her desk, pouring over mailing lists and telephone directories and trying to cajole people over the phone into revealing their lives on camera.

The moment she arrived at the converted end of terrace house, the three storeys of which now accommodated Grassroots Productions, she walked up the narrow staircase to the second floor and tossed her bag on to her littered desk.

'Where's Karen?' she asked Maisie, noticing that her boss was not at her desk. Twenty-four-year-old Maisie was a fellow researcher, stick thin and unreservedly trendy, whose wildly back-combed flame-red hair stuck out in all directions.

'Conference room,' Maisie said, tugging down the hem of her lime-green crocheted mini-dress through which her white bra and pants were clearly visible. She pulled a wry face and added, 'Liam's with her. On the war path as usual. Apparently he's come up with a brilliant new idea.' She said this in an ironic tone which matched her raised, thinly plucked eyebrows. 'They want you down there pronto, by the way.'

'Great,' Nina muttered, 'more leg work. I wonder what it is this time – children divorcing their parents? – battered husbands? – scrofulous sheep?'

Maisie looked bemused. 'What'us sheep?'

'Never mind.' Nina shook her head and hunted through the debris on her desk for a notepad and pencil. 'I'll let you know all about it when I get back.'

Flaking white paint was the general theme of the Grassroots Productions world. It covered the outside of the building and the interior walls like an unidentifiable skin disease and most of the steel and wood furnishings were decorated in the same fashion. Therefore, it always came as something as a shock to employees when they entered the meeting room.

Visitors to the company were led to believe that the world of television was comprised of contemporary designer decor and plush carpeting. In the meeting room, which was the only part of the building visitors were allowed to see, blue and black ergonomically fashioned chairs were grouped around an ebony wood amoeba-shaped table. Daffodil yellow cushions provided extra comfort and yellow vases containing blue silk tulips were dotted about the room, contrasting perfectly with the black furniture and matching ankle-deep carpet.

Karen and Liam were already seated side by side at the table, Nina noticed as she entered the room. Karen was slim, bordering on fashionably thin, with a glossy curtain of regularly trimmed ebony hair that fell midway down her back. With a quarter of the blood flowing through her veins of Spanish origin, she was petite and dainty,

INTIMATE DISCLOSURES

with a well-defined bone structure, almond-shaped brown eyes and a neat, sharply pointed nose and chin. Today, she was wearing a trouser suit of red crushed velvet. She looked fashionable, smart and – though small – she had the air of someone who was totally in control.

In contrast, Liam, Grassroots' proprietor, looked slightly seedy and dishevelled. He always reminded Nina of the archetypal tabloid hack and today was no exception. Jacketless, the sleeves of his off white shirt rolled up to the elbows and the hem struggling free of the too-tight waistband of his dark trousers, he looked as though he had slept in the meeting room and just woke up. His florid, jowly face was shiny with perspiration and his thinning mousy hair lay flat to one side of his square head and stuck up in an obstinate tuft at the other.

Off-putting though he looked, he still managed to charm Nina with his open smile as he waved her towards the vacant seat opposite him.

'Nina, love,' he said in his broad cockney accent, 'I thought you was never coming.'

'It's only five past nine,' Nina pointed out, glancing at her watch for emphasis.

'Well, don't worry yourself about being late,' he said, irritating her without meaning to, as he did with everyone, 'you're here now that's the main thing.'

He pushed a black folder towards Nina. It had a large red X on the front and the words INTIMATE DISCLOSURES in smaller red block type.

'Our new baby,' he said, 'a real stunner of an idea. Came up with it meself.' He gave a self congratulatory smile and visibly annoyed Karen by asking her to fetch coffee while he filled Nina in. He compounded his *faux pas*, Nina noticed with a flicker of inner glee, by patting her on the behind as she stood up.

While Karen was out of the room, Nina flicked through the proposal inside the folder. Liam's idea, which she had to admit to herself seemed like a good one for once, was based entirely around the sex industry.

'We want the punters to tell us where they go for sex. What they do. And who they do it with,' Liam enthused. He leaned forward and clasped his hands on the table. 'When I started thinking about this, it began to dawn on me how many different ways people get their kicks these days. Wife swapping, sex clubs, porn mags and films, S&M, all that, and more. Then there's the oldest profession of course. Not to mention table dancing, transvestites, hostess clubs and peep shows and the like.'

'It's certainly a thriving industry,' Nina agreed, trying not to look as revolted as she felt as she drew out a copy of a magazine called Mega Jugs from the folder.

'Some knockers eh?' Liam said with a leery grin.

'Hm, yes, quite.' Nina hastily stuffed the magazine back in the folder and closed it with relief. She was even more pleased that Karen chose that moment to walk back into the room carrying three cups of coffee on a black lacquered tray.

As she sipped her coffee Nina listened intently to Liam, while he explained to her and Karen how he wanted the documentary to go.

'To get a real insight, you'll have to get out there and get involved,' he said, ignoring Karen's alarmed expression. 'Talk to the people and get them on your side. Offer 'em blanked out faces, changed voices, sitting behind a screen, anything, just so long as you can get them on camera. And don't take no for an answer,' he advised, jabbing a finger at both Karen and Nina. 'I don't want no poncy git presenter on screen telling the viewers all about it, like it's an Open University lecture or something. I want real people, who really do the things we're talking about. Get under their skins and see what you can come up with.'

'It might be a little difficult,' Karen ventured hesitantly, 'people can be—'

INTIMATE DISCLOSURES

Liam's face became flushed and his round eyes popped slightly. 'Don't give me that load of old bollocks,' he said, banging his fist on the table and slopping his coffee into the saucer, 'if you're telling me you can't cut it I'll find someone who can. Tony Rawlings for instance—' He left the name hanging as a threat.

Nina watched as pink spots appeared in Karen's cheeks. Everyone at Grassroots Productions knew that Tony Rawlings and Karen Brady were sworn enemies. Mainly, Nina mused, because Tony Rawlings thought he was God's gift to TV and even better than that – in his own chauvinistic eyes at any rate – because he thought being a man automatically made him better than any woman.

'Tony has enough to cope with at the moment,' Karen said firmly, with a barely detectable quaver in her voice. 'He's still working on the Foreign Legion thing. Nina and I are quite capable of handling this. We'll get on to it right away.'

They left a few minutes later, Karen's heels marking an insistent staccato rhythm on the wood flooring of the corridor outside. In her hand she held a slim, red suede briefcase.

Nina followed in her wake, carrying the black folder and her notebook and pencil. She felt apprehensive about this project and knew now why the package containing the pornographic video had mysteriously appeared on her desk the previous afternoon.

When they reached the second floor, she caught sight of herself in the glass partition that divided the corridor from the work space. A good three or four inches shorter than Karen, even in the spiky heeled ankle boots she was wearing, she looked dumpy, whereas her boss looked sleek and well groomed. And Nina's hair, which she hadn't had time to dry properly that morning, had dropped into a centre parting and fell around her shoulders in unruly waves. Worse still, according to her own eyes, the black, ankle-skimming dress – which she'd believed she looked good in when she put it on only a couple of hours earlier – now appeared to make her the spitting image of Dracula's mother.

When they reached Karen's desk – a stark, neat and tidy contrast to Nina's own – Karen turned to her and said, 'Start hitting the phones, would you? Get lists of clubs and membership forms if necessary. And contact all the porno publishers, get them to put media packs in the post.'

'What will you be doing?' Nina ventured to ask.

Karen gave her a stony glare and glanced pointedly at her watch. 'I've got a good contact who may be useful,' she said curtly, 'I'll give him a ring and see if we can meet for lunch.' Rudely turning her back on Nina, she dismissed her without saying a word.

Nina returned to her own desk feeling exhausted already. This project would involve hundreds of phone calls and hours of dispiriting leg work. Plus, she didn't fancy having to deal with 'those types' as her mother would call them.

She was no prude but blatant sleaze appalled her. Whenever she was with Tom she would encourage him to drive miles out of their way, rather than venture into some of the more salubrious areas of the city. The sight of street girls bothered her. She found the gaudy images of naked women outside strip joints and proclamations of THEY'RE NAKED AND THEY MOVE acutely disturbing. And the only advantage to being so short, she believed, was being able to avoid looking at the magazines displayed so blatantly along the top shelves of every newsagent's.

By five thirty, she felt mentally exhausted and physically dirty. She longed to get back to the safe haven of her flat and soak in a hot bath. The grime of seedy sex seemed to have ingrained itself in her pores. She wanted to cook Tom a special dinner and watch a comedy film with him. Then make love before going to sleep. Tonight she didn't want a fuck, she wanted tenderness.

INTIMATE DISCLOSURES

Tonight though, she reminded herself, with a dispirited glance at the leaflet on her desk – which Liam had thoughtfully dropped off for her before he left – she would have to put all her romantic notions on hold and go back out to work. Provided Tom was willing to partner her, tonight they would be going to their first ever swingers club – The Bold and Brazen.

Chapter Two

'Now, whatever you do, don't go telling anyone that I'm involved in the media,' Nina warned Tom for the umpteenth time.

Tom sighed and ruffled her hair. 'Don't worry, sweetheart,' he said, 'as far as anyone is concerned, we're just Nina and Tom, your average kinky couple.'

'Absolutely.' Nina leaned forward over the dressing table and peered at her face in the mirror. Picking up her mascara she zigzagged the brush through her upper lashes and then stroked it carefully across the lower ones. 'OK,' she said, straightening up and appraising her reflection, 'I think that's me done.'

'Done and looking gorgeous, as always,' Tom said. Grabbing her by the waist he spun her around to face him. 'I love that dress, by the way, when did you get it?'

'After work,' she said, tugging at the hem of the black figure-hugging sheath, 'I thought I ought to look suitably raunchy. God, this is so short!'

Taking a step back, Tom appraised her. A smile spread across his face as his gaze took in her curvaceous legs clad in sheer black nylon and the sinuous curves of her hips, waist and breasts. Finally, his gaze landed on her face which had flushed to a very becoming shade of pink.

'Do we have to go out?' he asked meaningfully.

Nina smirked at him. 'Get your mind out of my stocking tops and go and bring the car round, I can't walk out to the garage in these heels.'

He saluted her. 'Yes, sir. Or should I call you madam?'

'Are you implying that I look like a tart?' She pretended to frown.

Sensing that she was about to have second thoughts about the dress and spend another hour going through her wardrobe for something less revealing, Tom shook his head.

'I'm saying you look fabulous and I'm going to get the car right now,' he said, 'wait for me on the front step.'

Even though it was a warm evening, Nina covered the skimpy dress with a thick black wool coat, picked up her bag and tottered out to the lift. On her feet she wore a pair of black patent leather stilettos. The shoes had an impossibly high heel which threw her body into an unnatural pose, making her back arch and her generous breasts and buttocks thrust against the tight fabric of her dress. She felt like sex on legs and while half of her longed to run back into the flat and put on something less revealing, the other half felt a small thrill at the knowledge that she looked really good.

The swinger's club was held at a bar in Bayswater and Tom dropped her off outside while he went to park the car. When he came sauntering back, his hands thrust deep in the pockets of his black trousers, which he wore with a ribbed black tee-shirt and pale green jacket, he found Nina jogging nervously from one foot to the other.

'You took your time,' she grumbled, slipping her arm in his, 'I've been propositioned twice already.' She cocked her head in the direction of the bar. 'Some of the people going in there look really creepy.'

'I expect you get all sorts,' Tom said. He had no preconceived notions about what a swinger's club and its members might be like, although he was intrigued to find out. 'Come on. Let's go in.'

Nina had phoned the number on the leaflet to pre-book their tickets, explaining – as Liam had advised her to do – that she was a friend of Angie's. Liam hadn't bothered to elaborate on who Angie was and Nina hadn't liked to ask. It made her wonder if the boss of Grassroots Productions was a swinger himself. But she had met his wife, Georgina, and she seemed far too twinset and pearls for that sort of thing.

Nudged out of her reverie by Tom's elbow, Nina signed herself in and handed over thirty pounds for the tickets, to a man with thinning brown hair tied back in a ponytail. He seemed surprised when she asked for a receipt but produced a small preprinted pad and scribbled one out for her anyway.

The bar was on two levels, she discovered. The upper level, which had a buffet, some seating and a rack for coats, was almost deserted. But the continuous thump-thump of disco music from the lower level sounded more encouraging.

Slipping off her coat and hanging it on the rack, Nina took Tom's hand and they walked down the stairs. The lighting was very dim on the lower level. And as Nina's eyes became more accustomed to it she realised that the ground floor comprised a large square dance floor, another similar sized area with tables and chairs and, around the edge of the room, lots of little alcoves. The alcoves were unlit and in some of them Nina could make out the movement of indistinct figures. Across the width of the far wall ran a bar and it was on this she set her immediate sights.

Dragging Tom across the dance floor to the bar she ordered a large gin and tonic. 'I need this,' she explained to Tom as she hauled herself up onto a bar stool. Crossing her legs, she felt the slither of smooth nylon and heard it crackle. Her hem slid up her thighs to expose a glimpse of the dark welts at the tops of her stockings. As she sipped her drink she grinned at Tom with her eyes.

He smiled back at her as he sat on the stool next to hers and ordered a mineral water for himself. 'Just don't go getting so pissed that you can't do your job,' he whispered, leaning towards her.

Looking alarmed, Nina glanced around. 'Don't mention my job remember,' she said.

Just at that moment her attention was distracted by the sight of a lovely-looking young woman in a hot pink chiffon blouse and tight black skirt that clung to her neat hips and bottom. Small, dusky-skinned and with long black hair that curled as it reached her waist, she was accompanied by a rather nondescript middle-aged man. 'Gosh, she's beautiful,' Nina breathed to Tom, 'shame about her partner though. I wouldn't want to swap with them.'

Feigning surprise, Tom looked at her. 'I thought we were here to observe, not to participate.'

Nina's wink held a hint of lasciviousness which he found surprisingly arousing.

'Well,' she said glibly, 'you never know.'

About ten minutes later, the 'odd couple,' as Nina dubbed them, came over to the bar. The young woman stood next to Nina and turned to smile up at her.

'Hi,' she said in a sweet, husky voice, 'I'm Angel. You're new here aren't you?'

Nina nodded dumbly, then found her voice. 'Nina,' she said, 'and this is Tom.' She turned to glance at Tom who was regarding Angel, she noticed, with more than a passing interest.

Just as she was about to say something else to Angel, the young woman's partner stuck out a meaty hand and grabbed Nina's, pumping her arm up and down enthusiastically. His palm was damp and sticky and Nina dragged her hand away as soon as she possibly could.

'This is my husband, Brett,' Angel explained.

Nina found herself glancing from one to the other. Brett and Angel were such an unlikely couple. Though Angel seemed an entirely appropriate name for her, as far as Nina was concerned, she thought Brett should have been called Frank instead – short for Frankenstein.

He reminded her of Liam in lots of ways. Although Brett

INTIMATE DISCLOSURES

was taller and not quite as flabby as her esteemed boss, he looked altogether too seedy – and eager – for Nina's liking. His muddy brown eyes held the hopeful, predatory look she had come to recognise of old. Aside from all his other shortcomings this, she thought, was a complete turn-off.

'Is Angel your real name?' she found herself asking – her researcher's 'nose' twitching automatically.

Nodding, Angel said, 'Oh, yes. My family is from Argentina but I have lived in London for most of my life.' Then she added, 'Do you go to any of the other clubs?'

'No, this is our first time,' Nina said, 'I don't even know of any others.'

'You really should try The Jungle,' Brett cut in, 'it's really relaxed. The parties last the whole weekend and you can wear a towel if you want to.'

'It's naturist,' Angel explained to Nina and Tom when she caught their bemused expressions.

'Oh, well, maybe we'll give it a go sometime,' Nina murmured. She took a small notepad from her bag and jotted down the name and Brett supplied the phone number for her to call for more details.

Useful, her sideways glance said to Tom.

As the evening wore on, several more couples came over to the bar and introduced themselves. One of the couples, who had come all the way from Wales, Nina really liked. Once again, she found herself feeling more enthusiastic about the wife than the husband. Which made her wonder if she harboured any bisexual tendencies. Although she couldn't actually imagine herself kissing, or touching any of the women she met, she found them far more appealing on the whole than their men.

The Welsh woman, Laura, promised they would be back once she and her husband Davy had done a circuit of the room. 'Well, you've got to, haven't you?' she said in her lilting accent.

With a casual shrug, Nina smiled at her and replied, 'Oh, absolutely. See you later perhaps.'

The music gradually became more raunchy than disco and, relaxed by several drinks, Nina got up to dance. Tom remained on the bar stool, watching her with his slumberous eyes and slow, easy smile. She danced in front of him, getting more and more turned on by the way he was looking at her. It wasn't just the crush of people that was making her feel uncomfortably warm, she realised, it was pure desire.

There and then she made up her mind to enjoy the rest of the evening. If necessary, she would go into work late the next day. It would be understandable after all, she told herself firmly. She couldn't be expected to work twenty-four hours a day. And this *was* work.

Churning her hips in time to the beat, she leaned forward from the waist and shimmied at Tom. The movement granted him a generous eyeful of her jiggling cleavage. His expression darkened, as she hoped it would, becoming wolfish. And she felt the sexual thrill of his affirmation that she was desirable and had the power to arouse him without touching him at all.

She danced in a circle so that she could people-watch as well as tantalise Tom. Behind the dance floor, the alcoves had all become occupied. And around the tables, couples who earlier had been sitting and sipping their drinks as in any other bar, were now engaged in various levels of foreplay. Turning slightly so that she could observe them covertly, Nina watched two men and two women in particular who swapped partners continuously.

First one couple kissed and caressed each other. Then they swapped. Then the two women embraced. Only the men remained aloof from each other. Clearly, lesbianism was more acceptable than homosexuality, she thought, knowing that watching two women make love was almost every man's number one fantasy.

INTIMATE DISCLOSURES

At that moment Angel came dancing over to her. Thankfully, Nina noticed, she was without Brett for once and she felt no qualms about turning around so that she and Angel could dance opposite each other. As the music changed to a more soulful beat Angel moved gradually closer to Nina. Not wishing to seem stand-offish, Nina remained dancing on the same spot. She could smell Angel's perfume quite distinctly now. A musky, floral blend, it caressed her nostrils and delighted her senses.

Angel flicked back her hair, smiling directly into Nina's face. Then, before Nina could do anything to stop her, the young woman wrapped her arms sinuously around Nina's neck and kissed her.

Stunned for a moment, Nina felt the full lips pressing against her own and responded automatically. She felt their breasts pressing together and the hardness of Angel's nipples. The young woman's fingers entwined in Nina's hair and caressed her shoulders. At the same time she forced Nina's mouth open with her own and in darted an inquisitive tongue. Wet and warm it danced tantalisingly across Nina's gums and wound around her own tongue.

Coiled like snakes their tongues held onto each other. Tasting. Nina's senses reeled. Angel tasted sweet and minty, with the slight tang of the bitter lemon she had been drinking all evening. Nina felt herself go hot and cold all at once. Opening her eyes she struggled to look at Tom. He seemed entranced, she noticed. Leaning forward, his elbows resting on his knees, his chin cupped in his hands, his face wore a dreamy, far away expression. And his blue eyes were dark with lust.

He's fantasising about us, me and Angel, Nina thought wildly, still responding to the girl's kiss. Desire surged through her. More the desire to titillate Tom than genuine arousal on her own behalf. In truth, kissing Angel was not that different to kissing some of the men she had known. Except, Nina mused dazedly, Angel's kiss was perhaps a bit more tender. And the young woman felt softer, more malleable somehow than any man. Men's bodies were hard when you came into contact with them, she realised, and they held themselves more rigidly. Whereas Angel's body, though trim and well toned, was supple and completely relaxed.

To Nina, to hold the other woman and explore her with her hands was like clasping a bolt of the finest fabric. The texture was of velvet, overlaid with silk. The skin on the exposed portion of Angel's arms felt as luxurious as satin. And her hair was smooth and glossy, the black strands falling between Nina's fingertips with the fluidity and appearance of oil.

'I like you,' Angel murmured huskily in Nina's ear. Her hand swept around Nina's body to cup a breast lightly. The fingertips played with the nipple. 'You like me too?'

All sorts of conflicting thoughts whirled through Nina's mind. Yes, she liked Angel. But in what way did she mean? Like her as a person, or as a sexual partner?

'Mm,' Nina mumbled, trying to be noncommittal. She felt her nipple harden between Angel's fingers and felt flooded by a familiar warmth. A rush of moisture soaked the crotch of the black g-string she was wearing – her only underwear.

Smiling at Nina as though she understood her naïveté and her dilemma, Angel took one of her hands and placed it on her own breast. Much smaller than Nina's, it was firm and easy to cover with her hand.

Nina let her hand rest there as if frozen. She risked a glance at Tom. To her surprise, he wasn't watching her and Angel at all any more but talking to a large, burly guy with receding white blond hair. His back was to her as he leaned his elbows on the bar. The two men seemed deep in discussion.

Realising that any arousal she was feeling was entirely her own, and not because of Tom's reaction made Nina feel confused. Was she supposed to feel like this? Angel's

INTIMATE DISCLOSURES

fingertips tweaked her nipple, pulling at it through the stretchy material of her dress and at that moment she felt a hot spear of lust which melted her insides. Almost of their own accord her fingers began to massage Angel's breast, moulding the pliable flesh beneath the chiffon.

Angel was not naked under her blouse but wore a flesh coloured bodystocking. The chiffon crackled over the silk underwear. Tiny jolts of electricity stung Nina's fingertips and she slid her hand down Angel's torso, feeling the taut contours of her lithe body. Over Angel's narrow hip her hand slipped to cup a high, perfectly rounded buttock.

Warm breath tantalised her neck as Angel moaned softly. Ostensibly, they were still dancing but their caresses were becoming more intimate by the second.

Nina felt the silk of Angel's palm stroke her shoulder, sliding the strap of her dress down her upper arm at the same time. The neckline of her dress was low and with a little dexterity, Angel managed to free one of Nina's breasts. Shielded by their own bodies from the view of others, Angel stroked Nina's bare breast. Her fingers kneaded the succulent flesh, the tips of them pinching and rolling the hard nipple until it became swollen and fully distended.

'I want to suck your nipple so much,' Angel murmured in Nina's ear, 'do you mind?'

Shaking her head dumbly, Nina held her breath, waiting for that first moment when the young woman's naturally pouting lips would enclose the bud of flesh that burned at the tip of her aching breast. She willed the rest of the room and its occupants away. She wanted to share a moment of complete intimacy with Angel but they were in the middle of a lively bar. It was impossible.

Sensing Nina's reticence, Angel changed her mind and covered Nina's breast again. Then without saying a word she led her across the dance floor, past the packed tables to a small alcove which, miraculously, was empty. The alcove was in pitch darkness and contained a narrow banquette seat, padded and covered in a soft fabric. To Nina's exploring fingers, it felt like velvet, or velour.

'Sit,' Angel commanded softly.

She knelt in front of Nina and without saying anything else, freed both her breasts. The generous lightly tanned flesh spilled bountifully over the lowered neckline of Nina's dress and fell joyfully into Angel's hands. The young woman's hands and mouth were all over them immediately. Clasping. Kneading. Suckling.

Throwing her head back, Nina moaned. Pressing her palms flat upon the seat she arched her back and thrust her breasts more urgently into Angel's hands. Her breasts felt as though they were on fire, and the sex flesh between her legs throbbed with urgent desire. She moved her hips, parting her legs. She felt the soft brush of Angel's skirt on her inner thighs as the young woman shuffled forward on her knees.

Her hands and mouth were full of Nina's breasts. The nipples were so swollen and hard as she rolled them around on her tongue, her fingertips digging into the exquisite globes of flesh.

Nina reached for any part of Angel she could touch. Her hair. Her shoulders. Her breasts. Sliding her palms under the neckline of first the blouse and then the camisole she encountered bare skin. The first touch of a naked breast that wasn't her own. The erotic jolt she felt almost left her senseless. Everything, time, the people outside the secluded niche, even Nina's own inhibitions seemed superfluous at that moment.

Through heavy-lidded eyes, she could see over Angel's shoulder that Tom was searching for her. He stood among the tables and chairs, looking around, a bewildered expression on his face. Almost by telepathy she attracted his attention, unsure if he would be able to see her feeble wave through the darkness of the alcove. But to her relief he came over. Wordlessly, Angel made room for him inside the alcove and he sat beside Nina.

INTIMATE DISCLOSURES

Without saying a word, except to show her with his eyes how much he desired her, Tom slid his hand up Nina's dress. He massaged her thigh for a moment, his fingertips pressing into the flesh, then stroking in deliciously tantalising circles. As they moved inexorably closer to the heat of Nina's sex she opened her legs wider and wider, encouraging him to touch her more intimately.

Tom and Angel's fingers collided. They both reached for the waistband of Nina's panties and drew them down between them. It wasn't easy working them down her legs in the confines of the alcove but Nina aided them, raising her bottom and wriggling until the damp scrap of material was draped lewdly around one ankle. In perfect harmony, Tom and Angel spread Nina's legs wide apart, forcing up the hem of her dress until it was bunched around her hips.

The heat of pure lust swamped Nina. Under her bare bottom she could feel the richness of the velvet covered banquette. And Tom and Angel's fingertips upon her bare thighs were exquisitely featherlight. She couldn't tell which set of fingers belonged to which person as they whispered up to her groin and stroked her vulva. They spread her vaginal lips apart, stroking and exploring, prising open the petals of her most secret flesh.

She closed her eyes, hardly able to bear the sight of man and woman looking at her so intimately. Hot waves of shame flooded her as she felt fingers inside her that weren't Tom's. They explored delicately, knowingly touching the sensitive place behind her pubic bone which could make her come instantly. Tremors of lust shook her, rippling outwards from the core of her sexuality. Her thighs trembled, her buttocks clenched.

Opening her eyes she saw and felt a familiar dark head nuzzle her breasts. The silky ends of Tom's hair caressed her chest and torso as his mouth hungrily feasted on her desperate nipples. Further down more silk stroked her thighs and abdomen. Angel's head was buried between her thighs and just as Nina shuddered with expectation she felt the first soft brush of the young woman's lips on her inner thigh. Her sex quivered, the juices flooding her as Angel's fingers continued to slide in and out of her throbbing vagina.

The moment she felt the wetness of Angel's tongue lathe her swollen clitoris she cried out and jolted her hips in orgasm. Waves of lust swamped her. The sheer carnality of her state, her breasts in Tom's mouth and hands, her sex in Angel's, overwhelmed her. It was too lewd, too erotic, too blissful to comprehend.

'Mind if I join in?'

Nina's state of wanton abandon was shattered instantly. Brett stood in the doorway to the alcove, the bulk of his figure blocking out everything else. Despite the dim lighting she could see the greedy light in his eyes, the lascivious way his gaze took in the scene. She cringed as Angel moved away from her automatically, giving her husband an excellent view of Nina's streaming, wide open sex.

She uttered a single strangled cry, 'No!' and tried to cover herself. 'I don't want to, I'm not ready for that,' she said more plaintively.

'OK, sweetheart. It's OK.' Tom took charge of the situation, pulling the top of her dress up and the hem of her dress down. He untangled her g-string from around her ankles and slipped it in his pocket.

Nina smiled weakly at him. She hoped the gratitude she felt was evident in her eyes.

He turned to look at her and held out his hand. 'Fancy another drink, precious?' he said.

Nina nodded dumbly and then managed an apologetic smile for Angel's benefit. Somehow she made it to the bar on trembling legs. If it hadn't been for Tom's nearness, his command of the situation and the reassuring grip of his hand she thought she would have dissolved onto the floor. When she reached the bar he helped her on to a stool and ordered a large G&T for her. Then he turned to her and smiled.

'Did I ever tell you how fabulous you are?' he said.

This time, Nina managed a faltering smile. 'Yes,' she murmured, 'and so are you.'

They left the club shortly afterwards but not before they had managed to exchange phone numbers with Laura and Davy, and Angel and Brett. Both couples promised to let Nina and Tom know when and where several private parties were to be held.

On the drive home Nina found the courage to broach a question which she had been longing to ask.

'Tom?'

'Hmm?' He glanced briefly at her without taking his eyes off the road for too long. Even at two in the morning the London streets were still busy.

Nina took a deep breath. 'What did you think of that place – and me and Angel? Did you mind? Did you enjoy it? I don't know what to think.'

Her words all tumbled out in a rush and then she found herself gripping her hands tightly together in her lap. She glanced down. Her knuckles gleamed a stark white in the semi-darkness.

Slowly, a hand covered hers.

'It's OK, sweetheart,' Tom said gently, his fingers squeezing hers. 'You have a job to do but that's no reason why you shouldn't enjoy yourself while you're doing it.'

'But how much of myself should I give to it?' Nina asked, glancing sideways at him. 'I don't want to risk damaging us.'

She was relieved to hear Tom's gentle laughter and feel the reassuring squeeze of his fingers.

'We're two grown ups, sweetheart,' he said, sounding wise beyond his years. 'You're researching aren't you – you're not planning to elope with any of these people?'

'Yes, I know but—'

'No buts,' he said, 'I love you but I don't own you. I want you to do whatever you want. Just promise you'll come back to me.'

'Oh, of course I promise,' she said, the tremendous relief she felt leaving her body on a huge sigh. 'You and me,' she added with feeling, 'we're a team. Soul mates, lovers and best friends. As far as I'm concerned we're inseparable.' She hugged the certainty to her. Feeling it as tangibly as if she were hugging Tom himself.

'Me too.' She could sense him smiling in the darkness. 'Now let's go home and have a cup of tea.'

For the rest of the week Nina busied herself on the phone, joining various clubs and trying in vain to get the publishers of pornography to talk to her. Although their wares were blatantly loose, their tongues weren't, it seemed and Nina began to despair of ever getting off the starting blocks as far as this project was concerned.

The growing list of areas to cover and people to contact seemed to be expanding by the minute. The sex industry, she quickly discovered, was huge and diverse. And Nina was finding it difficult trying to prioritise.

At their regular Friday meeting, she explained her dilemma to Liam and Karen. Couching her doubts in positive terms as far as she possibly could. The last thing she wanted was for either of them to think she wasn't up to the job. She could feel the sharp darts of Karen's displeasure. As her immediate superior, Karen had already told her in no uncertain terms that they were not to cock this project up, otherwise it would be lost to someone like Tony Rawlings.

By the same token, Nina thought, trying not to fume as she listened to Karen and Liam discussing another project, the other woman hadn't exactly been knocking herself out to help the project along. Apart from a couple of 'lunches', which had brought absolutely no results, Karen hadn't lifted a finger.

INTIMATE DISCLOSURES

'Now, it sounds to me as if both of you are getting nowhere fast,' Liam said, returning abruptly to the subject that had occupied Nina's every waking moment for the past week.

'Well, I wouldn't say that, exactly,' Nina countered, hoping she sounded bolder than she felt, 'it's early days yet.'

'You've got three months max to get this project in the can,' Liam interrupted. His pronouncement shocked both Nina and Karen and for the first time that morning they shared a sympathetic glance.

'Three months is impossible—' Karen started to say until Liam cut her off abruptly.

'Three months is it,' he said, 'end of story.' He glanced from one to the other and made as if to reach for the telephone. 'Perhaps I should give Tony a ring, get him up here—' He let the words dangle threateningly.

'No, OK, you win,' Karen cut in with a defeated sigh, 'we'll double our efforts.'

Nina almost laughed aloud – what did she mean by that, four lunches a week instead of two? – but was silenced by Liam's reply.

'Take my advice and treble them,' he said. 'You two, get your arses in gear and cut out all this feminine faffing about. If two lookers like you can't get in there and do the business I don't know who could. Start batting those eyelashes and shaking those little titties at the right people. And get me some results!'

As he banged his fist on the table Nina and Karen went into mutual blush state and Karen, Nina thought, looked as though she was going to have apoplexy.

'Take this,' Liam added, calming down a bit. He handed Karen a sheet of paper, typed and double spaced. 'A few of my closest friends are on here. Speak to them nicely and don't fuck up. It's bad enough risking my business on you two, I'm not going to lose my mates into the bargain.'

As soon as they got back to the second floor Karen handed Nina the list.

'Ring them all,' she said curtly, 'set up meetings with them for both of us.' She allowed her sharp tone to dissolve into a conspiratorial smile. 'I think, in this case, it's a question of safety in numbers.'

In view of Karen's unaccustomed display of feminine camaraderie, Nina ventured a question.

'As a matter of fact, I'm going to a sex toys party tonight – some friend of Maisie's – do you want to come?'

Karen raised an imperious eyebrow. 'Me, go to one of those things? You must be joking!' She gave Nina a condescending pat on the arm. 'No, you and Maisie go, I'm sure it's right up your street. I'm going to a cocktail party with an actor who shall remain nameless. Still, have fun.'

Nina fumed all the way home.

Chapter Three

The table groaning with bottles of cheap wine, as well as plates of sausage rolls and other 'nibbles', made Nina wonder if Maisie had got it wrong and had actually been invited to a Tupperware party instead of one for sex toys. Rachel, their hostess – tall, thin, short auburn hair and dressed in brown leggings and a sloppy jumper – was all of a nervous flutter. She kept darting about, taking people's coats and ushering them into the through lounge, urging them to help themselves to a drink.

The suburban sitting room was lined with a motley assortment of chairs, some dining, some kitchen and some white plastic garden. And a blue velour sofa and two armchairs had been pushed back against the sliding patio door to make more space for everyone. In one of the armchairs sat a round, motherly looking woman in a red and white polka dot dress. Her plump legs were crossed neatly at the ankles and the pink and white fingers of her left hand, were wrapped like chipolatas around the stem of a wineglass. On her ring finger, a diamond etched gold band bit into the flesh and glinted as she waved her glass around to emphasise whatever she was saying. Beside her on the floor stood a large tan leather suitcase and next to her black loafer-clad feet was a stack of brochures.

'I'm Jenny, your Fun and Frolics rep,' she said brightly to everyone who entered the room. Her handshake was warm and comforting and grey green eyes sparkled from under a mop of mid brown hair that fell over her face each time she leaned forward to pick up a brochure. 'Have a browse through,' she suggested, 'see if there's anything that takes your fancy. You can try what you want on if I've got it in your size and of course, you can have a go of the toys. They've all got fresh batteries in.'

Every time she said this, her little speech was greeted by a round of raucous laughter which made Nina wonder if the other dozen or so guests had arrived already half sloshed. When it was her turn she accepted a brochure, smiled weakly at Jenny and instantly made a grateful dash for the refreshments table. What was needed here, she thought, was definitely a big glass of plonk. Red or white, she didn't care just so long as it numbed her mind and eased her inhibitions.

All-female gatherings like this one tended to make her feel very uncomfortable. Particularly this type, she mused, cursing herself for being a social snob. The trouble was, as a single working girl, she felt she had nothing in common with most of the women there. Drink, give me a drink, she begged silently, casting her eyes over the dubious choice on offer. She was very tempted to open the bottle of rather nice Chardonnay that she had brought with her but didn't dare – not while there were already several litre bottles open and still half full. Instead she poured herself a glass of the dry white and stood there sipping it and trying not to grimace at its acidity while she glanced around.

Maisie seemed quite at home, she noticed, sitting on the sofa and chatting away with a perky-looking blonde who had been introduced to the rest of the room as Shelley. Pausing only to top her drink back up to the brim, Nina walked across the room and sat down next to Maisie.

'Me, Shell and Rache go back a long way,' Maisie explained to Nina when she asked, 'we all went to the local comprehensive. Now I'm the only one who's not tied down with a couple of sprogs.'

'Lucky you, Maisie,' Rachel said, coming to sit down

INTIMATE DISCLOSURES

at long last on the arm of the sofa beside Nina. 'It's nice to be able to forget being a mum for once. So,' she added, turning her attention to Jenny, 'what have you got for us in there?' She nodded in the direction of the suitcase.

'Lots of new goodies,' Jenny said with a wink. 'And I've got a surprise for you all for later. Part of the management's new initiative, it's supposed to encourage you all to buy more. Oops!' She clapped a hand over her mouth. 'Shouldn't have said that. Still, never mind.'

Naturally, everyone pressed her to reveal the nature of the surprise but Jenny staunchly refused to say anymore. 'You'll see,' was her mysterious reply. And she wouldn't budge an inch.

Everyone craned forward to look as she clicked open the catches on the suitcase. Inside, it was an Aladdin's cave of delights. Frothy undies and saucy outfits designed to titillate, as well as an intriguing assortment of plastic objects. One by one, Jenny took them out and held them up for everyone to look at.

'Meet Mr Amazing,' she said, clutching a thick pink vibrator by its base and waving it around. 'Guaranteed to give hours and hours of realistic pleasure.'

Rachel took the vibrator from her and turned it over in her hands, her slender fingers caressing its stem lovingly. 'It feels so lifelike,' she commented. As she twisted the base, the vibrator whirred into life and she ran the tip of it along her forearm. 'Ooh!' She shivered with pleasure and grinned at the other women. 'Beats the hell out of the washing machine.'

Most of the other women laughed but Nina and Maisie stared at each other uncomprehendingly.

Shelley took pity on them. 'You two wouldn't know,' she said, 'but all us home bodies appreciate the wonders of the washing machine on fast spin. All you have to do is lean against it for a few minutes and—'

She rolled her eyes expressively and a nervous titter ran around the room.

'Imagine doing that in the launderette,' Maisie murmured with a thoughtful expression on her face, 'that'd cause a few raised eyebrows.'

Everyone laughed again and all at once it seemed to Nina, the nervous tension that had gripped the small gathering seemed to dissolve. Now all the women were behaving in a much more relaxed fashion and were keen to see and handle the wares that Jenny had in her suitcase.

Nina took possession of a small white plastic object, shaped like an egg. It had a little remote control box attached to it by a lead.

'What does this do exactly?' she asked Jenny.

'It's a love egg,' the plump woman replied, 'you put it inside yourself and it stimulates your vaginal walls.'

Switching it on, Nina allowed the egg to jiggle around in her palm. It was doing wonders just for the sensitive flesh of her hand, which made her wonder what it could do for that other, more intimate part of herself. Leaning across the sofa, behind Maisie and Shelley, Nina whispered to Jenny to put her down for one of them.

'No need,' Jenny whispered back, 'I always keep of few of those in stock, you can take one with you.' She and Nina surreptitiously exchanged the sample for one in a box, which Nina then slipped equally furtively into her bag. She and Tom could have some fun with that later, she thought, grinning to herself.

She got up and helped herself to another glass of wine and when she returned she found that Jenny had moved on to some of the items of clothing.

'This is Chantal,' she said holding up what purported to be a French maid's outfit. 'I think you'd look good in this Nina, why don't you model it for us?'

Nearly choking on her wine, Nina caught the scanty bit of shiny black fabric edged with white lace as Jenny tossed it in her direction. She held it away from her as if it were an unexploded grenade.

'Yeah, go and put it on, Neen,' Maisie urged, 'you can use Rachel's bedroom, can't she Rache?'

'Mm, oh, yes, there's a full length mirror up there,' Rachel said with a friendly smile.

Nina glanced warily around. It was clear they were all expecting her to make a fool of herself. Knocking back the rest of her wine she thought, oh, why the hell not?

Rachel's bedroom was quite large and decorated in different shades of blue and pink. One woman was already up there, trying to fit her ample form into a red PVC dress.

'Jenny said this was one size,' she grumbled, tugging at the zip.

'Here, let me help,' Nina offered. Dropping the maid's dress on the bed she reached for the zip. Though it stuck a couple of times, Nina finally managed to haul it up.

'It's not bad is it?' the woman said, eyeing herself in the mirror while she desperately tried to hoist up her mammoth breasts and then tuck some superfluous bits of white underarm flesh into the dress. It gripped her around the bust and thighs quite fiercely and Nina wondered how on earth she was going to manage to walk in it. 'My Danny'll go like jelly when he sees me in this.'

'I'd have thought you'd want him a bit harder than jelly,' Nina countered without thinking.

To her surprise the woman went as red as her dress and started spluttering with laughter. 'Oh, my God,' she said, wiping her eyes with the back of her hand, 'yeah, harder than jelly. I must go down and show the others and tell them what you just said.'

So saying, she tottered out of the room on spindly heels. A moment later Maisie's friend Shelley appeared.

'Jenny wants me to try this on,' she pronounced glumly,

holding up a wisp of blue satin and lace. 'She's a right bully that one, wouldn't take no for an answer.'

As Nina started to step out of her skirt she nodded. 'I think we've just got to go along with it,' she said.

'Well no one said we've got to do it sober,' Shelley countered. From under the pink jacket she was wearing she produced Nina's bottle of Chardonnay, already uncorked. She held it out. 'Fancy a swig?'

Grinning conspiratorially, Nina took the bottle. They sat down on the bed, Nina just in a black sleeveless jumper, hold up stockings and g-string. As she raised the bottle to her lips Shelley shrugged off her jacket, laid it across the bed and then began to tug the matching shift dress off over her head. Underneath she wore just a plain white pair of bikini pants.

'I guess these'll have to come off too,' she said. Bending forward from the waist she pulled them down to her ankles and kicked them off.

The first thing Nina noticed about Shelley when she straightened up was that she was not a natural blonde. A silky chestnut brown, her bush was neatly trimmed into a heart shape.

'My husband did it,' she explained when she caught Nina looking at her. 'He says he likes a pretty cunt to look at.'

Nina felt herself going pink. 'I, er, that's nice,' she mumbled, taking another hefty gulp of wine.

'You don't like that word much do you?' Shelley said perceptively, sitting down next to Nina on the bed. Apparently unconcerned by her nakedness, she reclined back and made nonchalant circles in the air with her feet.

'It's, er, well, it's a bit crude,' Nina admitted.

'Yeah, it is. So what?'

As Shelley smiled, Nina noticed the young woman's irises were green, rimmed with hazel. It was an innocent look, though an unmistakable hint of naughtiness lurked behind

INTIMATE DISCLOSURES

it. Noticing it, a small flicker of attraction zinged through Nina which she immediately tried to subdue.

'I always think talking dirty is lovely.' Shelley continued, 'With the right bloke it can be a real turn-on.'

'I suppose so.' Nina knew she sounded doubtful. Passing Shelley the bottle of wine she watched while the young woman drank some. All at once she decided to come clean. 'Look,' she said hesitantly, 'I don't quite know how to explain this but I'm actually here to do some research for a TV programme.'

Shelley took the bottle away from her mouth and gazed at Nina.

'No shit,' she said. After a moment she added, 'So what's the programme about then?'

While they shared the remainder of the wine, Nina told her all about *Intimate Disclosures*.

'Well, I never,' Shelley said when Nina had finished, 'I bet I could help you out a lot. I've got ever so many friends who get up to all sorts – escorting, table-dancing, hostessing, that sort of thing. Then I've got another friend Yvonne who works in films – you know, porno stuff? And then there's Booty, lovely girl, gorgeous bod and black as the ace of – well – anyway, she works a lot of the strip joints in Soho.'

'Really?' Nina sensed her eyes were like saucers and could feel the adrenaline pumping through her. This was really good stuff. With a bit of help from Shelley she could start to make some serious progress on her research.

'Uh-huh.' Shelley nodded and hauled herself unsteadily to her feet. 'We'll talk some more about it later. Perhaps I could be on your programme.'

Nina watched the young woman reach for the satin and lace body feeling as though she couldn't quite believe her luck.

'Come on, Nina,' Shelley said, bringing her out of her reverie, 'get that thing on. Then we can go downstairs and wow them together.'

* * *

Rounds of applause and catcalls greeted their arrival. Shelley entered the room first, as bold as brass and pausing once she stepped across the threshold to pose provocatively.

'What did I tell you?' Jenny cried enthusiastically, 'That body is sublime.'

'Do you mean the blue thing, or Shelley herself?' one of the women quipped.

Shelley had the grace to blush, then turned to look at Nina. 'Come on,' she said encouragingly, 'don't be shy. We're all friends together here.'

Feeling horribly self conscious, Nina walked through the door. The maid's dress, with its attached white apron, was incredibly short, revealing her stocking tops and a small portion of thigh above. And it was tight on the bust, pushing her breasts up and together so that they looked as though she had deliberately served them up as a feast.

Maisie whistled. 'Fabulous!' she exclaimed. 'Just wait until I tell the others at work.'

Nina had just flashed her a 'don't you dare' look when the doorbell rang. Jenny was the only person who didn't look surprised by the interruption.

'Oh, quick, quick, come in and sit down,' she urged Nina and Shelley.

With a bit of huffing and puffing Jenny hauled herself out of her chair and fairly flew across the room. She disappeared into the hallway and they heard the sound of the front door opening. Muted voices followed and all the women exchanged curious glances.

Nina longed to run back upstairs to change but Shelley was already propelling her towards the sofa. So she sat and waited.

In the next moment, Jenny's pink arm shot through the open doorway and flicked the light switch, plunging the sitting room into semi darkness. The only illumination came from the open serving hatch to the kitchen and a couple of table lamps. Next came the unmistakable beat of

INTIMATE DISCLOSURES

taped music – loud and funky. Then the *pièce de résistance* appeared through the doorway – a young black guy, dressed in a white tuxedo and black trousers, followed by another young guy who was white. Looking like a negative image of the black dancer, he was dressed in a black tuxedo and white trousers and had long straight corn-coloured hair that reached halfway down his back.

As the two men danced into the room, moving and gyrating to the music, all the women shrank back into their chairs instinctively.

Nina found herself holding her breath, her cheeks going bright pink with embarrassment. One glance in their direction told her that she and Shelley had not gone unnoticed by the dancers. Hardly surprising really, Nina told herself, considering the way they were dressed – or rather underdressed. Knowing she was fighting a losing battle, she tried to adjust her neckline so that it wasn't quite so revealing and at the same time pull down the hem of her dress to cover her stocking tops.

Despite her embarrassment she felt herself responding to the dancers' interested gazes. Particularly that of the blond dancer. Although she thought the black guy was extremely attractive, there was something about the blond one. Something base and raunchy. Quite simply, she thought, feeling her stomach tense and her heartbeat quicken, he oozed sex appeal. And she was a sucker for long hair.

It scarcely surprised her when the blond dancer bumped and ground his way over to her, removing his tuxedo on the way and flinging it carelessly at a woman who caught it and clutched it to her like a life belt. Nina glanced at the woman, her eyes quickly taking in the flushed cheeks, over bright eyes and stunned expression.

All at once her attention was diverted again to the dancers. Having dispensed with jackets, shoes and socks, they were now removing their shirts. Swaying directly in front of her, so that Nina had no option but to look at him, the blond dancer began to unbutton his shirt. His actions were slow and provocative, unfastening the buttons one by one to expose glimpses of a smooth-skinned, muscular chest. When all the buttons were undone he ripped the shirt wide open, revealing a well toned torso that rippled and gleamed enticingly under a thin film of oil.

Nina felt hot. She tried in vain to look away but felt her gaze rivetted to that expanse of golden glistening flesh right in front of her. The scent of him assailed her nostrils: musky, fruity, definitely all male. She felt her juices trickling from her, her breasts heaving and thrusting hard against the insubstantial bodice of the maid's dress. Hot all over, Nina felt as though her body was blossoming right out of the tiny dress. Through a haze of arousal she realised he was holding out his hand to her, inviting her to dance with him.

No. No, thank you. She shook her head wildly, feeling her churning lust battle against her unwillingness to put herself in a humiliating situation. But his grip on her wrist was firm and with an insistent, 'Yes,' he hauled her to her feet.

'Christ!'

Nina heard his exclamation as she stood up and saw him glance at his partner. The black guy nodded approvingly, his liquid brown eyes casting a seductive glance over her body before reaching for Shelley's hand.

Shelley tried to demur, like Nina but it seemed, her protests were also totally in vain. In a moment she was on her feet, her slim, sinuous body barely concealed by the scrap of blue satin and lace. The black dancer whirled Shelley around and then clasped her to him, his hand spanning the small of her back.

Trying to take her mind off her own embarrassment, Nina concentrated on watching Shelley instead. She couldn't help noticing how the insubstantial blue satiny fabric had worked its way between Shelley's buttocks and how delightfully they trembled as she danced.

INTIMATE DISCLOSURES

Less reticent now, the other women in the room began to clap and call out words of encouragement.

'Over here big boy,' one of them shouted. Followed by the communal cry of, 'Get 'em off.'

Feminism at its finest, Nina thought as she tried to ignore the way the blond dancer's hand was creeping up her thigh. Feeling aroused now by the sight of Shelley, she tried to concentrate on the other women in the room. Jenny was back in her seat, looking as pleased as Punch with her little surprise, Nina noticed. And several of the other women, Rachel included, looked as though they could cheerfully murder her and Shelley for being the objects of the dancers' attentions.

For a brief moment, the dancers left Nina and Shelley stranded in the middle of the room while they gyrated over to a couple of the other women and urged them to unfasten their trousers. Hesitant only for a split second, the women complied, egged on by their companions who all reached out to touch a portion of muscular abdomen and thigh.

Stripped to minuscule tanga briefs – white for the black guy and black for the white – the dancers returned to the middle of the room.

'Prove that it's true what they say about black men,' one of the women called out.

Then, 'Come on blondie, prove it isn't.'

The blond dancer leaned his head close to Nina's and whispered in her ear. 'Do you think we should?'

She giggled nervously. 'I don't think you'll get out of here alive if you don't.'

His next question stunned her. 'Then would you mind doing the honours?'

Glancing around nervously, Nina bit her bottom lip. She sank to her knees in front of the dancer and found her fingertips inching under the black elasticated band that hugged his slim hips.

'Do it, do it!' the women chanted.

With a sigh of resignation tinged with anticipation, Nina tugged hard and brought the tanga down to his ankles. The cock that sprang free was rock hard. It slapped against his belly and rebounded to tap her on the forehead. Almost unwillingly, she raised her eyes. God, what a sight!

Covered with fine blond hair, his scrotum was pink and wrinkled and his blushing cock seemed huge from where she was kneeling. It reared up proudly, almost to his navel. Suddenly, she felt herself being jostled. Glancing sideways she noticed that one of the women – who had seemed particularly quiet and mousy – was practically crawling up the dancer's leg.

Obligingly, and with only the slightest twinge of regret, Nina moved. She sat back on the sofa, desperate to catch the breath which seemed to have deserted her and watched wide eyed as the woman took the dancer's cock in her eager hands. With feverish hands, the woman caressed it only for a moment before feeding it centimetre by centimetre into her wide open mouth.

'I never knew Barbara could deep throat,' Nina heard one of the other women remark.

'Well,' said another, 'you know what they say. It's the quiet ones that are the worst.'

Nina was so engrossed in watching her first ever live sex show, she didn't realise straight away that Shelley and the black dancer were missing from the room. Slipping back upstairs to go to the loo, she passed Rachel's bedroom and thought she heard strange noises. When she opened the door the first thing she saw was a taut black bottom moving up and down rhythmically. Then she noticed the pale, slender legs wrapped around his waist and a familiar scrap of blue satin discarded on the floor.

At that point something strange happened to Nina. All her finer instincts told her to close the door quietly and go back downstairs. But for some reason she stayed, watching through the crack in the door. She could feel her excitement

INTIMATE DISCLOSURES

mounting, her heart hammering and the blood pounding through her veins as though it were she being fucked on the bed by the dancer and not Shelley. Her vulva throbbed insistently and she reached under the short hem of her skirt to cover it with her hand. As her knees sagged with unresolved desire, her fingers slipped between her slightly parted thighs. Through the thin silk of her knickers she could feel the heat emanating from her body. The crotch was damp with her own juices, almost steaming. So much so that she could smell herself.

A heavy cloud of sex seemed to hang in the room. The musky scent, the heat, the careless moans and groans of the two people on the bed, the rhythmic twang of bedsprings.

Nina was thoroughly engrossed, watching covertly and stroking herself, until all at once she became aware of someone behind her. A hard body pressed against her back, while two hands slid around her body to enfold her breasts. She guessed who it was but didn't want visual confirmation. Instead she kept her eyes fixed on the sight of the copulating couple while her own fingers massaged her swollen vulva and the hands around her breasts kneaded and rubbed until her nipples were swollen and straining at the material which covered them.

Warm breath and the touch of lips on her shoulder. A hand moving to sweep her hair out of the way, then sliding over her shoulder again and down inside her neckline. This time the hand cupped her bare breast, the fingers playing with the aching bud of her nipple. Stifling her moans, she kept on looking, kept on caressing herself. In a moment she would come. She could feel the telltale signs of her orgasm. The heat, the steady, growing, pleasurable ache that spread from her lumbar region to swamp her pelvis. Everything else was swept away into oblivion as she gave herself up to the heady sensation of the moment. The dark eroticism that enfolded and gripped her, dragging her down into the abyss of pleasure.

Rocking on her heels, she felt grateful for the steadying influence of the body behind her and the hands holding her breasts. She continued to caress herself, waves of warm desire coursing through her. Her muted cry as she came a second time was drowned out by the much louder groans of the couple on the bed. Then, after a moment, she removed her hand from between her legs and felt the hands around her breasts slide away. Leaving only a final kiss on her shoulder the body behind her melted away to nothing. Taking a step back from the open door, she leaned against the wall for a moment to catch her breath.

When her heartbeat had slowed to a gentle canter and she felt some strength return to her legs, she backed quietly away from the doorway and went to the loo just as she had intended in the first place.

By the time she returned to the bedroom she found Shelley there but no sign of the black dancer. Laying naked across the bed, her arms flung over her head, her legs splayed in reckless abandon, Nina thought Shelley looked well and truly fucked. She stifled a giggle then blushed when the young woman suddenly raised her head and looked at her.

'I got a bit carried away,' Shelley said carelessly, by way of explanation. Moving as though every muscle in her body ached, she began to gather up her original clothes and put them on.

Nina debated whether to tell Shelley what had happened to her in the meantime but decided against it. The whole episode had a dreamlike quality that she didn't feel like sharing. She would tell Tom, of course, when she got home but that was different. He was her best friend and her lover, he would appreciate the experience for what it was. Shelley, she suspected, would have a bit of a snigger about it and then rush downstairs to tell all the others. And Nina didn't want that. To her mind the erotic episode should not be sullied in any way and for now it was her secret – hers and the blond dancer's.

INTIMATE DISCLOSURES

After they had both changed into their own clothes, Nina and Shelley went downstairs to rejoin the party. The dancers were still there, fully clothed again and drinking orange juice. The blond one glanced up and gave her a conspiratorial wink. Nina blushed but tried to look nonchalant about the whole thing. It had happened, it was over, end of story.

After a while, conscious of their usefulness as possible subjects for the documentary, Nina gathered up all her professional aplomb and approached the two dancers. As succinctly as possible, she told them all about *Intimate Disclosures*.

Arrik, the black guy, told her that he and Kyle – the blond one – were professional strippers and often danced as part of a larger troupe which was similar to the Chippendales.

'We usually do hen parties and that sort of thing,' he explained, 'or office leaving do's, they're very popular. When it's all of us together – The Dream Team – we work the clubs.'

'Would you like to become TV stars?' Nina asked, pitching straight in.

Arrik glanced at Kyle, who shrugged his broad shoulders nonchalantly. 'Sure, OK, why not?' he said, treating Nina to a lazy smile. 'Can we do our routine on camera?'

She nodded enthusiastically. 'I was hoping you would. Then afterwards perhaps you could just talk to the presenter about the sort of venues you perform at. Pretty much what you told me in fact.'

With a grin, Arrik rubbed his hands together and said, 'Sounds like great publicity.'

And a giant step forward for me, Nina thought.

Shortly after that the dancers left, each had one of Nina's cards which she'd personally had to tuck in their trouser pockets, and she had theirs, just in case. Returning to the heart of the gathering, she found the atmosphere somewhat deflated.

'Come on,' she said, feeling quite lighthearted now, 'let's

all have another glass of wine and then try out some of these toys. Here, tell you what, Jenny, show me what that one does—'

Nina came away from the party with the vibrating egg and the French Maid's dress already bought and paid for. She had also ordered a couple of different vibrators and something which was 'Guaranteed to suck your nipples into blissful oblivion.'

'I've always wanted my nipples sucked into blissful oblivion,' she told Maisie as they shared a taxi across the river – Maisie lived in Clapham.

Maisie laughed. She hadn't disclosed the nature of her purchases but was very enthusiastic about Nina's success with Arrik and Kyle.

'That was a bit of luck, wasn't it?' Nina said. 'Oh, but I forgot to tell you some even better news. Your friend Shelley told me she knows lots of women who work in "the industry",' she made inverted comma signs with her fingers, 'anyway, I've got her phone number. She's going to arrange for me to meet some of her friends.' She sat back and sighed, feeling pleased with the way the evening had turned out.

'Shelley's a diamond,' Maisie said, 'she'll set you right and if you ever want an assistant you only have to ask. I haven't got that much on at the moment.'

Smiling at Maisie in the half light, Nina nodded. 'Thanks,' she murmured, giving Maisie's hand a quick squeeze of gratitude, 'I may well take you up on that.'

As she had predicted, far from being put out that Nina had managed to enjoy an erotic encounter that didn't involve him, Tom was wholly appreciative of the episode. He was even more enthusiastic about the maid's outfit.

'I know it's a bit corny,' Nina called out from the bathroom, where she had insisted on getting changed, 'promise you won't laugh?'

INTIMATE DISCLOSURES

When she emerged from the bathroom, once again clad in the short black dress, stockings and even higher heels than the ones she had been wearing all evening, Tom's expression was far from one of amusement.

She couldn't help noticing how the dark shadow of lust obliterated the expectant look on his face the moment she stepped through the doorway into the bedroom. He was reclining on the bed, wearing only a pair of blue jeans, his dark hair still damp and curly from the shower.

'My God, you look fucking gorgeous,' he said in a voice that was low and filled with admiration. 'Walk around the bed, let me look at you properly.'

Feeling as though they had never set eyes on each other before, Nina did as he asked. She walked unsteadily around the wide double bed, never taking her eyes from his. The dark eroticism of his gaze spoke volumes to her, making her body flame and moisten with desire. Far from feeling embarrassed, or idiotic in the little black dress with its lacy hem, she now felt voluptuous and tarty. Sex on legs all over again, she thought. But this time it was all for Tom's benefit and they had hours and hours until morning. Hours which they could fill with tender, sensuous lovemaking, or hot, raunchy fucking – whatever they chose to indulge themselves in.

Chapter Four

Several days later, Nina was surprised to get a phone call from Angel. She was at her desk, working her way down a list of sex shops which she had been systematically calling for mail order catalogues.

'Oh, hi, Angel,' she said, picking up the receiver on the second ring, 'I didn't expect to hear from you so soon.'

'Well, I'm in a bit of a spot really,' Angel replied, coming straight to the point, 'I'm hoping you can help me out.'

Nina sat back and put her feet up on the desk, crossing them at the ankles and knocking a stack of magazines and catalogues on the floor in the process. Glancing at the floor, she decided to ignore them for the moment.

'What's up?' she said into the receiver.

'A party,' Angel said, 'quite an exclusive one but I've got no one to go with. Brett's away for a couple of days on business and all my friends are otherwise engaged. Mind you,' she added, lowering her voice a couple of octaves, 'not that many of them know that me and Brett swing.'

Probably not the sort of thing you go around publicising to all and sundry, Nina thought privately, aloud she said, 'So you want me to go with you, is that it?'

'Yes,' Angel replied, 'well, you and Tom really, if he can manage it. You see the thing is—' she paused to clear her throat, 'this party is called Male Overload. The whole point is that there are supposed to be at least three guys to every female.'

'You mean Tom would be expected to participate?' Nina

felt ridiculous for asking the question but she wasn't sure how he would feel about it.

She heard Angel's laughter and felt like refusing outright. But, reminding herself that this was all part of her current assignment, she promised Angel she would speak to Tom about it and get back to her.

'Give me a ring when you get home from work,' Angel said, 'if you are going we'll need to be there by nine at the latest.'

'Me, go and fuck a load of strange women – are you sure that's what you want?' Tom's reaction was quick and exactly what Nina expected.

'I'm not sure if I do,' she admitted, feeling a certain nervousness churn away inside her, 'how do you feel about it?'

She could imagine Tom's shrug as he replied, 'I could cope with it, up to a point. Provided that I fancied them and everything but I could just as easily live without it. I don't want to do anything that's going to upset you, or spoil what we have together.'

Nina paused to mull over his reply for a moment. She was touched and grateful for his response. It was true that no job was worth putting their relationship on the line for.

'We could just go along and see what it's all about,' she suggested hesitantly, 'then if I can't cope with the set up we could make our excuses and leave.'

'Fine by me,' Tom said affably, 'you know me, I'm easy.' He gave a little chuckle. 'In a manner of speaking that is.'

A slow smile spread across Nina's face and she wished Tom was there right at that moment so she could hug him, and kiss him, and . . .

'Nina, is that a personal call?' Karen appeared by her side looking flustered and furious in equal measure.

'Uh-oh, got to go,' Nina muttered to Tom, 'I'll give Angel a call and tell her we're on for it. See you tonight.'

INTIMATE DISCLOSURES

'Yeah, see you tonight, sweetheart,' Tom said warmly.

As she put down the receiver, Nina glanced up at Karen, guilt written all over her face. Then she gave herself a mental slap, her call to Tom had been in the interests of the company at the end of the day.

'I was talking to my boyfriend, but it was business, sort of,' she said, 'another bit of research I intend to carry out tonight.'

Karen, she noticed, looked sceptical. 'Are you sure you're not enjoying this research a bit too much?' she demanded. Noticing the top shelf magazines and sex shop catalogues scattered on the floor, she stooped down and began gathering them up.

Nina felt herself colouring. 'No, of course not,' she insisted hotly, 'I'm just doing what needs to be done, that's all.'

'Hm.' Looking exceedingly tight lipped, Karen dropped the magazines disdainfully on Nina's desk, as though they were covered in maggots and turned to walk away. 'By the way,' she said, glancing over her shoulder, 'someone called Kyle telephoned for you while you were at lunch. He should be ringing back, oh—' she paused to glance at her watch, 'about now.' With that she twisted her pursed lips into a replica of a smile and stalked across the room to her own desk.

'Kyle, huh?' Maisie said, leaning across her desk and looking at Nina expectantly, 'he was the dancer at Rachel's party wasn't he?'

'The one and only,' Nina said, feeling exhausted for some reason. She realised why she felt so tired. The constant telephoning and saying the same thing time after time, coupled with the unremitting nastiness of most of the literature she had been sent were beginning to take their toll. Just then the phone rang. It was Kyle, of course, right on cue.

'Hi, babe,' he said, 'I thought you might be interested to

know that the Dream Team will be performing at Nirvana on Wednesday night, would you like a couple of free tickets?'

Nina did a double take – would she? 'I thought Nirvana was a gay club,' she said.

'It is mostly,' Kyle agreed, 'but on Wednesday nights the club's open to all-comers.' He sniggered at his unintentional pun.

'Well, I'd love to go,' Nina enthused, smiling down the receiver, 'could you pop the tickets in the post to me?'

'No need,' Kyle said. 'You can pick them up at the door. I'll make sure they're there waiting for you. We'll be going on at about midnight.'

'OK, I'll be there,' Nina promised. 'And thanks a lot. Remind me to buy you a drink when you finish.'

Putting the phone down, Nina turned to Maisie and told her about Kyle's invitation. 'If Tom isn't interested, would you like to go?' she offered.

Maisie's red hair, which today was uncharacteristically smoothed into a chin length bob, fluttered like bird's wings as she nodded enthusiastically.

'You betcha,' she said. 'I love it there, plus I fancy a bit of that Arrik for myself. Shelley told me he's a fabulous lay.'

'Well, she should know,' Nina said.

At this point she decided to abandon all pretence at working. Instead she spent the rest of the afternoon telling an open-mouthed Maisie all about what had happened upstairs at Rachel's house.

Steam rose from the bath in a thick cloud as Nina climbed into it. Wincing slightly as her toes touched the water and felt its temperature, Nina eased herself down slowly through the thick layer of bubbles. If she was going to be jumped on by several men that evening, she at least wanted to start off with a clean body. Plus she needed desperately to relax. It had been an exhausting day.

Just as she felt the tautness leaving her muscles and had eased herself back against the padded bath cushion with a long sigh of bliss, she heard the sound of the phone ringing.

'Damn!' She felt tempted to ignore it. Five minutes she had been in the bath at the most, five bloody minutes!

Foam dripped from her, sliding down her shiny wet body as she stood up and climbed out of the bath again. She left bubbly footprints on the carpet as she padded, naked and dripping, into the bedroom and picked up the extension phone.

'Hello, Nina Spencer.'

'Hi, sweetheart.' Tom's voice sounded low and seductive and Nina gripped the receiver, a slow smile spreading over her face. It matched the warmth that spread upwards from her toes and engulfed her.

'Tom, where are you – when are you coming home?' she asked.

'Sorry, darling, I'm at the office. Geoff called me in, then when I arrived he plonked a load of plans on my desk that need going over.'

Nina grimaced inwardly. Tom was newly qualified and only six months into his first full time job.

'Are you telling me you're going to be late?' she said, playing the toes of her right foot over a heap of bubbles on the carpet.

'Very,' he said, sounding glum now, 'I've just ordered in a pizza. I'll probably be here for another few hours at least.'

Nina glanced at the clock. It was almost seven.

'But we've got to be at the party by nine,' she said, frustration welling up inside her and lending her voice a plaintive note. At that moment she envisaged Tom running his fingers through his hair distractedly. He never liked to let her down and she could imagine how frustrated he must be feeling. 'Look,' she amended, 'don't worry about it. I'll go along with Angel and see what this thing's all about. I don't have to participate.'

'You do whatever you want to do,' Tom said gently. 'It's important for you and your job. I won't lose any sleep over it, I promise.'

'Are you sure?' Nina could never quite believe he could be so laid back about the sex side of their relationship.

'You know I am.' His voice sounded warm and reassuring. 'What we have is special and you know I never say anything I don't mean.'

Nina laughed softly, once again wishing that he was there so she could hold him. 'OK, my darling,' she said, 'I'll give you the full rundown when I get back.'

Angel was more put out by Tom's non-attendance than Nina. She flicked her hair over her shoulder and pouted her pretty lips.

'We need all the men we can get at these parties,' she said, 'especially good-looking ones. Some of them can be quite hideous.'

Nina immediately thought of Brett and uncharitably wondered how awful a man had to be for Angel to categorise him as hideous. It made her wish she hadn't bothered to come at all and a host of doubts surfaced and began clouding her mind. Despite them, Angel was already walking across the lobby of the hotel where they had arranged to meet, making for the reception desk.

Male Overload, Angel had told her, was always held in the penthouse suite of this particular hotel. Although nothing was actually said about the nature of the parties, the management turned a blind eye to the number of people arriving and going up to the top floor.

'Some of the others are already here,' Angel said, leading Nina over to the lifts. She glanced at her wristwatch, a delicate gold bangle with a black heart shaped dial. Her

INTIMATE DISCLOSURES

petulant mouth finally formed a smile. 'I hope they haven't started without us.'

While they travelled up to the penthouse in the lift, Nina reclined against the mirrored wall and studied Angel. Looking as petite and as lovely as before, this time she was wearing a long white cotton dress that reached the ankle strap of her gold sandals. The simple dress set off her olive colouring to perfection and Nina couldn't help feeling a rush of desire as her eyes swept over the young woman. Just for a fleeting moment she thought it was a shame that she and Angel weren't on their way up to a room which they were going to share – alone.

'I love your dress,' Angel said, making it clear that she too had been appraising Nina in the same way.

Nina glanced down and then at her reflection. For tonight's little adventure she had deliberately chosen to wear something that was both alluring and easy to remove. The plain red crepe dress had thin, shoestring straps and a swirly flirty skirt that ended a couple of inches above the knee. And she had teamed it with a simple pair of red high heeled sandals and matching soft leather bag. It was too warm to wear a coat so she had slipped her black leather jacket over her shoulders and now she shrugged it off and draped it over her arm.

'Thanks,' she said, responding to Angel's compliment with a warm smile, 'I was just thinking the same about you.'

She noticed that Angel looked as though she was about to make a move towards her and felt a tingle of anticipation. But right at that moment the lift bounced to a gentle halt and the door slid open.

'We're here,' Angel said needlessly, stepping across the threshold and giving Nina an inviting wink.

Flutters of excitement started up in Nina's stomach again as she stepped into a cream painted, square lobby. The walls were hung with simple watercolour prints and a coat stand stood in the right hand corner flanked by two doors.

'The bathroom and the sitting room,' Angel said as she waved her hand carelessly.

They hung their jackets up on the stand – Angel's was pale green linen – and then Angel asked Nina if she wanted to use the bathroom before they joined the party.

Nina shook her head. 'No, I'm OK,' she said, 'shall we just go in?'

Trepidation gripped her as Angel opened the door. But if Nina was expecting to be pounced on by a couple of guys the minute she walked into the room she was to be disappointed. About twenty guys were there but all of them were seated, either at the small bar which ran along the left-hand wall, or on large pale blue and cream upholstered sofas.

They were a mixed bunch. Some middle aged, a few young ones who looked barely out of puberty in Nina's opinion, and most of them who looked to be in their thirties or early forties. The three women who occupied the room stood out like sore thumbs.

One was about forty and was dressed in a tight black leather dress. She had shoulder length black hair with the odd wisp of grey and a plump but nicely proportioned face and figure. She was also heavily decked out in sparkly costume jewellery.

The second woman, who was seated at the bar, was young, very thin, with long, straight dark blonde hair and was dressed in tan suede trousers and a white short sleeved tee-shirt. And the third seemed to be a composite of the other two. Slender but curvaceous, with mid-brown hair knotted loosely at the nape of her neck. She wore a nice open expression which was as uncomplicated as her clothing – a predominantly red, wrap-over dress sprinkled with a multicoloured floral design.

'Shall we have a drink and I'll introduce you to the people here that I know?' Angel suggested, leading Nina over to the

INTIMATE DISCLOSURES

bar. She exchanged lingering kisses on both cheeks with the girl in the suede trousers. 'Nina, this is Liz. Liz, Nina.'

Nina smiled and shook hands with Liz.

'Drink ladies?' The barman interrupted them.

Angel glanced at him and then at Nina and Liz.

'I'm OK,' Liz said, putting a protective hand over her glass.

'Gin and tonic for me,' Nina chipped in. Glancing around the room again she felt the knot in her stomach tighten and added, 'Better make that a double.'

Stiff drink in hand, Nina then followed Angel over to one of the sofas where the raven haired woman sat, surrounded by men. One of them had his hand on her knee and another, who stood behind her, was sliding his hands suggestively across the pale expanse of her bare throat.

'Jim, Dave and Ricky,' Angel said, pointing to each man in turn, 'and Soraya, our hostess.'

Wafting a vague smile around, Nina decided that she quite liked the look of Ricky. He was one of the younger ones. Tall and lean with a shock of blond curls, he looked fresh faced and his face bore a 'where am I – what am I doing here?' expression. Despite this, his pale blue eyes hinted at a keen intelligence and the way he said 'Hello,' and held out his hand told Nina that he came from a middle class background.

Dave looked quite nice, she thought, turning her attention to the other two men. Nice that was in an average bank managerish, or teacherish kind of way, Nina decided, eyeing his mid brown short back and sides and puppy-like expression – excitable, yet repressed, just waiting to be let off the leash. Jim, as far as she was concerned, was a complete no no – too old, too fat and wearing too much of a 'Yes, let me get stuck in!' expression for her liking.

She shuddered inwardly just imagining what it might be like to have his naked body floundering all over her and was relieved when Angel moved quickly on to the next sofa. There, the young woman introduced the three men, Mark, Simon and John.

'How biblical,' Nina quipped, feeling slightly tipsy already on only one drink – there hadn't been time to eat when she got home from work.

Simon grinned, making her warm to him instantly, but the other two remained stony faced. Well, they're off my bonking list, she said to herself, giggling inwardly.

Soraya came over to them. 'Looks like that's it, ladies,' she said with a disparaging glance around the room.

'What, only five of us?' Angel exclaimed.

Nina felt Angel's words sinking in like a medicine ball in quicksand. Surely not, she told herself, there had to be more women attending this odd little soiree. She had carried out a quick head count and actually noted that there were twenty two men in the room.

'Four,' Soraya amended, looking glum, 'I've got my period.'

Angel made a hopeless gesture with her hands and sighed. 'We can't, Soraya. I know it's Male Overload and everything but honestly, twenty odd men between four of us—' her words tailed away on another sigh.

'Like it or lump it,' Soraya responded bluntly, 'if you want to stay on the guest list the bedroom awaits.' One of her bejewelled hands waved towards a door that stood closed behind the grouping of sofas.

Icy perspiration broke out on Nina's forehead and more trickled into the deep valley between her breasts.

'I'm not sure about this, Angel,' she muttered, gripping the young woman's arm.

Angel turned her head and gave Nina a reassuring smile. 'It'll be OK,' she said, 'I promise. If too many men come over to you, or you're approached by any you don't like the look of, just tell them to fuck off.'

Nina stared at her. She had only heard Angel's delightful lips form nice words before. Before Nina knew what was happening, Soraya was leading the way to the bedroom and Angel was taking her arm.

'Come on,' she said encouragingly, 'we'll share the same bed. It will be all right.'

Allowing herself to be led into the bright, white on white bedroom which contained two king sized beds, Nina was relieved when Soraya moved to the windows and drew the curtains. With the room cloaked in shadows, it didn't seem quite so daunting to take off her few items of clothing and lie down on the bed next to Angel. They began to kiss and caress and Nina hardly noticed as the men began to gradually filter into the room.

A male hand touched Nina's thigh and when she glanced over her shoulder she noticed that it belonged to Ricky. 'I hope you don't mind,' he said, sounding as unsure of himself as Nina felt.

With a slight smile of encouragement, she shook her head. Rolling over onto her back she appraised him for a moment, her eyes taking in the pale lean body that looked as though it had never seen sunlight and the light dusting of freckles across his hairless chest. She couldn't bring herself to look lower. The fact that he was about to fuck her in a moment didn't seem to register with her and she lay passively back as he leaned over her and kissed her.

The touch of his lips was light and pleasant. He tasted minty, as though he had just brushed his teeth and when Nina felt his fingers inching between her slightly parted thighs she didn't recoil but let him explore her body. He was inside her in moments, with hardly any preliminaries. Fortunately for Nina, her short-lived session with Angel had been enough to arouse her.

His cock slid inside her easily and he began to move rhythmically, without any urgency. Nina felt absurdly grateful for this. Somehow she had imagined herself as a kind of sexual cross Channel ferry – roll on and roll off. By turning her head she could see that far more activity was taking place on the other bed. As far as she could make out, it was just a heaving mass of bodies.

In contrast, the bed chosen by herself and Angel had only three other occupants: Ricky, of course, and two older men who were taking what looked like very good care of Angel. One was sucking her small, pointed breasts while another, with receding hair and a slight paunch was thrusting manfully away inside her slight body. At least Angel looks as though she's enjoying herself, Nina thought, deciding that perhaps she should make the effort to appear a mite more enthusiastic.

The trouble was, she mused as she gripped Ricky's shoulders and made a few groaning sounds, she felt almost completely numb. Far from erotic, the experience was not all that thrilling to her body. Tom had trained her – and she supposed trained was the right word – to appreciate sensuality. Sometimes it was a question of quality rather than quantity as they both had demanding jobs, but that seemed infinitely preferable to her. Particularly now, she thought, coming back to the present with a jolt. Ricky, who had obviously climaxed without her even noticing, was moving away from her and another man had taken his place.

'No,' Nina said, raising her head off the pillow, 'not yet, I want a rest.'

A subdued titter ran around the bed. More men had grouped around her and Angel now. Only half of whom appealed to Nina marginally more than a visit to the dentist. She was relieved when a rather stocky man with jet black hair caught in a ponytail elbowed his way through the group and placed a possessive hand on her thigh.

'You heard the lady,' he said, 'give her some space.'

Sitting down on the edge of the bed, he glared at the other men with beady dark eyes until they backed away, all at once looking unsure of themselves. He turned, his stern expression at once creasing into a smile that concertinaed his face and seemed to reach right to the roots of his hair.

INTIMATE DISCLOSURES

'Thanks,' Nina said, not knowing what else to say. All of a sudden she felt conscious of her naked state and her hands fluttered uselessly over her breasts and pubis.

'Don't,' he said, grasping her by the wrists, 'please.'

His entreaty was said so gently that Nina immediately felt herself relaxing and allowed her arms to go limp. In fact, she realised, her whole body felt limp. Whether it was with relief, or something else she wasn't sure. A slow warmth stole over her and she knew she was blushing when she allowed her gaze to meet his.

'This is my first time,' she said, feeling as though she offered him some kind of explanation. 'At one of these parties I mean.'

'It never crossed my mind that you were a virgin,' he responded with another smile.

Nina felt herself blushing harder as she smiled back at him. Out of all the men there she felt a connection with the stranger that she hadn't experienced in a long time. And it made her wonder why she hadn't noticed him before. She trembled as he stroked a lazy hand across her stomach.

'What's your name?' she managed to gasp out.

'Rob,' he said as he trailed artistically shaped fingertips lower, over her hip bone before lightly grazing her pubis. 'Short for Roberto. My father is Argentinian.'

Ah, that explains it then, Nina thought, and just managed to stop herself from making the observation aloud. From all she had read, and gleaned from two friends who had holidayed in Argentina, Argentinian men were renowned for their sensitivity to women, and macho attitude to other men. No wonder the others had backed off at the first glint of his hard black eyes.

She sighed and without realising it, undulated her naked body, inviting him to explore her further.

Slipping off his jacket, shoes and socks, he lay full length beside her on the bed. His shirt was silky, a bright buttercup yellow and his loose designer suit jet black to match his hair.

'So what brings you here?' he asked as he resumed stroking her breasts and stomach.

Nina debated whether to tell him the truth, then thought better of it.

'Curiosity,' she said, 'and an invitation from Angel.' She allowed her eyes to drift to the young woman next to her who seemed to be enjoying herself under a heap of masculine flesh.

'Ah, the lovely Angel.' Rob spoke as though he knew Angel well and Nina didn't doubt it. After all, they were both probably old hands at the swingers scene. 'You like her?' A silky black eyebrow arched inquiringly, yet his eyes indicated that he already knew the answer.

'Yes, I do. She is lovely.'

'And you have fucked her already?'

Nina felt her stomach clench. The question struck her as deliciously intimate and she liked the way he wound his vaguely foreign sounding tongue around the word *fuck*.

'Not exactly,' she said. Briefly, amid a lot of blushes, she told him how she and Angel had met and what had transpired between them. Then she laughed self consciously. 'Anyway, I'm not sure that two women can fuck each other.'

His dark gaze made her go all liquid inside, reminding her for a fleeting instant of Tom and the way he often looked at her. Which wasn't at all surprising, she realised, as her lover had more than a little Latin blood flowing through his own veins. Perhaps this was why she felt strangely drawn to him. Not just because he had acted like her knight in shining armour, saving her from the marauding hordes.

'Of course they can,' he said. 'It is a beautiful sight.' He appeared to be remembering something, a blissful expression suffusing his face. Then he added, 'I would very much like to watch you and Angel making love one day.'

Feeling as though her stomach had been turned inside out,

INTIMATE DISCLOSURES

Nina gazed back at him. Her head felt fuzzy, the thoughts inside softened around the edges as though partially erased.

'I don't think that's going to be possible,' she said, tearing her eyes away from his face to glance around the rest of the room.

His laughter was gentle and loaded with promise. 'No, of course not here and now,' he said, 'but perhaps some other time.'

'Perhaps.' Nina sighed as she lay her head back and stared up at the ceiling.

The fingertips playing across her breasts were starting to make her feel extremely aroused. Her nipples had hardened under his skilful touch ages ago but now she felt the insistent tug of desire from within. The threads of erotic passion tightening, passing urgent messages from one erogenous zone to another.

'May I fuck you tonight?' he asked solicitously. He paused to stroke the flat of his palm over her torso. It lingered at the apex of her thighs, just covering the soft bush of pubic hair but doing nothing more.

Silently, she nodded and allowed her gaze to travel over his body. Reaching out, she began to unfasten the buttons on his shirt, pausing every so often to explore each portion of newly exposed flesh with her fingertips.

It seemed strange really, she thought as she watched him shrug off his shirt and then unbutton the waistband of his trousers, that the rest of the room and its occupants seemed to have receded into insignificance.

Even Angel and her multiple lovers, who were just a few inches away from her and who occasionally brushed against her arm, or hip, seemed remote somehow. It was as though in the midst of an orgy, she and Rob had managed to create an oasis for themselves. As an alternative to mindless fucking with a series of complete strangers, Nina thought her encounter with Rob was the best thing that could have possibly happened to her that evening.

Chapter Five

The touch of Rob's fingertips on her inner thigh, circling, always circling, slowly and provocatively, made Nina's body tingle with anticipation. Someone had put on some background music – Mendelssohn's *Notturno* from A Midsummer Night's Dream – which went some way to drowning out all the heaving and groaning going on elsewhere in the room. And it was this that filled Nina's ears.

Closing her eyes, she allowed herself to drift along on the tide of music, allowing the delicate strains and the exquisite sensation of Rob's caresses to take over her mind and body to the exclusion of all else. She could feel her sex responding to him, her labia swelling and opening out, her clitoris tingling. Her vagina felt so wet. And so open. Rob's hands gently parted her thighs still further and as she felt the cool rush of air glance across her most intimate places she shivered.

'You have a lovely body,' Rob murmured, 'soft and curvaceous. All ripe and wet and ready. And what a gorgeous cunt you have, my dear. All the better for eating you.'

Nina stiffened slightly, then melted again. Her heart was hammering behind her ribs, her breathing coming in shallow gasps. It took every ounce of her willpower not to beg him to simply take her straight away. Part of her was concerned that someone else might come over and try to participate but if they did she wasn't aware of it. Orgies weren't for her. She hadn't thought they would be and she felt even more certain now. But this thing with Rob. The masterful way he had taken possession of her, repelling all invaders, was another matter. It excited her like crazy.

Reaching down with one hand she ran her fingers through his hair and stroked his shoulder. It was firm and muscular, the only part of his naked body she could reach. Her fingers gripped and kneaded the muscles frantically as her desire for him grew. She could feel the occasional brush of his thigh against her leg and hip. His flesh was warm and covered with soft, downy hair. Similarly his chest. When he moved and she managed to graze her fingertips across it, she felt the fuzzy texture for herself.

Everything seemed to be happening in slow motion and with a vague, dreamlike quality. She could hear Rob's whispered compliments and erotic phrases above the music and the other sounds in the room. 'So lovely. Such a pretty face. Mm, what a lovely, juicy little body—' The words made her tremble and flame with passion. Erotic desire swept through her, urging her to sit up and try to pull him close to her.

'Please, don't keep teasing me,' she murmured plaintively.

He slapped her inner thigh lightly, his fingertips whispering over her swollen outer labia as he did so.

'Don't be so impatient,' he admonished her in a low growl of a voice, which only made her body crave him even more. 'I will fuck you but all in good time. First I must touch and taste.'

She trembled at the promise of his words, her body issuing another trickle of moisture. And then she felt his fingers exploring her vulva. Light and deft, they stroked and tantalised her eager flesh, spreading her so wide open she bit her bottom lip as she felt her cheeks flood with the proof of her shame.

'You are aching for it, aren't you?' he said, his words drifting up from between her widespread legs, his words as tantalising as the warmth of his breath on her already

INTIMATE DISCLOSURES

heated flesh. His fingertips stroked around the outer edge of her vagina. Teasing, always teasing, while other fingers massaged her swollen clitoris.

'Yes,' she gasped, raising her hips and flexing her thighs so that she was even more open to him, 'please. I need to come. I want to feel you inside me.'

She gasped again as his fingers pinched her clitoris hard. It was painful yet, at the same time, she was surprised to feel a spasm of pleasure. It rocked her, and held her in its grip. She was so close to release that she felt her body straining towards it. Filled with an urgent yearning. Throbbing with unfulfilled desire.

'Lick me,' she begged, feeling so ashamed of herself, yet reckless. So achingly desperate that she would say or do anything.

He turned his head. 'Open your eyes and look at me,' he commanded gently.

Slowly, she opened them. Raising her head she felt her breath catch. His gaze was dark. His half smile wicked and wolfish. Desire coursed through her again. Barely restrained passion thundering along every vein and sinew that crisscrossed her yearning body.

'Now,' he said, more softly this time, 'lie back and concentrate. Feel my mouth on your cunt. My tongue inside you. Concentrate on how it feels to the exclusion of all else.'

Smiling faintly, feeling weak with arousal, Nina lay back again and allowed her eyelids to close. She was aware that others were standing around the bed. Disparate men hovering, looking at her wantonly displayed body with hungry eyes, desperate to touch but kept at arm's length by Rob's tacit command to stay away from her.

She didn't mind them looking. In fact it added to the eroticism, she realised. To know that they were watching Rob caress her most intimate flesh. Her passive acceptance that they were witnessing her total helplessness. The humiliation of being thus displayed and in the grip of her own burning desire for sensual gratification. All of it thrilled her to the very core.

Rob played her body like a maestro. His fingers, lips and tongue touching everywhere, delving into her most secret honeyed flesh, until her body felt consumed by the sheer pleasure of his caresses.

'Touch her breasts,' she heard him say to someone.

The protest rose up in her throat but Rob ordered her to stay as she was and to keep her eyes closed.

'Not knowing who is touching you is all part of the enjoyment,' he assured her. 'Don't try to fight it. Trust me.'

Feeling helpless in the grip of her need to come, Nina stayed silent. She kept her eyes closed and revelled in the warm, languid sensation of total helplessness. Even as strange hands cupped her breasts. Stroking. Squeezing. Plucking at her nipples until she felt her whole body would explode. Other hands stroked her torso, her hips, along her thighs. Different fingers stroked her vulva and delved into the wide open channel of her vagina. She knew they weren't Rob's and whimpered at the humiliation of not knowing who was touching her.

Yet despite her shame the heat was still building inside her. Her clitoris, under the direction of Rob's flickering tongue and sucking lips, was sensitised to the point of eruption. She felt him move his head away from between her legs, his hair brushing the oh so sensitive skin on the inside of her left thigh. Then she felt his fingers caressing her inner labia, pulling back the little hood of flesh that concealed the sensitive tip of her clitoris.

'Look at her clit,' she heard him say as he brushed a fingertip lightly over the pearl-like tip, 'like a little cock. So swollen and succulent.'

Oh, God no! She recoiled inside from the piquancy of his caress and from the appreciative murmurs of the men gathered around her. It was the worst kind of humiliation

INTIMATE DISCLOSURES

and yet the best kind. Rob's fingers stroked with precise dexterity either side of the throbbing bud, while more fingers probed inside her, plunging, scissoring, eagerly stroking the sensitive inner walls of her vagina.

'Watch her come,' Rob said, moving his fingers faster around her clitoris.

Nina felt her whole body flame. Then her orgasm was upon her. Driving her to the very peak of ecstasy. She tried to buck her hips but felt herself pinned down by so many hands. Warm hands. Cool hands. Broad. Slim. Gentle. Rough. Kneading her breasts. Plucking at her nipples. Stroking every inch of desperate flesh. Her stomach. Her belly. Her thighs. Even sliding into the cleft between her buttocks and fingering the shameful little aperture of her anus.

It was all too much. The whole shameful mass of sensation flooded her and she heard herself screaming into the darkness where she temporarily resided.

Before she felt the last waves of her orgasm recede, she sensed someone climbing over her. Moving between her legs. The hard knob of a penis touched her vaginal lips and then she felt its smooth entry. Flickering her eyelids open just a fraction she was able to reassure herself that the cock sliding deliciously in and out of her belonged to Rob. There were no others touching her now. Though she could still make out the indistinct forms of people standing around the bed, watching Rob fuck her.

Well, let them, she thought, closing her eyes again and giving herself up to the wonderful sensation of his thrusting cock. Let them eat their hearts out. With a surge of triumph she felt his movements quicken. His thrusts became deeper, faster, until she heard him let out a faint groan and felt his body shudder. His climax swept through her, triggering another of her own. Then they became still, their bodies sliding together on a slick film of perspiration. Rob stroked her breasts, murmuring verbal caresses in her ear and kissing her neck and along her jawbone until their rapidly beating hearts slowed and their overheated bodies began to cool.

She wouldn't let anyone else touch her after that. Not even when Soraya expressed her displeasure and Angel tried desperately to persuade her otherwise.

'No,' Nina insisted, getting up from the bed on shaky legs and reaching for her clothes. 'I'm going to get another drink. Then in a little while I'll go home.' She smiled ruefully but inside felt a steely determination. 'Sorry if that makes me a party pooper,' she said.

Angel gave way with a sigh and a disappointed shake of her head. It hardly mattered, Nina thought, watching the tiny young woman become instantly consumed again by a hoard of men. If that's her way of enjoying herself, fine, but it's not my idea of fun.

Only two people were in the sitting room of the hotel suite when she entered. Both were seated on the high chrome and blue leather stools at the bar. One she recognised as Simon and the other was Soraya.

'Sorry,' Nina said to her again as she sat down next to Simon. 'Please remember this is my first time at something like this. I didn't feel ready to go the whole hog.'

Soraya reached across Simon and patted Nina's knee. 'Don't worry about it,' she said, 'I'm just jealous because I can't join in. Although Simon and I have been having some fun. Haven't we Si?'

The young man nodded enthusiastically and then asked Nina what she would like to drink.

Just as Nina had started on her third gin and tonic, Rob entered the room, fully dressed again, followed by the woman in the red floral dress. Her hair was no longer primly knotted at the nape of her neck. Instead it draped her shoulders in a glossy brown curtain. They walked straight over to the bar where Rob turned to Nina and gave her an intimate smile.

INTIMATE DISCLOSURES

'Nina,' he said, 'I would like you to meet my wife Michelle.'

His wife! Nina felt her mouth drop open and quickly tried to reform it into a smile.

'Hello, Michelle,' she said hesitantly. The woman was all smiles in return, though Nina felt wary of her. After all, she had just spent the best part of the evening fucking her husband. 'Have you been enjoying the party?'

'Oh, what? I'll say,' the woman enthused in an accented voice that was unmistakably Australian. 'Rob, darling, get me a Campari and soda would you?'

Hoisting her neat bottom on to the stool next to Nina's she told her that she had taken on no less than eight men that evening.

Gosh, Nina thought, feeling tremendously impressed and very unsophisticated all of a sudden, no wonder she wasn't worried about what Rob was getting up to with me.

'Rob and I have been swinging for six years now,' Michelle offered conversationally, 'even our honeymoon was spent at an exclusive swingers resort in Antigua. His first wife hated this sort of thing. Poor dear. Didn't know what she was missing, did she, Rob?' She glanced up as her husband handed her the drink she had requested. 'I said poor Yvonne didn't know what she was missing out on.'

'My first wife was very unadventurous sexually,' Rob agreed, smiling at his wife and then at Nina, 'she couldn't understand my penchant for kinky sex.'

I'm not sure if I could either, Nina thought privately, feeling a twinge of compassion for his ex-wife. Still, Michelle seemed happy enough about the arrangement.

After a second drink, by which time they had chatted about a whole realm of inconsequential things, Nina decided to broach the subject of *Intimate Disclosures*. This time, she made it sound as though she was a swinger who just happened to find herself working on a project that encompassed the sex industry.

'You're talking to the right people here,' Michelle enthused, squeezing Rob's arm and beaming at him. 'Rob and I – well, Rob mostly because I've got the kiddies to look after – we run a whole chain of bars and shops and clubs and things.'

'What, sex ones?' Nina asked, realising how idiotic her question sounded.

Rob smiled gently at her. 'Of course, sex ones,' he said. Reaching into his trouser pocket he drew out a small white business card. 'You must come along to our club in Greek Street one night. Wednesdays are best. Not too many people. Just the good ones. The sort who really appreciate the entertainment we have to offer.'

Once again, Nina couldn't believe her luck. Though she was starting to realise that the people who were actively involved in the kinkier side of sex were naturally the sort who flocked together. One introduction led to another, which led to more introductions. Consequently, the whole thing was becoming much easier to manage that she could have hoped.

Nina promised Rob and Michelle that she would go to their club sometime and when they finally moved away from the bar, Simon immediately struck up a conversation with her.

'I couldn't help overhearing about your job and everything,' he said, 'it must be really interesting.'

'Mostly boring,' Nina admitted, 'though I must say, this project has a little bit more zing to it than previous ones.'

'Such as?' He raised an inquiring eyebrow and Nina giggled.

'The River's Authority scandal in West Yorkshire, blood sports and urinary infections, to name but a few,' she said.

'Wow, gripping stuff!' Simon responded, laughing along with her.

Nina studied him as she sipped her drink, deciding that she liked him more with each passing second. He was

INTIMATE DISCLOSURES

good looking in a very conventional sort of way, with short brown hair and unremarkable features. Yet he oozed charm and an easy-going charisma. Trustworthy, like a best friend's older brother, he made her feel very relaxed in his company. And now she felt a slight twinge of regret that she hadn't encouraged his advances while they had been in the bedroom.

'Sorry about allowing Rob to take over in there,' she said, cocking her head in the direction of the bedroom door.

Only a few stragglers remained in there now. Through the open doorway they could see glimpses of white buttocks and thighs. Angel was one of the women still going strong, as well as Liz.

Simon shrugged. 'There'll be other parties,' he said, 'has Soraya invited you to the one at her house in a couple of weeks' time?'

'No, I don't think she's very impressed with me,' Nina replied glumly.

'Rubbish,' he declared vehemently. 'Any woman who actually dares to come along to one of these things is a good sport. And Rob wasn't the only one who was taken with you. Ricky said you were a good lay.'

Nina had the grace to blush. 'That's all I did, lay there,' she admitted, 'I let him do all the work.'

To her surprise Simon leaned forward and pressed his lips to hers. It was only a fleeting kiss but Nina felt something stir inside her. Then Simon leaned back and let his hand rest on her thigh.

'With a lovely woman like you, it could never be work,' he said, 'it would always be a pleasure.'

'Oh!'

Nina didn't know what else to say. His compliment was delivered honestly and without any hint of a sexual overtone. Glancing shyly at him, she realised he was rapidly becoming very desirable in her estimation. Feeling terribly embarrassed and sluttish all at the same time, she glanced at the bedroom door again.

'Would you—' she said hesitantly, 'I mean, it's not too late, is it?'

A broad smile spread across Simon's face. 'Would I?' he said enthusiastically, grabbing her hand and pulling her off the bar stool, 'I'd be delighted.'

When she arrived at work the following day, Nina was surprised not to see Karen already at her desk. Particularly as she was so late.

'Big boss not here yet then?' she asked Maisie, 'Or has she gone to lunch already?' It was almost twelve and it wasn't unheard of for Karen to disappear for one of her famous three hour lunch appointments.

'She's in hospital,' Maisie replied bluntly, hardly glancing up from her keyboard. Her fingers tapped frantically and Nina had to lean right over her desk to attract her attention.

'Why – what's happened, appendicitis or something?'

Maisie finally pressed the SAVE button on her keyboard and looked up. 'I thought someone would have told you. She was knocked down by a drunk driver last night.'

'Oh, my God!' Nina sat down heavily in her chair. 'Was she badly hurt? Oh, stupid question, she must have been to end up in hospital.'

'Fractured tibia and concussion,' Maisie responded flatly. It was well known that there was no love lost between herself and Karen. 'They're keeping her in for observation. By the sound of it she got off pretty lightly, the driver's in a much worse state apparently.'

'Serves him right,' Nina said, her mouth forming a grim line, 'when will the stupid bastards learn that it's not only their lives they're putting at risk?'

Maisie nodded. 'I know, Liam's already talking about doing a programme about it. He wants to get the ball rolling as soon as possible so that Karen can go on camera with her leg in plaster.'

'Wonderful,' Nina said, marvelling at how much of an opportunist their proprietor was, 'I bet Karen will be over the moon about that.'

'According to Liam it's a question of doing right by the company at every turn,' Maisie corrected her, 'apparently Karen's quite happy to go along with it. She wants you to go and see her at the hospital, by the way. It sounds as though she's determined to still direct proceedings from her death bed.'

'Oh, don't joke about it, Maisie,' Nina said reprovingly, 'the consequences could have been much worse.' She glanced at her watch again. In all honesty the prospect of spending an afternoon hitting the phones didn't hold much appeal. 'I think I'll go there now, which one is she in?'

'Charing Cross,' Maisie replied, looking suitably chastened. She reached for her handbag, took out her purse and extracted a ten-pound note. 'Could you get her some flowers, or choccies or something from me?'

Nina smiled. 'Sure. No problem.'

It was with a mixture of relief and a feeling of inevitability that Nina found Karen sitting up in bed in a private room, looking bright and healthy and doling out orders to a bevy of nurses. All looked agitated and careworn. So much so that Nina flashed the last of them, a plump West Indian, a sympathetic smile as they bustled out of the room.

'Close the door,' Karen ordered briskly, 'we don't want the hoi polloi eavesdropping on our meeting.'

Oh, so this was a meeting was it? Nina thought, doing as she was instructed, then drawing up a chair so that she could sit at Karen's bedside. More fool her for thinking her hospital visit was an act of compassion.

'Liam's told me to take a month's sick leave,' Karen

said. 'Of course I tried to argue with him, told him I could soldier on despite this.' She tapped her plaster covered leg with glossy red fingernails. 'But you know what an old softie he is, wouldn't hear of it.'

'Probably a sensible precaution,' Nina offered, trying to look sympathetic. 'What should I do about this project we're working on – shelve it for now?'

Karen shook her head. 'I did suggest it to Liam but he was adamant that we continue. That is to say, you, Nina—' She paused to clear her throat. 'If you wouldn't mind stepping into my shoes for a few weeks.' She grimaced ruefully and glanced at her plaster cast again before adding, 'I shan't have much use for them.'

A smile touched Nina's lips. It was the first time she had ever heard Karen attempt to be humorous.

'Of course I will,' she said.

'Well, get Maisie to help you,' Karen instructed, 'she isn't too busy at the moment.'

Nina remembered watching Maisie's fingers flying over her keyboard and wondered what Karen would define as 'too busy.'

'I'm sure she'd be delighted,' Nina replied.

Leaning forward, Karen said, 'So, tell me, Nina, how is your research coming along?'

Unbidden, a blush rose to Nina's cheeks. Speaking hesitantly at first, anxious not to disclose exactly how in-depth her research had been at times, she outlined her progress so far.

When she had finished Karen honoured Nina's efforts by magnanimously offering her a chocolate.

'Excellent,' she said, 'I always knew I could rely on you to do your best.'

Maisie was delighted to be told that she would be working with Nina on the *Intimate Disclosures* project. 'Are we still on for tomorrow night?' she asked, referring to their proposed visit to Nirvana to see the Dream Team in action.

Nina nodded. 'Yes,' she said, 'Tom's away as from this afternoon so he can't go with me after all.'

'That's too bad,' Maisie murmured, looking pleased all the same, 'where's he gone?'

With a sigh, Nina told her new assistant how Tom had been instructed to go to Bilbao to survey a new fish processing plant that his company was designing.

'Lucky him,' Maisie enthused.

'Yes, lucky for him,' Nina said, 'but not for me. It's going to be very difficult having to visit some of the places I've got on my list without a man in tow. Plus, I'm going to miss him like crazy.'

Maisie gave her a smile that Nina supposed was meant to be reassuring. 'Never mind,' she said, 'you've always got me to rely on.'

As keen though Maisie was, Nina couldn't help feeling despondent that Tom wasn't going to be around. Since they had got back together again they hadn't been parted for longer than a day. She missed him already and he hadn't even left England yet. His goodbye to her before his departure for work that morning had been sensuous and passionate. Hence her reason for arriving late at the office – not because she had spent the best part of the previous evening cavorting around with strange men.

Tom had been wonderful about the whole thing. In fact, Nina couldn't help wondering if her stories excited him more than a little. He liked hearing all the details. What was said. How she felt. Afterwards, they had fucked like crazy for a couple of hours and then, this morning, it had been more of the same.

Swinging is doing wonders for my love life, Nina mused wryly, and she couldn't help wondering how she would feel when the project came to an end. It would seem very strange going back to total monogamy. Perhaps she and Tom would carry on swinging regardless. She laughed inwardly, thinking it sounded like the title of a comedy film: *Carry on Swinging*, starring Sid James and Hattie Jaques – except neither of the fabulous comedians were around anymore.

'Nina, Nina phone, for you!' Maisie interrupted Nina's weird and convoluted thoughts by waving the telephone receiver under her nose.

She was surprised to hear Michelle's accented voice. 'Hi, Nina, is that you?'

'Yes,' Nina said, sounding as astonished as she felt, 'what can I do for you?'

'More a question of what I can do for you,' Michelle said excitedly, 'I was thinking about what you told Rob and I last night and then today I had a word with my brothers.'

'Your brothers?' Nina wondered for a moment if she was still locked in her confused fantasy world.

'Yes, Shane and Michael, the darlings. They're really a couple of horny looking guys. Shame our family had principles. I wouldn't have minded a bit of incest when I look back on things.' She overrode Nina's shocked gasp. 'Still, that's not the point. The thing is, they make films. Not just porn but real erotica. You know, with a story and everything?' She laughed. 'Anyway, I told them about meeting you and what a looker you are and everything and Rob backed me up.' She laughed again, this time the tone was slightly raunchier and Nina felt herself cringing inwardly. 'Don't mind me, I do go on a bit. If you like I'll cut to the chase. If you're interested they would like you to audition for their next film. What do you think – are you interested?'

The sound of her own blood rushing in her ears made it difficult for Nina to respond. Eventually, she said hesitantly, 'I've never acted before, I wouldn't know what to do.'

'You know how to fuck don't you?' Michelle asked bluntly.

Glancing across her desk, Nina noticed Maisie watching

INTIMATE DISCLOSURES

her and consequently blushed profusely. 'Um, yes, of course,' she said, 'but—'

'And you can walk and talk and you must know what it's like to be in front of a camera, what with working in TV and all.'

'Yes,' Nina concurred, 'that's true enough. Though I spend most of my time away from the actual studio.'

'Doesn't matter,' Michelle said, brushing away Nina's doubts. 'If you can be at their place next Monday, say about ten-thirty, you'll be able to get your first crack at stardom.' She laughed again and then asked Nina if she had a pen and paper.

With shaking fingers Nina dutifully wrote down the address Michelle gave her. It was lucky, she thought, that Karen was away, otherwise she would have had difficulty finding an excuse for this appointment. As it was, under her changed circumstances she could leave Maisie in charge of the telephone and do her own thing for once.

All at once anticipation gripped her. That and an overwhelming sense of curiosity. This was something new and exciting. It wasn't exactly necessary for her to actually take part in an erotic film, interviewing other porn actresses would be enough. But what an experience it could turn out to be all the same!

'I'll be there,' she assured Michelle, when she had finished writing all the details down.

'Great,' Michelle said. 'Now, a word of advice. This is an erotic film remember, so dress sexily. Black stockings, really high heels, that kind of thing. Oh, and the boys said to be sure to wear a short skirt and a top with buttons down the front.'

'Right, short skirt, top with buttons.' Nina jotted it all down. 'Anything else?'

Michelle's laughter touched her ears one last time. 'Yeah,' she said, 'break a leg.'

Chapter Six

Standing in the paved passageway outside Nirvana, Nina tapped her foot impatiently and glanced for the umpteenth time at her watch. She had been waiting for the best part of twenty minutes for Maisie to put in an appearance. Now her attempts at ignoring the motley line of people queuing to get into the nightclub, by pretending to study the window display of the clothes shop opposite, were beginning to wear thin.

'Boyfriend stood you up, honey – why not come in with us?' The invitation came from a tall, black transvestite in a silver dress who stood near the head of the queue.

Glancing around Nina was relieved to see Maisie climbing backwards out of a black taxi at the end of the passage. She smiled at the transvestite.

'Thanks for asking,' she called back, 'but my friend's here now.'

The clomping sound of Maisie's heavy platform shoes on the paving stones attracted everyone's attention. That and the sight of her wildly back-combed hair and bright green lurex jacket and shorts, worn over red tights, kept them looking as she descended the short flight of concrete steps to join Nina.

'Sorry, I'm late,' she said, all smiles, 'I managed to lock myself out of my flat and it took me about three hours to track down the caretaker and get him to bring over a spare key.'

'No problem,' Nina replied, feeling relieved that Maisie

had finally turned up, 'we've got another half hour at least until the boys go on.'

With their guest status, they queue jumped with ease and found themselves in the dark, dimly lit club, their eyes travelling everywhere as they took in their surroundings and the clientele.

The club was on three levels, each level divided into different sections and all crammed to the gills with a motley assortment of people. Black, white, gay, straight, long-haired or bald, the crowd of predominantly young males was enlivened by a generous sprinkling of theatrical-looking 'trannies.'

Making straight for the loo, Nina jostled her way past an extremely credible looking 'woman' wearing a black sequined leotard and seamed fishnet tights. At over six feet tall 'she' was leaning over one of the hand basins, circling her pouting lips with a coat of scarlet lipstick. And Nina found herself envying the transvestite her lithe figure, long platinum wig and endless slim legs.

Feeling frumpish in her brown suede hipster mini skirt and white ribbed top that showed off a none too flat midriff, Nina locked herself inside the cubicle. When she emerged she found two other transvestites had taken the place of the first and were assiduously exchanging beauty hints.

'Oh, my dear, that colour is just too divine on you. It brings out the blue of your eyes to perfection.'

'Have you tried that stay-put lipstick by L'Oreal? It's wonderful. I keep recommending it to everyone.'

Smiling, Nina washed and dried her hands quickly, then went back outside to look for Maisie who had agreed to stand in line for the cloakroom while she waited.

'All done,' Nina said brightly, catching hold of Maisie's arm.

Maisie handed her a green cloakroom ticket which Nina tucked into the back pocket of her skirt. 'Which way now?' she asked.

INTIMATE DISCLOSURES

When they said they wanted to watch The Dream Team, a bare-chested guy with pierced nipples gestured to the darkened room behind him where the dance floor heaved with oddly assorted people.

Having grabbed a bottle of mineral water each at the packed bar, Nina and Maisie elbowed their way along the perimeter of the dance floor until they were near the front. Above them rose the stage which was roughly triangular in shape and had a backdrop of the Manhattan skyline at night. The widest part was the back of the stage and the two sides were bordered by mock iron railings.

The raunchy beat of rock music started up, which was almost drowned out by a cacophony of clapping hands and stamping feet. Then a few minutes later, just as the audience had reached a frenzy, on The Dream Team came – eight men gyrating their beautiful bodies through a similar routine to the one Kyle and Arrik had performed at Rachel's sex toys party.

When they spotted Nina and Maisie, Kyle and Arrik mouthed and gesticulated invites to them to go backstage afterwards. Grinning broadly, the two young women nodded their acceptance.

The end of the Dream Team's performance was greeted with loud catcalls and a few lewd suggestions from some of the men gathered around the edge of the dance floor. Two of them – stripped to the waist, with cropped hair and posturing like mad for the boys' benefit – were also invited to go backstage. Not knowing where to go exactly, Nina and Maisie followed the two men and found themselves in a narrow corridor which had several doors leading off it. A large gold star affixed to one of the doors told all four of them which one they should enter.

The small, airless room was crammed with naked, perspiring bodies. The entire Dream Team – eight in all – were sitting around, unashamedly displaying their nakedness and drinking beer straight from the bottle. To Nina's relief, Kyle came straight over to her and Maisie. He asked them what they thought of the show before dragging them off to meet the others.

Greg, Paul, Dino, Fabian, Stuart, Mich, the names went in one ear and straight out of the other as Nina smiled and nodded to each of the dancers in turn. They were all very different in appearance and yet at the same time they looked like clones – muscle bound hunks who were making the most of what they had, physically, before they got too old.

This, Kyle told her a little while later was around the mid twenties mark.

'A bit like models then,' she remarked, accepting a bottle of cold beer from him.

Kyle smiled as he nodded. 'Yeah, worst luck. But an appearance on your show might just give us the chance to hit the big time before then.' Tilting his head back, he drank some of his beer.

Nina watched the way his throat rippled and found her eyes travelling over the broad expanse of his chest and down over his taut stomach to where his cock dangled over a pink, wrinkled scrotum.

He caught her looking and winked.

'Fancy some more action?' he said.

Feeling her cheeks flood with colour, Nina shook her head. But she couldn't deny the way her body had started responding to the suggestion. It was warm anyway in the club but now she felt hot and bothered for a different reason.

'I don't suppose there's anywhere we can get some air, is there?' she asked. She fanned herself with her hand and rolled the ice cold beer bottle over her brow, then across the bare expanse of her throat.

Smiling even more broadly, Kyle wandered nonchalantly over to a chair on the far side of the room which was piled up with assorted clothing. His gluteus muscles, firm and hollowed under his hips, flexed as he walked, the sight of them making Nina's stomach clench with desire. Pulling out

INTIMATE DISCLOSURES

a pair of faded blue jeans from the middle of the pile, he stepped into them and pulled them up, buttoning the fly. Then he sat down and slipped his bare feet into a pair of tan, tooled leather cowboy boots.

'Come on,' he said, standing up again and taking her hand, 'I know just the place for us.'

They went out of the club's back entrance and found themselves in a narrow alleyway. It was lit only at each end by a single street lamp. Perversely, Nina shivered when she got outside and Kyle immediately put one of his arms around her. The heavy, musky tang of perspiration still lingered on his golden-hued skin and Nina found her body responding in a very primaeval way. Snuggling up close to him, she slipped her arm around his waist.

His skin was soft and slick with moisture and – though she reminded herself of her own mother by doing so – she asked him if he was worried about catching a chill.

Kyle laughed but not *at* her and assured her that he would be fine.

'We could always find ways of warming ourselves up again,' he said suggestively. His fingers massaged the top of her arm and he turned slightly and bent his head so that his lips grazed her mouth.

Nina returned his kiss automatically, her lips opening under his, her tongue flickering around the inside of his mouth. Desire rampaged through her. A sudden, desperate need to assuage her physical and erotic cravings. She had never had sex in the open air before, or in a public place where there was a good chance of discovery.

The illicit nature of the moment made her senses soar and she imagined herself as a cheap hooker entertaining a 'client' in a back alleyway. The Americanism made her situation seem more glamorous somehow and she found herself thinking, 'Eat your heart out, Hugh Grant,' as Kyle's hands slipped up under her skirt and pulled down her plum satin bikini pants.

Kicking them off, she gave a gasp of surprise as Kyle gripped her buttocks and lifted her into the air. Coiling her legs around him, she felt the hard tip of his cock nudging at her wet opening. In a moment he was inside her, grinding his hips as he worked his way deeper and deeper until he was buried inside her up to the hilt.

'Pull up your jumper,' he ordered gruffly, 'I want to look at your tits while I fuck you.'

The insolence of his words sent a frisson of lust coursing through her and she scrabbled hastily at her jumper, pulling it up until her braless breasts were exposed. Caressed by the cool night air, they jiggled and bounced while Kyle continued to grind away inside her.

He manipulated her easily, treating her body as if it were as light as a feather. And she groaned as she felt his fingertips digging into the soft flesh of her buttocks while he rubbed his bristly jaw over her aching breasts.

Holding onto his shoulders, with her legs still wrapped tightly around his waist, Nina tried to match his rhythm. A sensual heat was building up inside her. His cock was good and deep inside her grasping vagina, alternately grinding and thrusting, and she could feel the swollen bud of her clitoris rubbing deliciously against his pubic bone.

In the next few moments they came. Both of them crying out as they shuddered violently. And afterwards, she disengaged her legs and slid down him, sinking down to her haunches so that she could slip off the condom and take his still rigid cock in her mouth.

His fingers, entwined in her hair, gripped and pulled roughly as she mouthed him, lapping up their combined juices. And she felt her bared breasts stroking tantalisingly against his denim covered legs.

'You're one fucking horny bitch,' he said, withdrawing his cock hastily from her mouth when it became too sensitive to bear her ministrations any longer.

Smiling provocatively up at him, Nina stroked her hands

INTIMATE DISCLOSURES

over her breasts and tweaked the distended nipples before reluctantly pulling her jumper down. Her leg muscles protesting, she straightened up. Her eyes scanning the pavement where they stood, she realised she couldn't see her discarded knickers anywhere.

'I'd better go back inside and look for Maisie,' she said, deciding to give up the hunt for her knickers and suddenly remembering her colleague, whom she had abandoned in a room full of naked men. The image made her smile to herself. Somehow, she thought, she couldn't imagine Maisie complaining about her desertion for one minute.

In contrast to the frantic pace of her week, the weekend was passing far too slowly for Nina. Normally she would have enjoyed the break, taking time to catch up on some much needed rest and relaxation. But without Tom there she felt bored and anxious. The whole *Intimate Disclosures* thing, she decided, was becoming far too difficult for her to cope with. And she still had her 'audition' to look forward to on Monday morning.

Late on Sunday evening Tom rang her and she was overjoyed to hear his voice.

'When are you coming home?' she asked, knowing she sounded plaintive.

'I don't know sweetheart. The guys on the site here are so slow about getting anything sorted out. It always seems to be *mañana* with them. And the language barrier isn't helping. I could end up being here another week if they don't get their fingers out.'

Nina shivered, thinking about Tom's fingers and what they could be doing to her right now if he wasn't stuck in Spain.

'I could always come over and interpret for you,' she suggested, knowing full well that it was out of the question. 'My Spanish is a bit rusty but it's better than nothing.' She sighed and added wistfully, 'Oh, Tom, I miss you so much. I wish you were here with me.'

'So do I, precious, so do I,' Tom said gently. He paused for a moment, then added, 'Where are you, Nina?'

'In bed,' she said, stretching across the acres of empty space beside her – at least it seemed like acres when it was not filled by Tom's body.

'And are you wearing anything?'

Nina's heart picked up a beat. The tone of Tom's voice had changed. Now it was dark and suggestive, almost as though he were there beside her after all.

'No,' she said breathlessly, 'I just had a bath and then got straight into bed.'

'Well,' he said, drawing out the word on a thread of decadent promise, 'what do you imagine I want you to do now?'

Nina's reply was barely more than a squeak. 'Touch myself?' she asked excitedly. Her fingertips were already drifting over her breasts as she spoke. She kicked the duvet off, sucking in her breath as the cool night air wafted over her, inciting goosebumps to spring up on her naked skin.

'Yes,' Tom said darkly, 'I want you to touch yourself and imagine that I'm there touching you. Reaching all those naughty little places. You know the places I mean don't you, sweetheart?'

'Mm-mm,' Nina replied, feeling hot and cold with barely suppressed desire.

Skimming her stomach lightly the fingers of her right hand slipped between her parted thighs. Her sex flesh was moist and already swollen. The outer labia blossoming apart just at the merest suggestion of erotic gratification.

Her ears picked up the sound of fabric rustling.

'I've got my cock out,' Tom said, his voice slipping like treacle down the phone, 'I'm caressing it as I think about you, naked and wet and open. Are you wet and open, Nina?'

INTIMATE DISCLOSURES

'Oh, yes, Tom,' she gasped. Her clitoris was throbbing and she touched it lightly, caressing the soft folds of her inner labia with torturous restraint.

'Don't you dare come yet,' he warned, sounding slightly breathless now, 'I'm not ready and I want us to come together.'

'OK.' Nina kept stroking herself, tantalising the little bud that seemed to scream inside her head for mercy.

'Now,' he continued remorselessly, 'I want you to finger-fuck yourself. Come on, baby, put those fingers in that juicy little hole. Are you doing it?'

'Yes, yes I'm doing it,' Nina moaned.

She could feel how creamy her vagina was and smell her own arousal. The musky scent touched her nostrils and flooded her senses. Her body seemed to clutch at her probing fingers, the velvety walls so tantalising as she plunged the pulpy, succulent depths of her own body. It felt as though she were soaring above the clouds. Drifting along on the heady current of her own arousal.

Tom's whispered suggestions and intermittent gasps and groans transported her into the realm of ecstasy. At last, when he told her she could touch her clitoris again, she did so with relief, her body arching against her own fingers.

'Not yet,' Tom murmured darkly, 'keep it light, keep it going.'

'I'm nearly there!'

'Don't! String it out, sweetheart. Just gentle caresses. That's it. Keep it light, baby. Just teasing. Soft. Gentle. Teasing.'

Although his words were intended to calm her down, they had the opposite effect on her. Almost beyond the limits of her endurance, Nina began to pant and plead with him.

'I can't hold out, Tom,' she whimpered. 'Oh, God, I feel so hot. I want you now. I wish you were here, touching me, ready to fuck me—'

'OK, baby, you can come now,' Tom interrupted, to Nina's relief.

She caressed herself fervently, stroking the hard nub of her swollen clitoris until wave after wave of pleasure rolled over her. Crying out into the receiver, she felt the perspiration making her palm damp and almost dropped the slippery piece of plastic. Tom's own groan of release sent a frisson of renewed pleasure through her and she wedged the phone between her ear and shoulder so that she could caress her breasts while her fingertips still moved over and around her pulsating clitoris.

Stroking themselves softly, they panted down the phone to each other until they managed to get their breath back.

'Tom, that was fabulous. You are fabulous,' she said breathlessly.

Feeling languid now, she allowed her body to relax completely. It was difficult to stop the receiver from slipping off her shoulder so she held it again. She didn't want to lose a single precious second of the tenuous link with her lover.

'No, my darling, you are,' Tom replied softly, then, 'I can't wait to get back to you. I promise, when I do I will make love to you and fuck you every which way.'

Nina smiled in the darkness, feeling overcome by the need to sleep. 'I'll look forward to that,' she murmured, 'but I'll never forget tonight.'

After a few more minutes of shared endearments, they brought their conversation to a reluctant close. And not long afterwards Nina felt herself slipping into a deep, restorative sleep.

A bright blue sky greeted Nina's first waking moment on Monday morning. She lay there for a moment, still feeling tired even though she had slept extremely well. For a little while she allowed her mind to replay the erotic conversation she had shared with Tom the night before. And she was

INTIMATE DISCLOSURES

not surprised when her body began to respond in its usual fashion.

This will not do, Nina Spencer, she told herself firmly, get up you lazy cow and go to work. It was only as she threw the duvet off herself and halfheartedly slipped her legs out of bed that she remembered where she was supposed to be going that morning. Oh, shit! The last thing she felt like doing was auditioning for a porno movie. Although, she mused as she trudged wearily to the bathroom, was there ever a good day to take part in a skin flick?

Showering thoroughly, she then spent ages shaving her legs and armpits and trimming her pubic hair – just in case. She didn't really believe that she would actually have to take her clothes off or anything, not when she explained her real reason for being there. Because her appointment wasn't until ten thirty, she took extra time to dry her hair straight, so that it looked longer and thicker. She also took great care with her makeup, even going as far as painting all her nails – fingers and toes – a confidence boosting scarlet.

It was only while she was rummaging around in her top drawer for a clean pair of knickers that she remembered Michelle's instructions about what she should wear. And underwear, if she recalled rightly, was a definite no no. A tremor of anticipation swept through her. To be asked to go and see two strange men, while wearing no underwear, definitely hinted at something more nerve-racking than a cosy interview.

Nina Spencer, you're going to come clean the minute you get there, she told herself sternly as she slipped on a short sleeved, white silk blouse and a plain, straight black cotton skirt that ended mid-thigh. Glancing down at the revealing neckline of her blouse, she fastened another button. Moments later a swift appraisal in the mirror told her that her efforts at false modesty were pointless. The shape and fullness of her breasts showed quite clearly through the clinging silk. And the dark circles of her nipples and areolae were even more obvious.

Disregarding the warmth of the air temperature and Michelle's instructions, she hurriedly covered herself up with the jacket that matched her skirt. Sod them, she thought, rolling a pair of black stockings with lacy tops up her legs and then forcing her feet into an excruciatingly high pair of black stilettos, they'll have to take me as they find me.

Throughout the long taxi ride – she couldn't face the potential embarrassment of taking the tube in no underwear – the words 'take me' kept reverberating in her head. Is that what's going to happen? she asked herself as she stared blankly out of the window at the busy London streets. Will they pounce on me and ravish me the minute I walk through the door – before I even get a chance to explain my real reasons for being there? Another nervous shudder swept through her, her anxiety gripping her empty stomach like a vice. Vice! She thought wildly, her imagination working overtime now, that's what'll happen to me, I'll get picked up by the vice squad.

Arriving at the smart serviced office building and being met by a perfectly normal looking receptionist was a bit of a let down after all her feverish assumptions about the most likely scenario. The young, smart suited woman, who wore respectable-looking glasses and her brown hair in a plaited bun, greeted Nina as if she were visiting royalty.

'Ah, Miss Spencer, so kind of you to come,' she enthused, 'please take a seat. Can I get you anything, tea, coffee—?'

Nina smiled as she sat down at the end of a range of low blue seating. 'Coffee would be lovely thanks,' she said, 'white no sugar.'

While she waited, Nina flicked through a copy of *Variety*, her eyes skimming over the ads for chorus girls and bit part actors. Far from seedy, the location seemed so normal. With

INTIMATE DISCLOSURES

its pale blue walls hung with abstract prints, vases of fresh flowers and groups of potted plants, the innocuous reception area made Grassroots Productions' conference room look way out in comparison.

The receptionist returned a moment later with a cup of coffee for Nina and a yellow file under her arm. 'The script,' she said, tossing the file on to the empty seat beside Nina. Shane and Michael thought you might like to look through it before you go in.'

Pausing only to take a couple of sips of the scalding coffee, Nina set the cup down on the low glass topped table beside her and picked up the file. Opening it she found pages and pages of pure dross.

'Luscious Lavinia is a tart with a heart. Sexy, curvy, with pouting breasts and a wiggling bum she saunters casually into the room, stopping every so often to fling off an item of clothing – suggestion: clinging mini dress, thigh high boots, no knickers etc.

Her husband can't get it up so he gets Jed – tall, hunky and horny (blue jeans and bare chest?) – to oblige. Swaggering over to Lavinia he starts fondling her huge tits . . .'

Oh, please! Nina thought, closing the file quickly in disgust. It wasn't so much the script itself but the terrible clichés that went along with it that bothered her. There was nothing in it to excite a woman. It was all designed to titillate – and she grimaced at the word – the average male. It was no wonder, she thought dispiritedly, that most men thought real women were closet nymphomaniacs. Why did this sort of thing have to be so crude and obvious? And why couldn't the script make it clear that the luscious Lavinia had a high IQ to go with her pouting, mega huge breasts?

Sighing, she opened the folder again and plodded on. The dialogue, she decided, was even worse than the plot. She laughed aloud. Huh, plot! Clothes stripped off – bonk. Quick scene change – clothes half off – fellatio. Good God, poor old Lavinia didn't even get a look in on the oral sex front! Only the men in the cast enjoyed that pleasure.

Well, I'll soon set these two brothers straight on a few home truths, Nina decided, closing the file for once and for all and gulping down her – by now – lukewarm coffee. I don't care if they are related to Michelle and Rob and my job's on the line, I can't just sit there and pretend the script is great, I just can't.

'Miss Spencer, you can go in now.' The receptionist's voice interrupted Nina's thoughts.

'Oh, right, er, thanks.'

Nina stood up and hastily tugged down the hem of her skirt. Now that the moment of reckoning had come she felt keenly aware of the fact that she was wearing no knickers. Her lower body felt as acutely vulnerable as the rest of her. Her naked sex quivering almost as much as her knees.

Feeling full of trepidation she walked on shaking legs towards the door the receptionist indicated. Who knew what lay beyond? Conflict? Humiliation – for one side or the other? Taking a couple of deep breaths as she stood outside the door, hand poised on the handle, she decided there was only one way to find out.

Chapter Seven

Shadows cloaked the dimly lit room as she entered. The only illumination came from a bright shaft of sunlight which pierced the gap in the floor length curtains which were pulled across the windows on the far wall.

Like a spotlight Nina stepped into it, inadvertently, the door opening into the room and admitting her directly into the gleaming ray of light. Holding up a hand she shielded her eyes from its glare. She couldn't see anyone in the room but she could hear them talking – two, no, three sets of muted male whispers.

Who was the third person? she asked herself, sidestepping the shaft of light.

'No,' a familiar voice called to her from the shadowy depths of the room, 'go back to where you were.'

She complied automatically, her brain simultaneously registering the owner of the voice – Rob. With an inward sigh of relief, she felt her shoulders slump and immediately received a second command from him.

'Don't stand like that. Where's your posture? Stand tall. Shoulders back. Chest out!'

Chest out indeed, she fumed, nevertheless doing as Rob asked. In nervous schoolgirl mode she felt like giggling but managed to compose herself.

'Nina Spencer?' Rob rapped out.

Her reply was a pert, 'Yes, you know I am.'

'Answer the question.'

She sighed again. Good God, what was this – The People's Court?

'Yes, I'm Nina Spencer.'

'Good. Welcome Nina.'

There were some more whispers, then two more voices with vaguely American accents said, 'Hi, Nina.'

'Hi.' She was beginning to feel ridiculous, she thought, and her feet were killing her in the high heels. Shifting uncomfortably from one foot to the other she attempted to take control of the situation. 'I want you to know right from the start that I—'

'Please be quiet for a moment, Nina,' Rob interrupted her briskly. It infuriated her and she opened her mouth to say so but he interrupted her again, even before she had begun to speak. 'Turn around. Nice and slowly so that we can get a good look at you.'

Nina thought she could argue at this point, or walk out of the room and go to her office. Sod this playacting. But, foolish and irritated though she felt, something in Rob's tone of voice compelled her to obey. Moving slowly and gracefully, she executed a three-hundred and sixty degree turn.

'Lovely,' Rob said, 'now, please unbutton your blouse.'

This was too much! 'No, I—'

'Do it, Nina!' Then more seductively. 'Do it for me.'

Biting her bottom lip, Nina's fingers began to work the top button of her blouse. Her fingers were trembling, she noticed, as were her legs. In fact her whole body felt as though it could crumple onto the carpet at any moment. The button sprang undone and she started on the next. When her blouse was completely unbuttoned she glanced around nervously.

Now, she realised, she could just make out three indistinct shapes. One almost directly ahead of her and just to the right of the gap in the curtains, the other two seated together on her left. All three men were obscured by shadow, the only visual images a faint outline of heads and bodies – like silhouettes – and the odd flash of white shirt and blond hair when they moved.

INTIMATE DISCLOSURES

'Take off your jacket,' Rob commanded, 'drop it on the floor.'

Wordlessly, Nina shrugged off the jacket. As she did so she felt the edges of her blouse ease apart, especially over her breasts. Glancing down, she noticed the movement had exposed the deep valley of her cleavage and a thin column of her torso down to the waistband of her skirt.

'What now?' she asked, feeling anxious.

It was not so much the things Rob had asked her to do, nor even the fact that Michelle's two brothers were also there, watching her. What bothered her was the way she felt. A steamy sensuousness was creeping over her. And with it, a desire to shrug off her inhibitions along with her jacket and see just how far she was prepared to go with this charade. This was a charade, wasn't it? she asked herself, uncertain of her own motives now. She hadn't actually intended, subconsciously at least, to pretend to audition for the part?

'Don't be so impatient, Nina,' Rob admonished her gently. She thought she could make out the movement of him crossing his legs. 'You're not in a rush, are you?'

She shook her head defiant, horribly aware of the way her braless breasts wobbled as she moved. A flush of shame warmed her cheeks and throat.

'Not particularly,' she said, 'but my feet are hurting in these shoes and the sun is in my eyes. Can't I sit down?'

'No, not yet.' Rob's reply was as swift as it was firm. 'We're not ready for you to sit down yet.' He paused and Nina heard him sigh gently. 'Stroke your breasts over your blouse, Nina,' he said after a moment, 'get those nipples nice and stiff.'

She felt appalled at his suggestion and started to shake her head.

'Do it, Nina.'

Unwillingly, she raised her hands to her chest. She clasped her hands over her breasts, feeling their fullness and their warmth. For a moment she luxuriated in the sensation, adoring herself. She could feel her heart fluttering uncertainly beneath her ribs. Excitement trickled through her veins.

'Stroke your breasts,' Rob said again, adding, 'Silk was a good choice. You must be a sensualist. Feel how the material glides over your skin. Silk on silk, isn't it wonderful?'

'Yes.' Nina could hardly get the word out.

Her throat felt closed up, her mouth dry. She licked her lips. Then her fingertips sought her nipples as if by remote control. It was like all those times she had pleasured herself – either alone, or for Tom's benefit. Oh, God, Tom! What would he think if he could see her now?

Still caressing her breasts and nipples, she imagined Tom's face. He would be aroused by the sight of her and the situation she had found herself in, of that she had no doubt. If he was there now his eyes would be dark with lust, his cock stiffening moment by moment . . .

Without realising it a harsh whimper broke from her lips. Her breasts felt full and swollen now. Her nipples hard and distended, greedy for more. Was she normal? she asked herself, to be able to stand there and do that in front of other people – two of them complete strangers. And was it normal to be so turned on by it? Enough to make her uncovered vagina stream with the proof of her own arousal and her clitoris to throb remorselessly between her swelling labia. She could feel the trickles of her feminine moisture running down the insides of her thighs. Could they see? she wondered. What part of her were they looking at?

'Your breasts are beautiful,' Rob said, as though he could read her mind, 'I still remember them. Still fantasise about them. I told Michelle how luscious they are. She says she envies you – and me for having played with them. She would like to see them and caress you herself. You should have heard her, Nina, describing to me in minute detail what she would like to do with your lovely body. Can you imagine it, two beautiful women – you and my wife – pleasuring each other? I hope there will come a day—'

'Stop it!' Nina cried out, unable to bear any more of his verbal torment. She felt so hot and desirous it was taking every ounce of self control not to run to the cloakroom and grant her body the relief it craved.

'Ah,' Rob murmured with a slight hint of amusement, 'so you like the idea too? I thought as much.'

Anxious though she was to deny it, Nina found she couldn't. Her brief experience with Angel had taught her that there was more to her sexuality than she had previously imagined. Why not Michelle? she asked herself. She was an attractive, sensual woman. Why not take her pleasure with Michelle as well as her husband?

'Maybe,' Nina mumbled, flushing with embarrassment again, 'we'll have to see.'

She heard Rob's laugh and remembered the way his eyes crinkled at the edges when he was amused.

'Show us those lovely breasts now, Nina,' he said, resuming his previous commanding tone. 'Pull the edges of your blouse apart slowly. That's it, tantalise us as you reveal your body.'

Lust, like a heavy fist, struck Nina deep in the solar plexus as he spoke. Her heart was hammering now. Perspiration trickled from her hairline, misting her vision. With her cheeks flaming she inched her blouse apart, exposing her naked breasts slowly and seductively. Desperate for something to drink, she licked her dry lips again.

'Beautiful,' she heard one of the other men say.

Nina trembled. Oh, God, she thought, I can't keep on with this charade. I have to put an end to it.

'Cup your breasts for us, darling,' Rob murmured, breaking through her thoughts. 'Hold them. Play with the nipples. Do it lovingly.'

She did it. She did it because Rob asked her to and because she felt too far gone to argue. There was something so shamefully erotic about standing there, illuminated by a bright shaft of light and fondling her naked breasts. They were lovely breasts, she couldn't deny that, and they gave her so much pleasure.

The hard buds of her nipples were stiff between her fingertips, the breasts themselves heavy and voluptuous. They spilled over her palms, the flesh soft and warm and silken. Wrapping one arm around herself she supported them from beneath while her other hand travelled down her torso, the palm flat against her feverish skin.

'Christ, I wish I had a camera right now!' she heard one of the men say. 'Why didn't I think of that – why didn't you think of it, Shane?'

A flash of blond hair, told her Shane was shaking his head.

'Quiet,' Rob hissed, 'I think we're ready to move on to the next stage.' He fell silent for a moment and when he spoke again his words were directed at Nina, his voice now low and seductive. 'OK, Nina, let's have that skirt off. Slide it over your hips, slowly like before. Make us ache for it, darling.'

The faint sound of Nina's anguished whimper stroked the still air. Reluctant to comply, her shaking hands nevertheless reached behind her for the zip. Its refusal to budge for a moment, drew out the tension still further. Totally consumed by barely restrained desire she tugged at the zip and finally it gave. Then she held the material against her hips with the flat of her palms before easing the skirt over her hips. Her breath caught as the waistband snagged briefly on her pubic hair. It wasn't too late to preserve her modesty. She could just haul the skirt back up again, put on her blouse and jacket and walk out of there. Her palms guided the skirt down her thighs, allowing it to slip as slowly and seductively as possible.

'Show us, baby, show us.' Rob's voice was encouraging. Dark and sexy now, it made her whole body flame with erotic intent.

INTIMATE DISCLOSURES

She let the skirt go, feeling a thin whisper of air snake across her naked buttocks and between her legs where her sex was awash with her own juices. The flesh there must appear so ripe, she thought, desiring herself for a moment. Kicking the skirt away, she straightened up and stood proudly, arms by her sides, legs just slightly apart, chin up.

'You are so beautiful, Nina,' Rob said, 'so, so beautiful. What do you think, boys?'

'Uh, yeah, fabulous.' Michael's voice was familiar to her now, although she had yet to see him.

The other one, Shane, agreed with his brother, adding, 'I think she could be just perfect for what we want.'

'Didn't I tell you?' Rob said, sounding pleased with himself, 'and didn't Michelle say exactly the same thing?'

'Yeah, yeah, OK, you told us,' Shane said, 'you're right as always, Rob.'

'But can she act?' Michael cut in. 'I mean, yeah, she's gorgeous and everything but—'

Rob interrupted him quickly. 'Michael, shut up. I don't want to have to remind you who is backing this little venture.'

So, Nina thought, putting two and two together instantly, Rob was the money man, I might have known. She turned her head in his direction. Her eyes pleaded with him through the shadowy gloom to say something, do something.

'Nina, sweetheart, could you walk slowly towards me. Can you see where I am?'

'Yes,' she gasped, relieved to be allowed to move out of the shaft of light, 'I can see you, just.'

'OK,' he said, 'then come over to me, baby. Swing those hips as you walk. That's right. Wriggle it for Shane and Michael.'

His instructions were horribly shaming but she did it anyway, walking slowly in just her high heels and black stockings, rolling her pelvis just the way he asked her to.

He held up his hand when she almost reached him. With the sun no longer in her eyes she could just make out the shape of him and the movement of his arm in the dim light. Dressed in a loose, dark suit with a white shirt, she could see he was seated on a low two seater sofa. Black, she presumed, because she could hardly see it at all. And he was reclining, his legs crossed casually and his other arm stretched out across the back of the sofa.

'Stand with those legs a little wider apart please,' he murmured, 'that's right, just about hip width.'

She noticed he glanced across to the two brothers. At a fleeting nod of his head they got up as one and crossed the room to join him. Then they perched either side of him, on the arms of the sofa.

This Nina found distinctly unnerving. Now all three of them were real people, not just shadowy figures. Even though she still couldn't see them properly, she could feel their body heat and smell their aftershave. They were within touching distance, she realised, if they wanted to they could reach out and caress her naked body. She shivered involuntarily.

Rob's concern was immediate. 'Are you cold, Nina?'

'No,' she said, speaking hoarsely because her throat was still dry, 'just nervous.'

He laughed lightly. 'Of me?'

'No.' She shook her head.

'Of Shane and Michael?'

'Yes, a bit.'

'But why? They're not going to harm you. I wouldn't let them.' He paused and leaned forward before adding, 'I like you, Nina. I wouldn't let anything bad happen to you. I want you to enjoy this. I'm here to protect you.'

'I don't want them to touch me,' she admitted in a small voice.

He laughed again, but gently and with no malice. 'They're not going to touch you,' he assured her, 'you're going to be the one doing the touching. You're going to touch yourself.'

'I am?' She felt so gauche. Like a child again. Nervous and unsure of her situation.

'Yes,' Rob said, reclining back again, 'I want you to caress yourself, my darling. We want to watch you make yourself come.'

'Oh, I couldn't.' Nina's denial was immediate. Her shame at the mere thought evident by the warm flush staining her cheeks. She put her hands up to her face and felt how hot it was. Then she shook her head, her eyes downcast.

'You mean you've never done it before?' Rob asked. His voice was slightly mocking, tinged with incredulity.

Nina felt foolish. 'Of course I have but – but not—'

'But not like this,' Rob finished for her. 'I know, sweetheart, I know. But isn't this just the tiniest bit exciting? Can't you feel the sexual tension around us? Don't you feel beautiful knowing that the three of us are here to admire your body? Don't you?'

A nod of her head was all she could manage. Rob was so cruel in his assumptions, she thought. Cruel because he was right. She hated his knowing how she felt. In some ways it made her feel far more naked than simply being without clothes. He could see right inside her, read every dirty, shameful little thought that ran through her mind.

'I'll touch myself a bit,' she conceded, 'to please you. But I don't think I'll be able to come. Not in these circumstances.'

'Ah, Nina, Nina,' Rob said with a shake of his head, 'you don't realise how far you can really go, do you?'

Desperately, Nina tried to ignore him. Again he was probing too deeply, getting too close to the truth for comfort. Instead of speaking she skimmed her palms down the sides of her body, following the curves. Her fingertips glanced over the sides of her breasts where the nipples were still standing to attention. They bumped gently over her ribcage and almost met in the middle, at her waist. When they reached her hipbones she paused, drawing her breath in deeply, for courage and with the faintest suspicion of arousal. If she could just pretend that they – Rob, Shane and Michael – were not there. Or if she could simply imagine that this was an elaborate, erotic dream . . .

Her clitoris was pulsing beneath the closed purse of her outer labia. She stroked a fingertip down the slit between. Down the little vertical mouth and between her legs to the place where she was wet. Capturing some of the moisture on her fingertip she slid it back up again, pressing a little harder, forcing the tiny mouth to open.

The lips parted slightly and her fingertip encountered the familiar folds of soft flesh. Pubic hair, soft and blonde brushed the sides of her finger. She pressed harder, allowing the single digit to become embedded between the folds. By flexing the knuckle she managed to press the hard bone against her swollen bud. She moved her finger around slightly, making tiny circles.

With her breath sucked in and her eyes tightly closed she slid her finger further up until the soft pad of its tip came into contact with her clitoris. The sensation was familiar and wholly absorbing. This was familiar territory, the gentle stimulation, the pulling and circling of the little cowl of skin that protected her most delicate, sensitive part.

Bringing her other hand into play she allowed it to roam her breasts and torso at random. The questing hand ended up at the apex of her thighs, stroking her pubic mound. Two fingers slipped either side of her gently circling finger. They pulled her labia apart, wider and wider. She continued to circle, bringing another finger into play, and then another. Three fingers were her optimum amount. With three fingers working together she could achieve an orgasm in a matter of minutes.

'Oh-oh-ooh!'

INTIMATE DISCLOSURES

Great wracking tremors of lust gripped her pelvis, forcing her to grind it shamefully against her hands. She couldn't spread her labia any wider apart and yet she wished she could turn her sex flesh inside out. Bending slightly at the knees she rotated her hips lewdly, tilting her pelvis so that the wide open mouth of her vagina gaped at the three men. Creamy trickles of moisture gathered at its lip and trickled down the insides of her thighs. Beads of perspiration broke out on her throat and forehead. She had said she couldn't do it and yet she had. It had been easy. So shamefully, lust quenchingly easy.

A long moment of silence followed in the shadowy room. The three men sat still and spellbound, their eyes glazed and fixed, not to the sight of Nina's pinkly exposed vulva, but to her face. The dreamy, satisfied, other worldly expression she wore was far more fascinating than any amount of naked flesh.

'You may sit down, Nina,' Rob murmured, 'when you are ready.'

Nina blinked. Where was she? Colouring deeply as she opened her eyes and looked at the three men, she remembered. Then she snatched her hands away from herself, like a petty thief caught with her hands in the till.

'There's no need to feel ashamed, Nina,' Rob went on, 'you did what I asked you to do and you enjoyed it. Didn't you? What's wrong with that?'

'Where shall I sit?' Nina asked, ignoring his questions and the shameful implication behind the truth of what should have been her honest response. Of course she had enjoyed it. How could she possibly deny that?

Shane (or was it Michael?) got up and fetched her a chair. He put it down right next to her so that she was forced to remain in front of them. She sat and wanted to cross her legs but didn't have the strength in them. They felt wobbly and slightly deadened, as though she had been kneeling on them for some time.

'Could you do that in front of a camera?' Rob asked, when she had had a moment to compose herself.

'No.' Nina shook her head. 'No, or rather yes, probably, but I don't want to. I've gone far enough.' Then, leaning forward with her elbows resting on her thighs and hands clasped loosely in front of her, she told them the whole truth.

Fully dressed and with a cup of coffee in her hands, Nina sat on the sofa next to Rob and watched the door open. Through it stepped a couple of tall young men, with broad shoulders and taut, muscular torsos. They were naked to the waist and one had longish, floppy wheat coloured hair. The other looked foreign, possibly Greek or Spanish, Nina thought.

She realised she must have been staring at him because he turned around, glanced at her and then walked straight over to her.

'Luca,' he said, holding out his hand.

Nina glanced at it. It was deeply tanned and thick black hairs sprouted from the wrist. She smiled.

'Nina Spencer, I'm here to research a documentary, do you mind?'

He shrugged, his broad smile displaying even, white teeth. 'No, I don' mind,' he replied in broken English, 'Spanish men they have no hang-ups.' The bold statement was followed by another shrug and an even wider grin.

Nina wasn't sure if she believed him so she smiled enigmatically. Then her glance flickered to the other man, the blond one. 'What about you?' she asked.

Instead of shrugging, like his colleague, he tossed his head, flicking his long hair over his shoulder. 'Nah,' he said, 'why should I? If you've got it, flaunt it. And the publicity'll probably do me good.'

Nina sat back, feeling relieved. Rob had said the two actors wouldn't be a problem, and nor, he assured her, would the actress they had lined up to take part in a test

INTIMATE DISCLOSURES

scene that afternoon before Nina had appeared on the scene as a possible alternative.

It seemed neither Rob, Shane, nor Michael were particularly disappointed by her disclosure and her refusal to take part in the film they were making.

'You go a long way to make sure you get your foot in the door,' Shane had said with a good natured smile. 'I've got to hand it to you, Nina, you've sure got balls.'

'No, she hasn't,' Michael had quipped, 'not that I noticed anyway.'

Their laughter had relieved the final traces of tension that had lingered between them. And then Nina had been allowed to get dressed again. To her surprise, Shane and Michael had made a tactful withdrawal, as though now they knew she wasn't a porn actress, she was entitled to her privacy. Rob, she noticed, exhibited no such double standards. He had remained seated and watched her dress with as much interest as he had viewed her slow striptease.

'You look better without clothes,' had been his only comment.

Afterwards, all four of them had shared a quick sandwich lunch. While they ate Rob had explained what was going to happen that afternoon and asked Nina if she wanted to stick around. It seemed Shane and Michael were planning to screen-test a couple of actors with an actress. The scene would be one taken from the script and would involve one of the actors having sex with the actress, while the other – playing the actress's husband – watched on.

'Do you think they'll mind me being here?' Nina asked, to which Rob laughed.

'Not a bit,' he said, hugging her briefly, 'they're professionals. Why should they worry about an audience?'

Nina didn't have a good answer to that one and so she simply smiled and accepted Shane's offer of a second cup of coffee.

A few minutes later the door opened a second time and

in walked a tall, leggy blonde with huge breasts. Nina tried to stop herself gawping but couldn't. Barely restrained by a low cut pink Lycra dress, the jutting orbs seemed to defy gravity.

Shane and Michael pounced on her immediately, leading her to the sofa on the far side of the room and gesturing to her to sit down between them. Moments later, all three were involved in an animated discussion that involved a lot of laughter.

'Boob job,' the blond actor confided to Nina out of the corner of his mouth, 'notice how they don't wobble when she laughs.'

Nina noticed. Then she tried a little laugh for herself and immediately felt her own breasts jiggle in response. She smiled at the actor. Just looking at him made her feel good. With his corn coloured hair, sky blue eyes and warm, lazy smile he was like a summer's day.

'Which one of you gets to play the paid lover?' she asked.

'Me of course,' he said, jabbing his finger at his chest, 'poor old Luca's the business man husband who can't get it up.'

Flashing a sympathetic glance at the Spaniard, Nina was rewarded by a sexy wink. It helped to remind her that the whole thing was about acting.

Shane came over, rubbing his hands together enthusiastically. 'I think we're ready to roll, Grant,' he said.

The blond actor nodded. 'Right oh, do you want me to get my kit off?'

Nina felt a tremor of anticipation and realised she was looking forward to seeing him naked. In fact, the whole idea of watching the scene being acted out and filmed had filled her with a warm glow of shameful excitement.

She turned to Rob. 'Can I make a suggestion?' she asked tentatively.

He treated her to one of his slow, seductive smiles

INTIMATE DISCLOSURES

and his hand moved to her thigh, squeezed it and then stayed there.

'Sure,' he said, 'fire away.'

Nina took a deep breath. It wasn't really her place to interfere and Rob, Shane and Michael had already been more understanding than she could have hoped.

'It's just that I read through the script while I was waiting,' she began, 'and I couldn't help noticing how one-sided all the action is. I mean,' she went on hurriedly, 'apart from being – er – fucked and fondled a bit, the actress doesn't seem to come off too well in the pleasure stakes.'

Rob looked mystified. 'I'm not with you,' he said, shaking his head.

Nina cleared her throat. Now she had started, she was finding it difficult to continue. 'I just thought,' she said, 'that it wasn't very fair for her to have to do all that oral stuff and not get any in return.' There she'd done it, she'd said her piece. She sat back, feeling satisfied and relieved.

For a moment Rob was silent. He stared at her wordlessly until Nina felt her stomach knotting and then turning to water. Then he said, 'You know something? You're absolutely right.' He glanced over to the other side of the room. 'Hey, Shane! Come over here a minute.'

Shane, Nina noticed, looked reluctant to leave the actress's side but rushed over to speak to Rob anyway. After Rob had repeated what Nina had said, the young man turned to look at her.

'It sounds a bit gratuitous to me,' he said bluntly. 'If we put in some oral for her, we'll have to cut a bit out somewhere else.'

Nina felt herself blushing as she replied, 'Couldn't they spend a bit less time fucking? I mean, does it add anything to the film to have them performing in so many different positions? Surely the audience would get more turned on by seeing the female character actually enjoying herself, instead of having to act it.'

'She will enjoy herself,' Shane protested. 'Grant's a very well hung boy.'

Pursing her lips, Nina gazed levelly at him. 'Ever heard the phrase, size isn't everything?'

'She's got a point, Shane,' Rob cut in, much to Nina's relief – she was beginning to think she was a minority of one, in a world of macho misconception. 'You know as well as I do these actresses are always complaining that they're too dry to perform properly. I think if tantalising Tanya over there,' he cocked his head in the actress's direction, 'was truly sexually aroused it would come across brilliantly on film. And we could dispense with the KY.'

Listening to the exchange, Nina couldn't help marvelling at it, and at the fact she was there at all. It was all a very long way from the damp-walled bedsits and noisy neighbours of her previous research. She was startled when Michael suddenly leaped to his feet and clapped his hands loudly.

'OK, people,' he declared, his sweeping glance taking in everyone in the room, 'five minutes. Then we'll go into the studio. We've got to get moving, time's money.' His glance landed meaningfully on Rob who nodded.

'May I use the telephone?' Nina asked, suddenly remembering her responsibilities. 'As it looks as though I'm going to be here for the rest of the day I ought to phone my assistant to let her know.' She felt very grand referring to Maisie as her assistant.

As usual, Rob was all smiles and geniality. 'Of course,' he said, 'use the one in reception, then ask Sarah to show you through to the studio.'

A few minutes later, as Nina gave Maisie a censored version of what had transpired that morning, she reflected on the true situation. Even now it was difficult for her to believe that in a short while she would be watching three complete strangers having sex.

Chapter Eight

Nina was familiar with studios but the one she entered, after she had made her phone call to Maisie, seemed very odd. She supposed it was because the studio was not purpose built but merely a room that had been left bare, save for the set itself and a few apt director-style chairs scattered here and there.

The set was a bedroom. On two sides, hardboard walls were covered with pale blue emulsioned anaglypta and the raised floor area was carpeted in a deeper shade of blue. The kingsize bed was the only piece of furniture. Draped in navy satin, Nina could see straight away what an excellent backdrop it would make for what was about to take place on it. She let her mind take flight at the imagery of golden limbs and torsos writhing about on the dark satin.

As far as Nina could recall, the scene to be shot was a simple one, with little dialogue and a lot of fucking and sucking. She shuddered at the thought, realising that if she had continued with her charade it could have been her and not Tanya, alias Lavinia, who would have been the star performer.

At the moment Tanya and the two actors were sitting down. Instead of chatting among themselves they were gazing into space. Nina supposed that they must be psyching themselves up for the parts they were about to play. As the only spare seat was next to Luca, she walked over and sat down.

He turned his head immediately and fixed her with

a penetrating, sloe-eyed stare. Then, very deliberately it seemed, his eyes travelled the entire length of her body, right down to the tips of her toes. Equally slowly, they travelled back up until they met her uncertain gaze again.

Nina felt mesmerised. Her body had begun to tingle all over as Luca appraised her and she realised, with a sinking feeling of fatality, that she was hopelessly attracted to him. Like a magic potion, the clichéd tall, dark and handsome combination was weaving its erotic spell on her yet again.

'At first I thought you were the actress,' he said in a low voice, leaning sideways so that only she could hear him, 'my disappointment stabs me like a sword.'

Nina laughed nervously. Honestly, she thought, these Latin men can be so dramatic. Nevertheless, she felt flattered and told him so.

'Maybe after,' he suggested, 'you and me, we 'ave our own rehearsal, yes?'

'Um—' Nina stalled. From the corner of her eye, she was relieved to see Rob making his way toward them.

'Shane and Michael are ready when you are,' Rob said with a pointed glance at Luca and then the others.

Appearing not to be at all put out by Rob's interruption, Luca smiled evenly. Bracing his large, tanned hands on the arms of the chair, he pushed himself up. Deliberately pausing to flex his shoulder muscles he glanced at Nina. He looked pleased with himself, she noticed and cursed herself for staring so blatantly at him when it was obviously what he wanted.

Unlike Luca, Grant leaped to his feet with athletic vigour, tossing his floppy haired head. And Tanya rose more gracefully, only allowing her nervousness to show when she began twittering to Shane and Michael about camera angles and getting her best side.

'Yeah, up her fat arse,' Grant mumbled unkindly, earning himself a reproving look from both Rob and Nina.

'Less of that,' Rob warned, 'I don't know what you've

got against Tanya but it better not come across on camera, otherwise you're off the picture.'

Grant postured a bit. 'No worries, boss,' he said, sliding his hands into his back pockets and thrusting his bare chest out, 'I can make out like I enjoy fucking any woman. You know that. God,' he paused to toss his head again, 'what an actor!'

As he wandered off, still swaggering, Rob turned to look at Nina. His expression was rueful. 'It's all true, unfortunately,' he said to her, 'Grant Cheyenne, if you can believe such a name, is one of the best erotic actors in the business. Seeing him in action I'd defy anyone to guess that he's gay.'

'Gay!' Nina blushed as the word shot out of her mouth. Hastily, she lowered her voice, 'Sorry, I mean, gay? Are you sure?'

Rob nodded and patted her hand. 'I know, it's incredible isn't it? Still,' he added, looking thoughtful, 'all the best ones are. Even Señor Macho over there.'

Nina shook her head as she followed Rob's gaze to the edge of the set where Luca stood. 'Oh, no,' she asserted, 'he's definitely not gay. He tried to chat me up just now.'

'Poor, innocent little Nina,' Rob mocked kindly as he sat down beside her in the seat Luca had vacated, 'can't you tell the difference between acting and realism?' He smiled at her. 'No,' he went on, 'I don't suppose you've ever had to before. At least, not consciously.'

Ignoring Rob's sarcasm, Nina found her gaze rivetted to Luca. Gay? He couldn't be. Surely not?

Just at that moment, as if to confirm the validity of Rob's claim, she saw Luca reach out and squeeze Grant's left buttock. The two men shared a knowing smile which made Nina sit back and reassess her opinion of the world and everyone in it. In a way, she decided in that instant, it was fortunate that Luca wasn't heterosexual. At least it meant she wouldn't have to do battle with her conscience about whether to turn him down or not.

Shane shouted to the actors to take their places then hoisted a large video camera on to his shoulder. Michael was similarly equipped and when Nina turned to Rob and asked him why there was no sound man, he told her that the soundtrack would be dubbed on afterwards.

'They'll still speak their lines now though,' he told her, 'otherwise we'll lose continuity.'

It pleased Nina that Rob spoke to her as one professional to another. Though he could be patronising at times, mostly he treated her with respect and made his interest in her as a woman more than clear. If it was only for the fact that he was useful to her research she would want to see him again. All at once, Nina realised that because she had been thinking so hard she had missed the start of the action. When she finally turned her attention back to the set she noticed that Luca was strutting about, giving his orders to Grant.

'I want you to kiss my wife,' Luca was saying, 'kiss her hard and fondle her over the top of her clothes. Then I want to watch you strip her naked. She likes it, the bitch, I can tell she's hot for you.' He cast a narrow-eyed glance at his 'wife'.

Tanya, playing the part of Lavinia, pretended to protest. 'Pedro no, you know I don't want it like this.'

'You do as I say, bitch,' Luca growled. Grabbing her by the arm he thrust her toward Grant. 'You say I am not enough of a man for you, then take this guy. Let me see him fuck you the way I used to.'

As Luca took a deliberate step back, Grant pulled Tanya tightly against him.

Unable to help her curious gaze straying, Nina fancied she could see a distinct tumescence straining at the crotch of Grant's tight jeans. It was so convincing she found herself marvelling at his acting ability. Despite what Rob had told her, she found it difficult to believe that either man was gay – even though she had insisted to Tom that most porn actors were homosexual only a couple weeks earlier. At least these

INTIMATE DISCLOSURES

two were good-looking, she reminded herself, not like the men on the film she and Tom had watched. Tanya though, she mused wryly, was typical of the porn actress breed, if only for her tumbling mane of platinum hair, pouting lips and stupendous chest.

With the vaguest stirring of arousal, she watched as Tanya's breasts were crushed against Grant's chest as he pulled her roughly into an embrace. The actor kissed her passionately, scrunching up her hair in one hand while the other hand massaged her buttocks. His hand slid under the hem of Tanya's shocking pink dress and he pulled down a tiny, white-lace g-string.

'Panties!' Luca snapped, his dark eyes flashing at Tanya, 'I told you no panties. Why must you always disobey me, Lavinia? Now you will have to be punished.'

While Grant stood and gawped, Luca stepped forward and yanked Tanya out of his arms. Turning, he sat down on the end of the bed and pulled Tanya with him, positioning her over his lap, face down. Nina felt her libido kick in as she watched Luca raise the back of Tanya's dress and deliver a series of stinging slaps to her well-rounded bottom.

As if galvanised into action by the erotic sight, Grant unzipped his jeans and took out his cock. Nina marvelled at how stiff it was and watched enthralled as he began to masturbate furiously. All the time his eyes were fixed to Tanya's squirming behind, which was becoming redder and redder as Luca continued to slap it.

Tanya was whimpering by now and Nina felt her mouth becoming drier. She shifted uncomfortably on the chair, only too aware that her naked vulva had begun to swell and moisten in direct response to the scene being acted out in front of her. A moment later she felt Rob's hand slip over her thigh and inch under the hem of her skirt. She glanced sideways at him and noticed that he was not looking at her but at the set. Parting her thighs wider, she gave into the irresistible desire to be caressed intimately.

Rob's fingers probed her streaming vagina, driving in deeper and deeper until Nina was panting quietly. She tried desperately not to attract the attention of the others, or to disturb their professional concentration. It wouldn't be fair, she told herself, moaning shamelessly inside her head. Then, oh God, Rob, just don't stop touching me!

Luca pushed Tanya roughly off his lap. She sprawled on the floor at his feet, legs spread wide and her hair in disarray. She looked thoroughly wanton, Nina thought, desiring the young actress herself and simultaneously shocking herself with the realisation.

As Shane moved in with the camera, Tanya opened her legs wider, displaying her swollen vulva to the glass eye of the camera lens.

'Wider,' Shane muttered, 'and lift your bum up a bit. I want to come right between your legs and get a good close up of your cunt.'

Hearing Shane's instructions and then watching Tanya comply with them as if it were the most natural thing in the world, Nina felt her breath becoming short. She spread her own legs wider, as wide as the arms of the chair would allow, and raised her own hips just a fraction so that Rob's hand would have greater access to her body. Her whole vulva was throbbing by now, the rest of her body tingling with sensual excitement and demanding fulfilment.

Nina though it incredibly lewd to watch Shane kneeling between Tanya's thighs with the camera trained on her most intimate parts. And to see the expression on Grant's face as he continued to masturbate himself. But it didn't stem the flow of her mounting arousal, quite the reverse. With an inner quiver of shame, Nina realised that the more humiliating the situation, the more turned on she became.

Michael was filming the whole scene from a slight distance and now he changed position as Shane stood up and walked backwards until he was just beyond the edge of the set.

INTIMATE DISCLOSURES

At a nod from Shane, Luca said, 'Get up, you whore, and suck him.' He nudged Tanya with his toe. 'Go on, do what you do best, get your pretty little mouth around his prick.'

Crawling on her hands and knees, with her naked, glowing bottom swaying from side to side, Tanya went to Grant. Kneeling up in front of him, she reached for his cock and caressed it for a few moments before feeding its entire length between her glossy, sugar pink lips.

As Tanya mouthed Grant, Nina sucked in her own breath. It was becoming harder and harder for her to breathe normally. Rob's fingers were doing magical things to her hungry sex and she was fast reaching the point of no return. She groaned softly as she felt his thumb circle the tip of her clitoris. After a few moments of this she began to grind her vulva eagerly against his hand. Even though it was a struggle, through heavy lidded eyes she forced herself to concentrate on the filming while Rob's fingers stimulated her.

Michael, she noticed, was squatting down, his camera capturing every lick and suck, as well as the assured manipulation of Tanya's fingers on Grant's stiff shaft. Slender and pink-tipped to match her lips, they played his cock like a musical instrument.

In the meantime, Shane had moved around the set to film the rapturous expressions on both actors' faces.

'I take it this is all going to be edited together?' Nina gasped, glancing just for a moment at Rob's profile.

'Oh, absolutely,' he said, 'without editing, most films just look as though they've been made by an amateur. This is a quality production.'

Nina wanted to say something complimentary but her breath caught as, in the next moment, she watched Luca haul Tanya to her feet, rip off her dress and throw her naked on to the bed.

'He's very masterful isn't he?' she groaned, hardly bothering to disguise the note of longing in her voice.

'He's supposed to be,' Rob murmured back, 'that is the part he's playing. Lavinia is submissive you see?'

Feeling idiotic, Nina shook her head. 'Not really,' she confessed, 'I haven't got around to that side of things on my research yet.'

She heard Rob laugh. It was low and throaty but not mocking.

'How old are you?' he asked rhetorically, adding with a smile, 'You haven't begun to live yet have you, darling? I can't help wondering how much kinkiness you would have got round to discovering if you hadn't been assigned to make your documentary.'

Nina fell silent, considering his words. It was true, she thought. Even though she had previously considered herself as sexually sophisticated as the next woman, she realised now that her erotic education had huge gaps in it. She was only just starting to find out that there were so many things she hadn't experienced before.

'Can you point me in the right directions?' she asked him, 'I want to learn everything.'

The movement of his fingers quickened inside her, causing her to gasp. 'I love the way you do that,' he confessed.

Nina felt confused. 'Do what?'

'Ask me for my help and place your trust in me,' he answered. 'Somehow it makes me think of you as virginal.'

She laughed as she squirmed her body against his touch. 'I don't think I behave like a virgin, do you?'

This time, Rob favoured her with a glance. His eyes were dark and lustful, as penetrating as his fingers. 'Virginity is a state of mind, not of body,' he said enigmatically. 'Now concentrate on the filming or I won't make you come.'

Biting her lip to stem the flow of the reply that sprang immediately to her lips, Nina turned her attention back to the film set.

The first thing that struck her was how flattered she felt

INTIMATE DISCLOSURES

that Shane and Michael had taken her suggestion on board. True to Nina's concept, Tanya now was laying on her back with her knees drawn up and apart while Grant lay on his stomach and lapped at the swollen pink flesh of her vulva.

'Go on, eat her,' Luca urged, ad-libbing. He sat at the head of the bed, stroking Tanya's hair with one hand and the jutting orbs of her naked breasts with the other. 'Come on, superstud,' he taunted Grant, 'get your tongue right inside her. That's it, now lap up all that cream.'

Nina felt sure her groan of lust matched that of Tanya's. Right at that moment she would have given anything to swap places with the young woman on the bed. Her own clitoris felt so swollen she was certain she couldn't hold back her orgasm much longer and yearned desperately to feel a tongue flickering over it. Yet however much she wanted to come, she dreaded the thought of doing so because she knew she wouldn't be able to keep quiet about it.

Just watching the young actress thrashing about on the bed, with Grant's blond head buried between her thighs, was enough to make Nina orgasm. But when Rob suddenly began tapping her clitoris repeatedly with the pad of his forefinger she felt a familiar onrush of lustful sensation. Moments later, by luck more than judgement, she managed to time her muted cry of release to coincide with Tanya's much louder moans.

While Nina was allowed to bask in the afterglow of her orgasm, Tanya was afforded no such luxury. Getting right back to the script, Luca ordered Grant to, 'Put that prick in her and fuck her hard.'

Reclining back languidly, with her legs still splayed apart, Nina watched enthralled as the gaping red mouth of Tanya's vagina beckoned to Grant.

In an instant, Grant turned Tanya around so that she was positioned on her hands and knees, her back arched and bottom thrusting high into the air. Then he knelt behind her and slid his hard cock straight into her wet opening.

Nina had never witnessed such close up fucking before. Even during her visit to the swappers' club and her experience at Male Overload she had been far too preoccupied with her own enjoyment to take much notice of what else was going on around her. Now though she was able to luxuriate in the spectacle of Grant thrusting into Tanya.

Each time he withdrew slightly she saw how his shaft glistened with the young actress's juices and the way her swollen flesh seemed to grab at his cock and draw it back in again. The whole thing was so erotic it made Nina ache to be a part of it.

Occasionally, her view was obscured by either Shane or Michael going in for a close up. But most of the time they filmed from a slight distance. Nina could understand this. Tanya and Grant's expressions were too sensational not to capture on video tape. And the sight of the young woman's dangling breasts was as alluring as those of her churning hips and moist sex.

Nina felt as though she was burning up with desire as she witnessed the scene. Particularly when she saw how wet Tanya had become. This wasn't just acting, she told herself, no woman could get that aroused purely for professional reasons.

She was startled by Rob's whisper of encouragement.

'Why don't you go over there and touch her?' he said, 'I can tell you want to.'

Nina tried to deny it by shaking her head but she couldn't ignore the way her heart suddenly started to pound at his suggestion.

'I couldn't,' she muttered lamely, 'it's not in the script.'

Rob caught her chin, forcing her to turn her head and look at him. His eyes glittered. 'Forget the film,' he said, 'just follow your instincts.'

On shaky legs, Nina got up. As she walked across the narrow divide between her chair and the edge of the set she felt as though she were moving in a trance. All she could think about as she walked was the young woman on her hands and knees. She wasn't interested in the sight of Grant's hard cock, or even Luca's macho appeal, but excitement pounded inside her as her gaze raked Tanya's blushing sex, nicely rounded bottom and pendulous breasts.

She ignored Shane's look of surprise as she skirted around him and sat on the edge of the bed. Reaching out she cupped one of Tanya's dangling breasts in her hand. It felt hot and heavy and in comparison to the size of the breast its nipple seemed delightfully tiny. Nina caught the hard little bud and toyed with it gently, rolling it between her thumb and forefinger.

The actress's delighted whimpers were all the encouragement Nina needed to climb right on to the bed and position herself so that she could caress both breasts. Even knowing that they owed a lot to silicone, she still couldn't help feeling a huge surge of desire as her hands roamed them sensuously.

After a few moments and still feeling vaguely trance-like, Nina allowed her fuzzy gaze to follow the sinuous contours of the young woman's naked body. Golden skin gleamed on the generous curves and as her hands left Tanya's breasts to roam her back and hips, Nina revelled in its silky smooth texture.

Glancing up she noticed that Shane had his video camera trained on the movement of her hands. She blushed, feeling that she shouldn't be doing what she was doing, especially not when it was being filmed, yet feeling hopelessly unwilling to stop.

'Take your blouse off,' Shane whispered to her, 'press your naked breasts against her back.' He motioned to Grant to move out of the way.

Nina watched Grant's cock slide out of Tanya's body while her fingers scrabbled with the buttons on her blouse. She felt feverish – hot and cold at the thought of what she was about to do and yet full of yearning for the sensation of her flesh against that of the young woman. Her awareness that Shane's camera was trained on her as she shrugged off her blouse and dropped it on the floor was acutely thrilling. It was horrible. It was arousing. It was, oh God . . . !

As Tanya knelt upright Nina flung herself at the actress. Clasping her arms around the young woman, Nina cupped her full breasts with eager hands and pressed her own breasts and torso against the young woman's naked back.

Tanya's flesh was hot and silky, her hair brushing Nina's bare shoulder as she flung her head back. She was moaning hoarsely and though Nina couldn't see the young woman's face, she could easily imagine her blissful expression.

In front and to the side of Nina and Tanya, Shane and Michael were avidly filming, their video cameras capturing the sensual reality of both women clasped together in a natural, erotic embrace.

Nina sensed Rob coming up behind her and heard him mutter something unintelligible to Luca. 'Improvise, Luca,' she then heard him say in a louder voice, 'just use your brains and do your best.'

In the next moment, Nina felt a finger trace the length of her spine. She knew it belonged to Luca and, as his hands slid down over her buttocks and began to massage them, she had to remind herself that the actor was gay and just doing his job.

Luca's fingers sought the zip on her skirt and pulled it down.

Nina tried to protest but her arguments were feeble and without conviction. The truth was she was hot for this. Burning up with lust.

'No!' The single word came out as a gasp as her skirt was already slithering over her hips.

'Don't fight me, *chica*,' Luca murmured in a voice that was loud enough for Rob to hear and make a note of for the soundtrack. 'You want this, you know you do.'

Feeling helpless in the grip of her own passion, Nina

helped him to remove her skirt completely. Then one of his hands slid between her slightly parted thighs as he turned the rest of his attention to Tanya.

'You did well inviting your friend to join our little party,' he said confidently to her, as though the words had been scripted, 'I will make sure you are both rewarded.'

Nina shuddered with barely suppressed anticipation and she felt Tanya's heartbeat quicken beneath her ribs. As Luca's hand caressed her vulva expertly and her own hands stroked and massaged Tanya's breasts, Nina found it difficult to remind herself of the facts. Her only motivation was pure lust. An overwhelming desire for sensual gratification. It made no difference to her that the cameras were rolling, recording every inch of her exposed flesh. Nor that the people involved were acting.

Somehow, she didn't believe for one moment that Tanya was not enjoying herself. Her arousal was too obvious. By slipping a tentative hand over the young woman's mound and between her thighs, Nina could feel how hot, wet and swollen she was. Grant hadn't come so she knew the juices that coated her fingers were all Tanya's.

Remembering Grant, Nina flashed a curious glance at him. She smiled inwardly as the phrase 'spare prick at a wedding' sprung instantly to mind. His was wilting, she noticed and wondered if there was anything that could be done for him. She and Tanya were far too engrossed with each other to pay him any attention, and Luca was busy caressing her.

'Why don't you do something to excite Luca?' Nina murmured to Grant, 'I'm sure he'd love it if you did.'

The smile Grant gave her in response was one of relief tinged with gratitude. In an instant he was crawling around the perimeter of the bed, making sure he remained in shot. In the next moment, Nina felt the slight brush of his fingertips on the back of her thigh as his hand sought Luca's crotch.

She sensed fumbling, then heard the sound of a zip being

lowered. Something hard and fleshy slapped against her buttock and all at once Luca's fingers began stroking her more urgently. Without having to look, Nina knew that Luca's increased fervour was due to Grant's ministrations.

A few moments later Luca came all over her buttocks. The warm, sticky sensation of his semen spurting over her was unmistakable. Just for that brief moment Luca's fingers stopped caressing her vagina and at the same time Tanya turned around in her arms. Lips, breasts, torsos and thighs met, one body of feminine flesh churning against the other.

Nina felt her senses reeling. Luca retreated from her, his fingers sliding easily out of her vagina and she and the actress fell as one to lay full length on the bed. Shane's camera zoomed in as Nina spread her thighs to allow Tanya's hand to slide over her desperately throbbing sex.

'Wonderful,' she heard Shane say, 'fan-fucking-tastic! Just get those legs a bit wider apart, Nina baby, I want to get this in close up.'

Nina felt her cheeks flood with mortification but it didn't stop her doing as Shane asked. She felt too far gone now. Her body was aching for release and all she cared about was the light touch of Tanya's fingers on her desperate flesh.

'Christ, you're wet,' Tanya murmured in her ear as her fingers delved into Nina's vagina.

It was the first time Tanya had spoken to her and Nina felt as though the words would become ingrained on her memory for ever. The sense of shame she felt as Shane positioned himself on his elbows, the camera trained right between her legs was nothing compared to the strength of her arousal.

'Work those fingers, baby,' Shane urged to Tanya and, a moment later, 'let's see that pretty pink mouth of yours on her pussy.'

With a small gasp of surprise, Nina felt Tanya's long hair brushing her stomach, followed by the agonizingly sweet touch of her lips. Unable to help herself, Nina began whimpering with desire as the young actress kissed her way down her torso, over her belly and into the light thatch of her pubic hair. Feeling thoroughly wanton, she raised her hips and made an offering of her burning sex. She was desperate to feel the cool caress of Tanya's mouth.

'Spread those pussy lips open wide, Tanya honey,' Shane urged the actress in a low voice, 'I want to see you giving her clitoris a good tongue lashing.' In preparation, he shifted the camera on his shoulder and leaned over them both.

Nina moaned at the humiliation and tried halfheartedly to close her legs. But Tanya was positioned between them with her knees braced against Nina's thighs to keep them wide open.

'Show momma what you've got,' the actress murmured as her fingertips spread Nina's labia apart and began to stroke her swollen clitoris. 'Mm, you are a delicious mouthful aren't you, my love.'

Nina felt faint. Faint with a surge of lust so strong she was grateful to be lying down. Tanya's caresses were featherlight, so achingly, tantalisingly gorgeous that she felt her whole body going into meltdown before spiralling into a vortex of carnal frenzy.

She felt strange hands on her breasts. They stroked her shoulders, stomach and thighs. It seemed they were everywhere. I'll see all this happening on film later, she thought vaguely, lost in the throes of the sensuality that enveloped her. It seemed so unreal she didn't protest when a strange cock slipped inside her empty vagina, nor when another pressed itself against her half-open lips. As her entire body was consumed, so her senses were filled with a medley of unfamiliar scents: floral perfume, male musk and the sweet and sour tang of perspiration. And her eardrums throbbed to a wonderful harmony of ecstatic moans, soft whimpers and harsh, ragged breathing . . .

In the far off distance a voice said, 'Cut.'

Then louder, 'Cut. That's it. You can stop now. It's a wrap!'

Nina surfaced slowly, as if from the bottom of the deepest ocean. She glanced around in confusion. The others, Luca, Tanya and Grant were moving away from her and from the bed which made her feel suddenly bereft. Shane and Michael, she noticed, were no longer filming. Only Rob stood silent and apart from the others. He was watching her with a strangely intense expression on his face.

'All done?' she asked shakily, pulling the sheet of blue satin close to her and wrapping it around her naked body. She sat huddled in the sheet, her trembling knees drawn up to her chest. All at once she felt exhausted and a little shell shocked. A tremulous smile crossed her lips as Rob came over and sat down beside her.

'It's a wrap,' he said gently, his hand reaching up to stroke her hair. The sheet slipped from her shoulder a little and Rob moved his hand down to caress the bare skin thus exposed. Allowing her head to drop sideways, Nina rested her cheek on his hand.

She felt bereft of speech and it was only when Rob finally asked, 'Are you OK?' that she finally found the strength to speak.

'Yes, of course.' She smiled up at him. 'A bit tired I suppose.'

The look he gave her was a knowing one. 'I'm not surprised,' he murmured, 'would you like to get dressed and go for a drink somewhere?'

Nina was surprised by his invitation and yet grateful. She had half-expected him to want to continue where the others had left off. Considering his suggestion for just a moment, she raised her head and shook it regretfully.

'Normally I'd love to,' she said, 'but I think all I want to do now is go home and soak for hours in a warm bath.'

'That sounds like a good idea. You'll be stiff in the

INTIMATE DISCLOSURES

morning,' he joked. He stood up and held out a helping hand to her.

As Nina rose slowly to her feet she allowed the satin sheet to fall. It pooled around her feet like a dark blue puddle. She couldn't help but notice the dark flash of desire in his eyes as he looked at her, nor the answering tug in the pit of her stomach. Yet she didn't feel right about changing her mind. Home seemed the best place to be at that moment. With a bit of luck Tom would ring her later, with news of when he would be coming home, she hoped.

All at once she couldn't wait to get dressed and be ready and waiting when his call came. Experimental sex was okay in small doses, she decided, but there was nothing to compare with the slow, sensuous and even sometimes humorous lovemaking she and Tom enjoyed.

Chapter Nine

Seated at her desk at a quarter past ten on Thursday morning, Nina felt as if nothing interesting would ever happen to her again. It seemed inconceivable, she thought, idly tapping her pen on the notepad in front of her, that Monday's highly charged events could be followed by two and a bit days of mind-numbing boredom. And she had nothing, apart from a long list of telephone calls to make, to amuse herself with for the rest of the day.

Is this what happens, she asked herself, when a person starts to expand their sexual horizons? Does everything else begin to pale into insignificance? Was that why some people set out to find kinkier and kinkier outlets for their desires? Putting down her pen and clasping her hands behind her head, she leaned back in her chair and stared at the flaking white paint on the ceiling. If that was the case, she mused, where did it all end?

Idly, she glanced around the busy open-plan office. Everyone there was absorbed in his or her work: talking on the telephone, hammering away at a keyboard, or drinking coffee and making notes. How many of them, she wondered, harboured a sexual secret or two? Did some of them go home at night and transform themselves into avid swingers, or bondage queens? Were there a few closet gays among her colleagues? Did the men visit prostitutes – or even the women come to that? Maisie, as she knew only too well, was sexually voracious and was probably typical of most of the younger women who worked there. She made no secret of her many boyfriends and often talked about 'shagging the guy I met last night.'

As if she could read Nina's mind, Maisie called out from her desk behind Nina's.

'Nina, I've got a woman called Clementine on line eight for you. She says you left a message on her answering machine.'

Nina racked her brains to remember who the woman was. She picked up the receiver hesitantly and pressed the button which would connect the call.

'Hello, Nina Spencer here, how can I help you?'

The answering voice was low and husky, as though its owner smoked too many cigarettes. 'I think it's more of a question of how I can help you,' the woman said. 'I believe you called me from my ad in *Penthouse*.'

That rung a bell. Nina had spent the whole of the previous day combing the small ads in men's top shelf magazines, hoping to speak personally to the assorted women who advertised 'a discreet massage service.' Grabbing the copy of *Penthouse* from the pile on her desk, Nina immediately found Clementine's advertisement. It simply said, 'Beautiful, sophisticated lady offers discreet massage in luxury central London apartment.' Followed by the phone number.

'Yes,' Nina said, feeling relieved that at last one of these women had deigned to speak to her, 'I'm really grateful to you for returning my call.'

Standing in a public call box in a side street in Shepherds Market, Nina drummed her fingertips impatiently on the little metal shelf beside her. It was almost two hours since she had spoken to Clementine and she was late. Traffic congestion and then realising she had picked the only taxi driver in London who hadn't done 'the knowledge,' meant that the success of her secret assignation was hanging in the balance.

INTIMATE DISCLOSURES

To her relief, the phone was picked up at the other end, though it was a strange voice that enquired, 'Yes, how can I help you?'

'My – my name's Nina Spencer,' Nina stammered into the receiver, suddenly feeling nervous, 'I spoke to Clementine earlier this morning?'

She ended on a questioning note that prompted the voice at the other end to reply, 'Oh, yes, I know who you are. OK, I'll give you directions on how to get here. They're quite simple, you won't need to write them down.'

Nina concentrated on the instructions and when she left the call box she headed across the street, turned left and then left again into a little alleyway. At the bottom of the alleyway was a three-storey house with a basement. It was the basement flat that was her ultimate destination. She realised the young woman whom she had just spoken to on the phone was Clementine's 'maid'. From what she had gleaned from her research, most professional call girls had personal maids who answered calls, took bookings from clients and looked after them until the call girl was able to see them personally.

Stone steps, with a black wrought iron balustrade and railings, led down to a minuscule patio which was crammed with terracotta pots of flowering plants. On the wall by the glossy black front door was an intercom. Pressing the buzzer on the intercom, Nina waited until her call was answered then spoke her name into the metal grille.

'Oh, yes,' came the reply, 'turn the handle on the door and push.'

Nina's feet sank into soft, deep pile carpeting as she entered the reception lobby. It was quite large and square, with a range of low comfortable seating covered in a hardwearing peach fabric. All around her, the pale cream walls were hung with abstract prints. Nina got the impression that she had entered a very feminine domain. Her surroundings struck her as being more like a beauty salon than any of her preconceived notions of 'seedy massage parlours.' Indeed, she thought, walking over to the light ash reception desk on the far side of the room, if she didn't know better she could quite easily imagine coming here herself for a massage.

The woman seated behind the desk stood up and introduced herself as Nina approached. She was tall and slender, with short dark hair and was wearing a smartly tailored black and white check suit, the jacket unbuttoned over a red blouse. Reaching across the desk she held out a slim hand to greet her. The nails, Nina noticed as she glanced at the woman's hand, had recently been treated to a French manicure.

'Hi, Nina, I'm Laura, Clementine's maid,' the woman said.

Nina smiled up into deep brown eyes and shook the proffered hand. Laura was not young, she realised, noticing the crow's feet at the outer corners of the woman's eyes and the fine lines around her mouth and nose, but she obviously took good care of herself. Her makeup was as perfect as the rest of her.

'I don't know how much Clementine has told you,' Nina ventured.

Laura smiled back. 'Everything,' she said simply, 'Clementine and I have no secrets. In our line of business, trust is vital.'

'Of course.' Nina sat down on the edge of one of the seats, opened her bag and automatically took out her notepad and a pen.

'Put that away, for God's sake,' Laura hissed immediately, looking alarmed. 'Do you want to frighten all of our clients away? Word soon gets around you know.'

Nina pulled a wry face. 'Sorry,' she mumbled, hastily shoving the notebook and pen back in her bag, 'I wasn't thinking.'

Looking relieved rather than annoyed, Laura sat down again behind her desk.

'Look,' she said, leaning forward and clasping her hands together, 'you must understand Clementine's taking an enormous risk letting you come here. This is a very tricky business for lots of reasons. The men who come here rely on complete anonymity. They trust us to be discreet. One word to the press, or the vice squad, and their whole lives could be in ruins. Not to mention mine and Clementine's.' She let out a long sigh as she sat back again. 'Do you know how hard we, or rather I have to work to keep trouble off our backs?'

Nina shook her head.

'Bloody hard,' Laura said. 'Every call we get from a new client could be a ruse. The press are worse than vice. The police don't really mind about this sort of thing you see. Provided that they don't get any complaints about Clementine they leave us alone. But the press, Christ, they're the real thorns in our side.'

'In what way?' Nina asked, feeling horribly aware that she was one of the loathsome breed to which Laura was referring.

As if she realised who she was talking to, Laura gave a rueful laugh. 'Oh, don't worry,' she assured Nina, 'Clementine has a brilliant nose for trouble. She actually believes you could do us, and the industry as a whole, a bit of good with your programme.'

'I hope so,' Nina said, butting in, 'I want to get the message across that what Clementine is doing is actually of benefit to society rather than a problem.'

'Yes, she told me you said that,' Laura said. 'Anyway,' she went on, 'your job, for the time being, is just going to be to sit there and keep *schtum*. Observe by all means but you must not question any of our clients, is that understood?'

'Oh, absolutely,' Nina agreed, nodding.

'If anyone asks,' Laura continued, 'you're here to learn the business. A trainee maid, got that?'

'Yep, no problem.' Nina nodded even more enthusiastically. 'You can rely on me.'

Laura regarded her levelly. 'I hope so,' she said, her tone and expression deadly serious, 'otherwise we're all in the shit.'

After fifteen minutes or so of no activity, a couple of things happened at once. First, the telephone rang. Then, while Laura was speaking to the caller the intercom buzzed. Asking the caller on the phone to hold for a moment, Laura invited the visitor to come in.

Nina glanced up as the door opened. She was keen to see a real 'client' for herself and had to admit that the man who entered was something of a surprise.

Over six feet tall, dark haired and well built, with a finely chiselled face which was spanned by designer sun glasses with black rims, Nina thought the man looked just like a film star trying to stay incognito. He had announced himself as Jay on the intercom which made Nina wonder if it was a pseudonym, or even just his initial. If nothing else, his appearance made Nina think again about the sort of men she had always assumed used call girls.

As he sat down on the next but one seat to her, Nina flashed him a wary smile and was rather put out when he didn't respond in kind. He gazed stonily at her for a moment through the dark lenses of his glasses before turning his head abruptly away to stare at the print on the opposite wall.

The blue and red lines and swirls of the abstract print taunted Nina. Obviously, they were of more interest to him than her. Shrugging inwardly, she glanced at Laura to see if her expression would give anything away but the other woman was busily engaged in typing something on her word processor.

When she had finished, Laura stood up and walked around her desk to stand directly in front of the visitor.

'Coffee, Jay?' she asked, smiling brightly.

INTIMATE DISCLOSURES

'Yes, thank you, Laura and a digestive or two if you have them,' he said.

His accent was very upper middle class. Nina glanced at his clothes and noticed that the dark blue suit he was wearing was well tailored, if conservative. And his black leather shoes looked as though they were handmade. The cuffs and collar of his blue and white striped shirt were very white and the cuffs were set off by square, gold, diamond-cut cufflinks. Dark hair protruded from the cuffs and on his left wrist he wore a Rolex oyster watch.

'Have you quite finished?' he asked suddenly, turning to look at Nina again.

Startled, she jumped. 'Oh – er – sorry, I didn't mean to stare,' she floundered, 'I just—'

He waved a hand dismissively at her. 'Don't bother,' he said, 'I am not really all that interested.'

Well! Nina felt like exploding at him. Not interested? How bloody arrogant could you get? She opened her mouth to offer a quick retort, then closed it again just as rapidly. You're here to observe, she reminded herself, not to tear a strip off one of Clementine's clients. It galled her to sit in silence and wait for something to happen. But sit there she did until eventually the door beside her opened and another woman appeared.

This must be Clementine, Nina thought as she eyed the woman up and down. Unlike her maid, Clementine was quite short and not at all slender. Though she wasn't exactly the sort of shape that Nina would describe as fat. Voluptuous would be a more apt description, she supposed. With her long cascade of auburn hair and large violet eyes set in a rounded but pretty face, Clementine was certainly an arresting sight. And she simply exuded sex appeal.

Nina felt the pull of instant attraction for this woman and could easily imagine that she was a popular call girl. She could well imagine men flocking to her establishment in their thousands crying, 'Take me, take me, the money's no object!' She smiled to herself at the illusion and caught an answering smile on Clementine's face.

'You must be the trainee maid?' she said, holding out her hand to Nina, just as Laura had done. But, whereas Laura's nails were long and well manicured, Clementine's were short, unpainted and rounded at the tips. She glanced at the man seated next to Nina. 'Five minutes, OK?'

Nina couldn't help noticing how he seemed to lose his composure when Clementine spoke to him. His cheeks flushed and he had to clear his throat a couple of times before answering.

'Yes, of course. Whatever you say, Clementine,' he mumbled as he stared down at his feet.

Nina had to smother a smile. She stood up as Clementine beckoned to her to follow and found herself entering the older woman's inner sanctum.

For some reason, she had expected Clementine's consultation room, as she called it, to be stark white and clinical. Instead, it looked more like a room in an old-fashioned bordello, with heavy red drapes at the windows to match the counterpane on the large brass bed. A long, gold velvet covered ottoman stood at the foot of the bed. This piece of furniture matched the ornate chaise longue that stood on bowed mahogany legs in the deep bay in front of the window.

'Fabulous, isn't it?' Clementine enthused, whirling around gaily.

She was dressed in an ankle length kimono, patterned predominantly in red, gold and blue. When she spun round, the kimono parted at the front to reveal surprisingly shapely, cream stocking-clad legs.

Nina grinned as she nodded enthusiastically. 'You really love all this don't you, Clementine?' she asked perceptively, before adding, 'I can't tell you how much all my preconceived notions have been shattered to smithereens already.'

INTIMATE DISCLOSURES

Clementine laughed and led Nina over to the ottoman. They sat down side by side. Crossing her legs, Clementine turned to face Nina.

'First of all,' she told Nina in her husky voice, 'only my clients call me Clementine, to my friends I'm simply Clemmie. That's still not my real name of course, only my relatives and gynaecologist know that.' Pausing for a moment, she patted the kimono, located a pocket and drew out a pack of Benson & Hedges. She tipped one out and lit it, then inhaled deeply. 'Yes,' she said with a theatrical sigh, 'I indulge myself in all the vices.' Her laughter turned into a cough and she pulled a wry face at the cigarette.

'Life's too short not to, I suppose,' Nina observed, smiling warmly.

'Too right, darling,' Clemmie said as she patted Nina on the shoulder. Leaning back against the brass bedstead she gazed up at the ceiling as she smoked. Occasionally, her mouth formed an 'O' and puffed out a perfect smoke ring. 'I don't know if you're going to get all that much of interest out of this visit,' she went on after a few thoughtful puffs. 'I try to make my involvement in this business as glamorous as possible. I couldn't do it otherwise. But even so, it can still become as boring and repetitive as any other job.' She paused to laugh again. 'I call it the daily grind.'

Nina chuckled along with her. 'I must remember that.'

With narrowed eyes Clemmie said, 'Better not. I'd hate my clients to think I didn't enjoy every minute. They all believe they're special to me, you see. It's a knack you've got to have if you want to be successful at this. Each one of them believes that he is my special number one client.'

'I can imagine him out there thinking that,' Nina murmured, inclining her head toward the wall that divided them from the reception area. 'He strikes me as a bit of a bighead.'

'Big head, small dick,' Clemmie said lightly, eliciting a surprised glance from Nina. 'Oh, yes,' she added, 'the arrogant ones are the worst for that. I suppose they've got to compensate somehow. But I wouldn't take any notice of Jay, he's a pussycat in tiger's clothing. One of my favourites actually. He likes to go down on me.'

'Is that unusual then?' Nina asked, marvelling at the woman's frankness.

As she got up to stub out her cigarette in a brass ashtray which stood on top of a little antique dressing table, Clemmie glanced back over her shoulder.

'I'll say. With most of them it's half an hour of pouring out their hearts to me, followed by a quick wank or whatever. Most of them don't give a fuck about giving me any pleasure. That's what makes Jay so special. Out of all of them he really is my number one client, bless him.'

Nina couldn't help but notice the note of fondness in Clemmie's voice and was prompted to ask, 'Do you dislike any of your clients?'

'Oh, no, not dislike,' Clemmie said, shaking her head emphatically. She started to preen herself in front of the mirror. 'They are all special to me in their own way. It's just that some I enjoy being with more than others.'

Nina glanced at her watch. 'Am I holding you up?' she asked. 'I don't want my being here to interfere with your business.'

Turning round, Clemmie leaned back and rested her hands on top of the dressing table.

'I suppose I should get on,' she admitted, as though she had a stack of letters to type. 'Would you like to stay and observe?'

'What – really?' Nina was amazed.

Clemmie laughed again and waved a hand toward a screen in the far corner of the room. Covered in red felt, with a gold scroll design, it was draped – deliberately, Nina assumed – with a pair of sheer black stockings and a suspender belt.

'You can sit behind there and play the voyeur,' she

said. 'Go on, it doesn't worry me,' she added when Nina hesitated. 'Unless you don't want to—'

'Oh, no, I do,' Nina interrupted hastily. She walked across the room and glanced back over her shoulder as she reached the screen. 'I can't tell you how grateful I am.'

'Shut up,' Clemmie admonished, straightening up and reaching for the door handle. 'Don't bother to thank me. Just make sure you give us working girls a good representation on your programme.'

Nina felt her heart beating fast as she sat on the low padded stool which she found behind the screen. By positioning herself just so, she was able to look around the edge of the screen while remaining unobserved. From the place where she sat, she could see most of the bed and the chaise longue by the window.

It excited her to know that she was going to be witnessing a very private scene and that one of the people she would be observing would have no idea she was there. Placing a hand against her rib-cage she felt her rapid heartbeat for herself. I am becoming such a wicked person, she mused, Tom won't know what's hit him when he comes home tomorrow.

She couldn't wait to see Tom. There was so much she had to tell him. Since their last long, highly charged phone call they had only been able to speak to each other a couple of times. And even then it had only been for a few minutes on each occasion. The night before though, Tom had rung her briefly to say that he would be catching a flight home around lunchtime on Friday. Nina, anxious to see him again after so long apart, had promised to go and pick him up from the airport.

Just as she was pondering the sort of fun she and Tom could enjoy the following evening, she heard the door open and Clementine inviting Jay to go in and make himself comfortable. From her vantage point behind the screen, Nina watched Jay walk up to the bed.

For a moment he simply stood, looking down at it. Then he turned around and sat down, quite tentatively, on the edge.

'Come on, Jay, relax,' Clementine urged, coming briefly into view. She moved away again and Nina heard the chink of glasses. 'I'm going to have a glass of champagne, Jay, will you join me?' she added.

Jay's plummy voice was hesitant. 'Yes, er, that would be lovely.'

He still looked uncomfortable, Nina thought, and she couldn't help wondering how many more times he would have to visit Clementine before he learned to relax in her company.

Clementine didn't seem to notice his ill ease and chattered away inconsequentially as she poured their drinks. A moment later she walked back over to the bed and handed Jay a tall flute glass. Touching the rim of her own glass to his she said, '*Santé*,' in a seductive voice.

'Cheers, bottoms up,' Jay responded with just the merest flicker of a smile. 'You know, Clementine,' he went on, 'I have had one hell of a week.'

'Have you, my love?' Clementine sat down beside him and reached up to his face to stroke back a thick hank of hair. 'Why don't you slip off those shoes and socks and lie back? Then you can tell me all your troubles.'

Jay did as she suggested, plumping up the pillows behind him and reclining back. And for ages it seemed he talked and talked. Much of his conversation was about his business, which was demanding too much of his time. His family, which by all accounts was similarly demanding. Then, finally, he mentioned his wife Sarah.

Nina, who had almost fallen asleep by this time, suddenly sat up and began to take notice. So now she was about to discover why a man like Jay should find it necessary to

INTIMATE DISCLOSURES

visit a call girl, she thought, aching to take out her notepad but not daring to. On this occasion she would have to rely totally on her memory.

'Is your wife still seeing her therapist?' Clementine asked.

Jay sighed. 'Yes, bloody quack. You know I have told her she is wasting her time seeing him but she won't listen to me. Oh, no. According to her the sun shines out of his backside. Mr *Marvellous* Manderley, what a name!' He paused to sigh again and take a long swallow of champagne. 'I am convinced Sarah is having an affair with him.'

Nina saw Clementine was trying hard not to smile. Instead, the older woman pursed her lips and took Jay's empty glass from him.

'I've told you before that's probably not the case,' she called over her shoulder as she walked over to the other side of the room. 'Women quite often get fixated on their therapist, or doctor. It's very normal. I mean when you really think about it you—' She paused as if reconsidering what she was about to say.

'Go on,' Jay prompted, with a slight edge to his voice.

Clementine walked over to him again and handed him a replenished glass of champagne.

'I was going to say,' she said softly, 'that your wife's therapist provides a similar function to me. Apart from the sex, of course.' She laughed lightly. 'Oh, come on, Jay,' she added, giving his arm a friendly punch, 'you know as well as I do she's not sleeping with him. He's just someone who listens to her. You pay me to listen to you. Why would you be here now otherwise? If it was just sex you were after you could bed just about any woman you wanted. You're a good-looking man.'

'This is entirely different,' Jay said, ignoring her compliment and looking as truculent as a schoolboy.

'No.' Clementine smiled as she shook her head gently. 'It isn't, Jay. It's exactly the same. Everyone needs someone to talk to. Someone they can trust and who won't judge them. There is no difference.'

For the first time Nina noticed Jay offered Clementine a genuine smile. And all at once she knew what stance she would take with this particular part of the *Intimate Disclosures* programme. She watched, feeling her stomach clench with anticipation as Jay sat up, put down his glass and reached out to Clementine.

'Come here, you wonderful woman,' he said in a voice that was thick with emotion, 'I simply do not know what I would do without you to talk some sense into me.'

Discreetly untying the belt on her kimono, Clementine allowed it to slide off her shoulders as she moved to straddle Jay's legs which were stretched out on the bed. Underneath she wore a cream lace basque, the suspenders framing a thick bush of glossy auburn hair.

'That's enough talking for now, my love,' she said huskily, reaching forward to undo the buttons on his shirt, 'I think we can find a lot more interesting things to do to pass the time.'

The time of which Clementine spoke seemed limitless in that sequestered room. The womb like decor enhanced the feeling of warmth and sensuality. Feeling a part of the proceedings yet apart from them all at the same time, Nina found herself squirming uncomfortably.

As Clementine undressed him, Nina couldn't help noticing what a lovely body Jay had. Well built but nicely toned, it was faintly tinted with the soft golden glow of a suntan. And his well-defined chest and shoulders were covered with a fine down of dark hair. Underneath his trousers he wore a pair of red Calvin Kline briefs which seemed a startling contrast to his sober outer wear. Tight and stretchy, they clung to deliciously taut buttocks like a second skin.

When Clementine pulled these down over lean hips and equally lean, hard thighs, his cock sprang free. Already erect

INTIMATE DISCLOSURES

it pointed straight up to his navel from a thick nest of dark hair. As Clementine had said, Jay's penis was below average size but still looked to Nina as though it was capable of giving a woman a lot of pleasure. And beneath it, his scrotum hung like two furry plums just waiting to be plucked and enjoyed.

As though she could read Nina's mind – or perhaps she and the older woman were simply on the same wavelength – Clementine immediately reached out and cupped Jay's balls in her hands as if weighing them. She caressed them in a way that was gentle and reverent, then bent forward to nuzzle and lick them.

Wearing an expression of pure bliss, Jay fell back against the mound of pillows at the head of the bed, one long leg dangling over the edge, the foot touching the floor. The other leg was bent up, the knee almost touching the bed. It was a position that exposed his manhood in such a way that it struck Nina as both trusting and vulnerable.

She envied Clemmie, she realised, as she fought to keep her breathing silent and even. Her erotic senses were stirred by the situation and at the sight of Jay's glorious body. Playing the voyeur was all very well, Nina thought, except that it didn't offer her much in the way of physical release.

Throwing caution to the wind, Nina felt under the hem of her dress. A plain sky blue, the cotton sun-dress ended just a couple of inches above her knee. Spreading her thighs apart, her hand immediately sought the moist warm place between them. She was wearing only the flimsiest pair of lace panties and with one hand holding the crotch of them to one side, she was able to caress herself with the other.

Her heart was beating rapidly. On the other side of the screen she saw Clemmie kneel up then crouch low over Jay's prostrate body. Her long auburn hair brushed enticingly over his bare chest and stomach as she lathed his nipples with her tongue.

Jay was groaning quietly, his hands mindlessly roaming the generous curves of Clementine's hips and milky white bottom. Working continuously, his fingers dug into the rounded globes, easing them apart then together again in a steady rhythm.

Clemmie was squirming, her pelvis churning with obvious excitement. Nina had often wondered if call girls simply went through the motions with their clients. But it was clear to her that the older woman just beyond the screen was enjoying every moment of her encounter with Jay.

And little wonder, Nina thought, watching one of his hands caress Clemmie's plump, sticky sex. He was obviously a skilled and enthusiastic lover. His fingers were working deeply inside her now and Nina used her own fingers to simulate his caresses on herself.

Her own vagina was creamy wet with arousal and her fingers slid in easily up to the knuckle. Stroking the velvety walls, she found the sensitive spot behind her pubic bone and began to caress it, her thumb simultaneously rubbing the swollen bud of her clitoris.

Knowing her body as well as she did, Nina sensed that orgasm was only a few strokes away. Anxious to delay it for a little while longer, she moved her thumb away from her clitoris and simply teased the sensitive folds of her labia instead. Without direct stimulation of her clitoris the burning lust that had threatened to overwhelm her ebbed a little. Even so, Nina could feel her heart palpitating rapidly and inwardly cursed the sound of her short, jagged gasps of pleasure.

Thankfully, these were muffled by Jay's elated groans and Clemmie's frequent moans and whimpers. The older woman also kept up a running commentary of lascivious comments, mostly remarking on Jay's beautiful physique, the impressiveness of his erection and the effect his caresses were having on her body.

Again, Nina didn't doubt she meant every word. She

INTIMATE DISCLOSURES

could see quite clearly the effect Jay was having on Clementine.

Her breasts were swollen, the nipples huge and juicy-looking. And the ivory flesh swung from side to side like pendulums, grazing Jay's bare skin as she moved to lick and caress every part of his body.

All at once Jay, who until that point had remained relatively passive, suddenly sat up and pushed Clementine over backwards. Her shapely legs sprawled wide on the bed and Nina felt her breath catch as the gorgeous man swooped between them to claim the pouting flesh of Clementine's vulva with his mouth.

The saliva in Nina's mouth dried instantly. And a slow but inexorable warmth spread over her. Once again her thumb sought the hard nub of her clitoris which pulsed insistently. She circled the tip slowly. Each caress was agonizingly poignant and yet pleasurable in the extreme.

Under the skilful onslaught of Jay's lips and tongue Clementine came in a rush, her generous mouth opening wide to emit a scream of, 'Oh, God, yes—'

Now it was obvious that Jay was in control. His demeanour and deft movements dominated Clemmie who lay panting and submissive under the languorous weight of her partially spent passion. Scooping her up from the bed, Jay carried her over to the chaise longue. Once there he put her down, positioning her knees on the soft fabric so that they were spread wide apart.

She faced the back of the sofa, her arms resting on the polished wood. In that position, with her back arched and her bottom thrusting out, she appeared even more shapely. Her waist seemed sharply indented and her hips flared out into generous and enticing curves.

Jay stood behind her. He held himself erect, his torso hard and muscular, his buttocks tight and rounded. For agonizingly delicious moments, Nina watched his hands follow the sinuous contours of Clemmie's body. His hands cupped her breasts, fingers toying idly with the nipples, before sliding down over her stomach and between her parted legs.

Nina gave an involuntary moan which matched that of the older woman. She was past caring that she might be discovered behind the screen. And she believed Jay was too intent on caressing Clementine's body to take any notice of what might be going on around him. Sliding both her hands between her legs, Nina cupped her sex. She felt its wet stickiness coating her fingers, and delighted in its warmth and the strong throbbing of her clitoris.

The most exquisite foreplay was that which she viewed from behind the screen. The sight of Jay's hard cock sliding into Clemmie's moist vagina almost made her come immediately but she pressed her palms against her hot sex, willing herself not to capitulate yet. There was more to enjoy. And she knew her final pleasure would be all the more exquisite for making herself wait.

As Jay gripped Clementine's hips and thrust into her with long, measured strokes, so inspiration struck Nina. Beside her in a wrought iron candelabra was a long white candle, unused. With only the merest hesitation Nina plucked it from its holder. Holding her vaginal lips open with the fingers of one hand, she guided the end of the candle into the wet channel of her vagina. Deeper and deeper she pushed it in, until it would go no further. Then she began to simulate Jay's thrusts, sliding the pale stick of wax in and out until she felt her internal muscles convulse around it.

Rocking and writhing on the stool, she managed to ride out the hot waves of her orgasm in total silence. Only when Clemmie let out another long scream of ecstasy did Nina allow herself to let go completely. And when she did her cry of release was rent silently, the echoes of erotic passion reverberating throughout her entire body.

Chapter Ten

Frustration of a non-sexual kind gnawed at Nina the following morning. She was desperate to take her time getting ready to meet Tom later that afternoon and was nervous about driving to the airport. She drove so rarely and was unsure of the route she should take. And she found Heathrow hellish at the best of times. All of this conspired to make her feel resentful about having to go into work that morning.

As it was Friday she was committed to the usual end of week conference with Liam. And she knew that, barring holidays and serious illness, her boss would accept no excuses for nonappearance.

Reluctantly, Nina dragged herself out of bed, under the shower and then into her clothes – a short, flirty skirt in sky blue, white ribbed tee-shirt and thong sandals. By the time she managed to flag down a taxi she had already walked halfway to work and consequently arrived looking and feeling totally frazzled. The last person she needed to see, looking her old bright and efficient self, was Karen.

'Nina, hello, we were beginning to wonder if you were going to make it.' Karen glanced pointedly at her watch as Nina entered the conference room.

Nina glanced at her immediate superior, noting the pristine white plaster encasing her leg and the pair of crutches propped up against the wall behind her. She couldn't help marvelling at the way Karen managed to look disgustingly chic despite her disability. She was dressed in a tailored navy gabardine shorts suit. The shorts looked more like a mini skirt and were cut high enough to allow for the plaster cast.

'Isn't she a trooper?' Liam enthused as he came into the room just as Nina sat down. He beamed fondly at Karen, then flashed Nina a look that demanded her wholehearted agreement.

'Oh, er, absolutely,' Nina mumbled as she tried to smile brightly. She reached down beside her where she had placed a stack of paperwork on the floor. 'Fortunately,' she added, not wishing to linger on Karen's wonderfulness, 'we in research haven't been too handicapped by the situation.'

Knowing her remark sounded vaguely bitchy, Nina avoided eye contact with Karen. Instead, she concentrated on sorting through her paperwork. When this was done she handed Liam a freshly typed copy of her notes and an update of the progress she and Maisie had made so far.

Liam spent a while reading through them. Then, when he had finished, he glanced up and nodded approvingly.

'You really seem to have got a handle on all this, Nina,' he said. 'Congratulations are in order.'

Looking daggers at Nina, Karen smiled sweetly at Liam and leaned across the amoeba-shaped table.

'May I see?' she asked, reaching out for the notes. Unlike Liam, Karen was less than enthusiastic about Nina's efforts. And she flicked through the paperwork with obvious disdain. She clearly wasn't happy about the implication that she was not indispensable. 'I agree with Liam,' she said finally, looking directly at Nina with an insouciance that made Nina want to slap her finely-hollowed cheeks. 'This is good stuff for a beginner but there are some huge gaps.'

'We're barely halfway through,' Nina responded through gritted teeth. 'All the major legwork has been done. Now we're working on the follow through.' She leaned forward and all but snatched the papers away from Karen's slender hands. 'As you can see, I've got quite a few signed appearance agreements. We've got a good two hours of television here.

INTIMATE DISCLOSURES

With the extra guests I still need to recruit, the whole thing will edit down very nicely.'

'You don't think there might be too much to work with?' Karen countered.

Nina clenched her hands tightly in her lap. 'No,' she said, 'not when you consider how diverse the sex industry is. It's like opening one of those Russian dolls, you know?' She glanced at Liam who nodded.

'Good alliteration,' he said, beaming broadly, 'we might use that. In fact,' he went on, 'I think we should just let Nina carry on with this. I was going to put you back on the case, Karen, but all things considered I think the project's progressed too far. And we've got loads of new ideas that need investigating. You can get on to those instead.'

Glancing sideways at Karen, Nina noticed the other woman was fuming beneath her pasted on smile. For a moment Nina thought Karen was going to try to argue with Liam but instead she widened her smile – which failed to touch her eyes – and said, 'Of course, Liam, whatever you decide is best.'

Karen wasn't to remain quite so amenable, Nina discovered when they finally closed the meeting. Halfway up the staircase on the way back to their office, the other woman stopped in her tracks and turned to face Nina. Her eyes blazed.

'You think you're so bloody clever don't you, you little bitch?' she hissed angrily. 'How dare you take advantage of my accident to suck up to Liam to improve your chances.'

Nina was taken aback by the vehemence of her attack, and the injustice of it. 'I – I wasn't, I haven't—' she stammered.

The response was a disparaging sigh. 'It's my own fault,' Karen continued, 'I obviously underestimated you.'

All at once Nina regained her *sang froid*. 'I think maybe the real problem is you overestimate yourself,' she replied boldly. 'All I ever wanted was to do my job to the best of my ability.' It suddenly occurred to her that sometimes she had taken her obligations a little too far, or let her enthusiasm get the better of her. 'Liam's no fool,' she went on, ignoring the nagging voice in her head. There was no reason to admit how far she had gone in the name of research. 'And I think he was right to keep me on this project. It makes sense not to upset the applecart at this stage.'

'Any more clichés?' Karen sniped back. 'You and your "it's really like a Russian doll,"' she mimicked Nina's voice, 'you make me sick.'

Fed up with the way the conversation was going, and anxious to get on her way to Heathrow to meet Tom, Nina pushed past Karen and made to climb the rest of the stairs. Really, she fumed, a remark like that didn't deserve to be credited with a response.

Then, as an afterthought, she stopped abruptly and glanced over her shoulder. 'If seeing someone else do a good job and getting the credit for it makes you sick, Karen,' she said, glaring at the angry face behind her, 'then perhaps you should think about readmitting yourself into hospital. I don't think anyone around here would miss you all that much.'

Regretting her outburst, even though she felt it was justified, Nina shook all the way home in the taxi. And when she got behind the wheel of her car she had to sit and take several deep breaths before she felt calm enough to set off. She hated confrontations like that at the best of times and was surprised at herself by the way she had reacted to Karen's verbal attack. Nevertheless, she told herself firmly, there had been no good reason for such nastiness. Superior or not, Karen didn't have the right to slate her for doing a good job in her absence.

Thankfully, the traffic out of London was light and Nina made it to the airport in good time. Having parked the car

INTIMATE DISCLOSURES

in the multi-storey car park, she entered the cosmopolitan milieu of Terminal One.

Watching all the people coming and going she felt a pang of envy. They were lucky to have the freedom to travel. All she wanted to do right at that moment was get on a plane and take off somewhere. Anywhere would do as long as it was away from Karen, Grassroots Productions and the sexually confusing world she had become embroiled in.

Seated in a blue plastic chair in the arrivals' lounge she fantasised about meeting Tom, turning him around and heading straight for the ticket desk for a flight out again. 'Don't ask questions,' she would say, 'let's simply throw caution to the wind and go somewhere exotic.'

Straight away she realised it was a futile dream. She and Tom were both too committed to their careers to do anything that impulsive. They had to juggle time constantly simply to be together. A spur of the moment holiday was out of the question.

Just as she was debating the hopelessness of her situation, Nina heard the tannoy announce that Tom's flight had arrived. In front of her the arrivals' board clicked out its confirmation. Tom's plane had landed at long last. In a short while he would be through customs and baggage claim and she would be able to put her arms around him again. It was a wonderful prospect.

The next fifteen minutes seemed to drag by but eventually, as she stood just beyond the barrier at the arrivals' gate, she saw Tom emerge. He was surrounded by a throng of other people but in Nina's eyes he stood out head and shoulders from them all.

'Nina, my precious girl!' Tom called out, his face lighting up when he saw her.

She felt her legs go weak. Tom in the flesh was far more poignant than her memories of him. In a moment he had rounded the barrier and flung his bags to the floor.

Wrapping his arms around her he picked her up and held her in a bear hug.

With her toes dangling inches above the ground, Nina sighed with pleasure as his mouth sought hers for a deep, lasting kiss that was full of emotion.

'God, I've missed you,' she managed to gasp out when he let her go.

Grinning, he ruffled her hair and bent to pick up his bags again. 'I've missed you too, baby,' he murmured, 'I can't wait to get you back home.'

'Mm, me too.' Nina smiled at him and took his arm. She could hardly keep her hands off him and had to touch him constantly to reassure herself that he really was there with her at long last.

As they walked toward the lift that would take them to the car park she kept glancing at Tom's profile. He seemed no different and yet the flesh and blood reality of him was so intense it was almost surreal. Thinking back over her experiences of the past couple of weeks she realised that, while she had had some fun times, they had merely served as a substitute for Tom. Now he was back with her in the flesh all she could think about was the two of them alone together.

'Tom,' she said, clutching his arm urgently as they reached the parked car, 'I don't want to wait until we get home. Let's go somewhere. All I can think about is having your cock inside me again.'

Looking pleased but a bit bewildered, Tom glanced around the deserted car park. Without saying anything he unlocked the car and began stowing his bags in the boot. All the time he was doing so, he was also thinking.

'Right,' he said decisively, slamming the boot lid down. He looked Nina up and down, appraising her. In one swift movement he put his hands round her waist and lifted her up, depositing her on the boot of the car. Then he yanked off her panties.

INTIMATE DISCLOSURES

'Wha – what are you doing, Tom?' Nina giggled nervously as she glanced around in confusion. Looking down she saw that Tom was pushing her legs wide apart and at the same time fumbling with his fly.

Excitement coursed through her. Even though her whole body was trembling she could feel the heat rising within her. Immediately her sex flesh began to tingle and she felt the proof of her passion trickling out of her.

'This is crazy, Tom,' she protested feebly, half laughing, half moaning as he grasped her hips and pulled her right to the edge of the boot lid. She put her feet on the bumper and braced herself with her hands so that she could raise her hips slightly to meet his advancing cock.

'I don't care if it is crazy,' Tom said gruffly as he thrust himself inside her, 'I've been dying to do this. It's all I've been able to think about during the flight back. You and your horny little body, your lovely wet cunt—'

'Oh, God, Tom!' Half out of her mind with passion, Nina rammed her pelvis hard against him, meeting him thrust for thrust. 'Fuck me hard, Tom. For God's sake fuck me hard!'

She could feel her swollen clitoris mashing against his pubic bone, his rhythmic thrusts dragging at her sensitive labia. Their lust was so carnal, so basic that she thought her mind and body were going to explode in tandem.

He was looking down at her. At the place between her legs where their bodies were joined. Her eyes travelled down. She could see her own widespread flesh and almost swooned at the sight of Tom's cock sliding in and out of her body.

'Harder, Tom, harder—' she groaned. Wrapping her legs around his waist she welded herself to him. At the same time she threw her head back, thrusting her breasts provocatively at him.

Bra-less and shielded only by the thin white tee-shirt, their outline could clearly be seen. They looked full and luscious, the nipples hard and bullet-like beneath their scanty covering.

With an anguished groan Tom grappled with her tee-shirt, pulling it from the waistband of her skirt and pushing it up over her full breasts. Lowering his head he took one nipple in his mouth. He sucked it hard. Greedy, like a baby suckling its mother, his lips tugged at the distended bud until it grew to twice its original length. Then he got to work on the other one.

Nina arched her back further, pushing as much of her fervent body against him as possible. Her vagina felt wet and hot and hungry, it gripped the full length of him yet grasped for more. She could feel the hard metallic boot beneath her bare bottom, her buttocks squirming on the slick film of her own juices which had pooled beneath them. And her breasts felt huge, as hot and swollen as her sex. Carnal gratification was everything at that moment. The desire to fill and be filled, fuck and be fucked.

Her climax was almost upon her now and she risked moving a hand so that she could put it between her legs. For a moment her fingers lingered on the hardness of him. They delighted in the feel of the stretched, sticky flesh of his stem each time it withdrew from her gaping vagina. Then she moved her hand, her fingers working quickly and rhythmically over her clitoris.

A moment later she came, with a huge cry and a shudder that almost put Tom off his stroke. But her vaginal muscles were strong. They gripped him tightly. And as the waves of her orgasm swept through her she felt herself convulsing around him, precipitating his own orgasm.

For a while he continued to move in and out of her. Then, reluctantly, he withdrew. Tucking his cock back inside his trousers, he stroked his other hand between her legs. When he raised his hand his fingers glistened with their combined juices.

'Wanton little hussy,' he said, smiling directly into her

INTIMATE DISCLOSURES

eyes, 'I ought to take you home and give you a good spanking.'

Her eyes twinkled devilishly. 'If you think you're man enough.'

The challenge was issued on a wave of soft laughter which was snatched away from her in an instant as he suddenly raised her legs and pushed them back toward her chest. Pinning them back with his forearm, he raised his free hand and slapped her upturned bottom smartly.

'That's what you get for being cheeky,' he said, releasing her legs again. 'Now, put your panties on, you little madam, and get in the car.' He turned to give her a mock frown which quickly dissolved into a smile as he added, 'And let that be a lesson to you.'

Even though she had just orgasmed, Nina felt a fresh surge of excitement. The humiliation of being thus treated only seemed to add an extra frisson to her reawakened desire for Tom in the flesh. She didn't have time to ponder her feelings, or to suggest second helpings because, in the next moment, a sudden clatter followed by an echo of voices told her that they were no longer alone in the car park.

Scrambling hurriedly off the boot of the car, she grabbed her knickers from the aerial where they hung, flag like, pulled down her skirt and rushed around to the passenger door. As soon as she was inside the car she put her knickers back on again.

'That was close,' she said, smiling at Tom as a couple of men in dark suits and a woman walked up to the car parked just three spaces away from them.

Leaning over the centre console, Tom clasped her face in his hands and kissed her. 'I really am glad I'm back,' he said when he broke away. His expression was, for once, completely serious.

'So am I,' Nina replied hoarsely, gazing back at him while trying to get her breath back. 'Believe me, so am I.'

* * *

With the edge taken off their initial frustration they chattered freely as they drove home. Every so often Nina would break off to rub her bottom and give him a rueful glance.

'It's still stinging,' she said when they reached Hammersmith. 'I don't know how some people can bear to be whipped and caned and things.'

'You still haven't got to the bottom of that yet then?' Tom punned intentionally.

'Idiot,' Nina countered pertly, punching him lightly on the arm. 'No I haven't as a matter of fact. I thought I'd wait until you got back so that we could visit a fetish club together.'

Tom raised his eyebrows in mock resignation. 'Oh, God,' he murmured, 'now I remember why it was such a relief to be away. It's a hard life being a TV researcher's boyfriend. Only joking,' he added quickly, just in case Nina thought he was serious.

'I know,' she said. She slipped down further in her seat and turned her head to look at him. 'This project has been hard work though, believe it or not. And I am glad you're back. Not just because I want to drag you off to meet a load of wierdos.' She let a few moments slip by and then added, with an expression of pure innocence, 'The funny thing is, although I think it's a pretty odd thing to admit to, I quite enjoyed being spanked.'

Nina was sorry she had to leave Tom at the flat to go back to the office for a little while. She would have preferred to join him in the shower and then drag him off to bed for what remained of the day. Instead, she had no choice but to leave him lying on the sofa with a bottle of cold beer and a sandwich and trek all the way back to work.

There she found a stack of phone messages waiting for her. The one that interested her the most was an urgent entreaty from Rob to ring him back as soon as possible.

As soon as Nina sat down she picked up the phone. In the

INTIMATE DISCLOSURES

middle of dialling, she remembered something and turned her head to glance at Maisie.

'Could you be a love and sort out those fetish club details for me?' she asked.

'Sure thing, boss.' Maisie grinned as she gave Nina a mock salute. Then she lowered her voice and added, 'Karen's been in a foul mood all day today. Even worse than before. What did you do to her this morning?'

Rob's number was engaged so Nina put the receiver down and swivelled round to face Maisie. Even though Karen wasn't at her desk she too kept her voice deliberately low.

'She's pissed off because Liam said he wants me to stay on this project. He's taken her off it and put her on to other things.'

Maisie shrugged. 'Well, big deal,' she said, 'what can she expect when she's been away for a while? She knows as well as anyone how fast things move around here.'

'She's annoyed because I didn't make a total cock up of this,' Nina replied. 'I honestly think she was expecting everything to fall apart in her absence. As far as she's concerned, it's a bit galling to come back to work to find everything still running like clockwork.'

'Silly cow,' Maisie muttered. She shuffled through a stack of papers and drew out the ones Nina wanted. 'Here you go,' she said, leaning over her desk and holding them out.

'Thanks.' Nina took the lists and glanced through the names and addresses of all the fetish clubs in the country. 'I didn't realise there were so many to choose from,' she commented, glancing back up at Maisie who laughed.

'Well, there are a lot of pervy people about,' she said, 'I should know, I once had this boyfriend who—'

Nina stopped her in her verbal tracks. 'I'd love to hear all about it, Maisie,' she said, smiling, 'but perhaps some other time, eh? I've got to try and get through to all these people before they pack up and go home. Lucky bastards,' she added, knowing she still had a good couple of hours work ahead of her.

'Course,' Maisie said, 'don't take any notice of me and my runaway mouth.' She stood up. 'Coffee?'

'Love one.' Nina watched Maisie walk away, then turned her attention back to the phone. She pressed re-dial and was relieved to hear the phone ringing at the other end. A moment later it was answered by Rob.

'Nina, you gorgeous hunk of woman,' he enthused, 'where have you been? I've been trying to reach you all day.'

'In a meeting and then out,' Nina said. She felt herself smiling as she reclined in her chair. 'So, Rob, what can I do for you?'

His laughter was instantaneous. 'Want me to give you a list?' The tone of his voice was seductive and Nina could feel herself starting to glow with pleasure. 'What I was really calling about,' he went on, 'is a party tomorrow night. It's for a good friend of mine who's just come back from Argentina. He and his wife have been swinging for years. The place is fabulous, by the way, with every sort of luxury you can imagine. Do you think you could make it?'

Nina only had to think about it for a second. 'We'd love to,' she said, stressing the 'we'.

'Great, so Tom's back then,' Rob said, sounding not in the least disappointed. 'Michelle is looking forward to playing with him.'

A somersaulting stomach took the place of Nina's earlier glow.

'Oh, well, wonderful,' she managed to gasp out, 'do you want to give me all the details? I'm ready when you are.'

She made a note of the address, the time of the party and the names of the host and hostess. Then she and Rob chatted for a few minutes. He told her the film they had shot was currently being edited and she would be able to view 'the rushes' in a few days. So much had happened since then, Nina had almost forgotten about the film. And

INTIMATE DISCLOSURES

she wasn't at all sure that she wanted to see the finished product. Somehow, she mused, she couldn't imagine the video tape version looking half as good as the real thing.

After she had said goodbye to Rob and put the phone down, she sat forward in her chair and rested her chin in her hands. Staring off into space, with her thoughts miles away, she hardly noticed when Maisie put a mug of coffee down on the desk beside her elbow.

What she was having difficulty getting to grips with – now that she had reverted her mind to it – was not watching the video film but the idea of Tom fucking another woman. And in front of her. If she could look at it rationally, she realised, it would be no big deal.

She had done enough playing around lately and while it had been fun at the time it had meant absolutely nothing. Somehow, though, she couldn't quite bring herself to feel so blasé about sharing the man she loved with another woman – or women. There were bound to be others at the party who would want to join in the fun.

What was doubly difficult was that she couldn't think of another living soul in whom she could confide. Because she worked such long and erratic hours she had few close female friends. And those she did have were totally 'straight'. If any of them knew what Nina had been up to lately, she realised, they would either be shocked, or incredulous, or both. Even Maisie, she thought, who was very laid back about all things sexual, probably couldn't relate to Nina's predicament. She had already freely admitted that – in her words – she had never been stupid enough to fall for a man.

When she finally got home later that evening, she entered the flat wearing an extremely glum expression. Even though she thought she had managed to disguise her feelings Tom's instant, 'Hi, babe,' followed by, 'hey, what's up?' told her that she hadn't managed to do a very good job of it.

Walking into the sitting room, she sat down and told him

all about it. She spoke honestly, leaving out nothing at all, not even bothering to disguise her feelings which – she freely admitted – were probably horribly hypocritical.

'Well, I don't need to fuck other women,' Tom said candidly, when she had finished, 'so if you don't want to go, we won't go.'

Though she felt grateful to him, Nina sighed. 'It's not that simple though is it, Tom? If I'm going to do this job properly I have to go to these things. And—' She broke off and looked sheepish.

'And despite everything, you quite like the idea,' Tom finished for her.

Nina glanced up at him. Their eyes met and held. Oceans of understanding passed between them. Eventually, she glanced down again.

'I'm so stupid, aren't I?' she mumbled.

Cupping her chin, Tom raised her face to look at him again. 'No,' he said gently, 'not stupid, human.' For a moment he paused, thinking about the dilemma. 'Look,' he added finally, 'why don't we just go along and see how things pan out? Then, if at any point you're not happy about going with the flow we can just make our excuses and leave. It makes no difference to me either way.'

'I wish I could be as laid back as you about things like this,' Nina admitted, feeling overwhelmingly grateful to him.

Tom smiled gently at her and pulled her into his arms. 'If we were all the same,' he reminded her, 'think what a dull old world this would be.'

'Well, we certainly can't say our lives are dull at the moment,' Nina said, giving him a rueful smile in return. She snuggled up close to him and let her hands travel over his body, one hand seeking and enclosing his cock. 'Now that's enough talk. I think we've got some catching up to do.'

Chapter Eleven

The address Rob had given Nina was for a flat in an exclusive residential street in Mayfair. Tom drove into the private driveway and then had to spend ten minutes or so trying to find somewhere to park. There were a lot of cars, mostly of the prestige variety. While he was negotiating their modest little number into a space between an Aston Martin and a Daimler Nina felt her stomach knotting.

It was a lovely summer's evening. The air was still and balmy, enfolding Nina's bare arms with the light warmth of a cashmere shawl. She was wearing a plain white stretchy dress that clung to every curve and had a lacy panel sewn into a deep plunge neckline. She wore no underwear and through the lace the generous swell of her cleavage was enticingly visible. As she swung her legs out of the car she felt the soft breath of air caress her bare skin and whisper between her thighs where her naked sex tingled in response. Her hand trembled as she stooped to pick up her bag from the footwell. She was nervous and yet as excited as hell by the prospect of the forthcoming evening.

Tom guided her by the elbow as they walked up to the Georgian facade of the building. He located the right buzzer on the intercom panel by the front door and when Michelle's voice answered Nina took over and announced her and Tom's arrival.

With a *click* the front door opened and they entered a large square vestibule. The floor, walls and ceiling were all white. The flooring was marble, veined with thin threads of blue and greyish green and from the high ceiling hung a sparkling crystal chandelier.

Directly in front of them a wide mahogany balustraded staircase beckoned invitingly. Rob and Michelle's apartment was on the top floor and Tom and Nina decided to climb the four flights of winding staircase instead of taking the lift. Impressed by the way their feet sank into the thick cream and floral patterned carpeting that covered the stairs, they glanced at each other.

Nina tried hard to quell the excitement that mounted inside her with each step she and Tom took. The knowledge that Michelle fancied her seemed both strange and exciting. If Michelle had been a man she would have thought hardly anything of it but because she was a woman . . .

Recollecting her limited experiences with Angel, Nina knew instinctively that her anticipated liaison with Michelle would be far more sensuous and rewarding.

On the upper landing the front door to the apartment stood wide open. Wondering why she felt so out of her depth all of a sudden, Nina took a couple of deep breaths to try and calm her nerves. She gripped Tom's hand as he walked confidently up to the door.

Several exquisitely dressed couples could be glimpsed through the open doorway and Nina immediately felt demoralised by the sight of them. Her choice of outfit, which she had believed was appropriately provocative for such an occasion when she had put it on, now seemed cheap and tarty in comparison to the beautifully cut designer dresses the other women were wearing. She glanced at Tom and was about to whisper to him that she wanted to go home when Michelle suddenly appeared in front of them and welcomed them in.

As soon as they stepped over the threshold Michelle said, 'Nina, darling, so good of you to make it,' and took both Nina's hands in her own. She squeezed them warmly and smiled directly into Nina's eyes.

INTIMATE DISCLOSURES

Embarrassed by the unexpected display of affection, Nina lowered her gaze. She noticed that the fingers which were wrapped around her own were slender and artistic, with long red painted nails. And on the third finger of Michelle's right hand a large ruby balanced out the sparkling diamond of the engagement ring on the left.

On this occasion Michelle's hair was pinned up in a soft, slightly bouffant style from which a few stray tendrils escaped. These meandered down the sides of her face enhancing its delicate bone structure. And her slim, fine boned body was draped in a flowing ankle-length sheath of cream silk. The dress seemed to emphasise the satiny, bronzed skin of her shoulders and arms, while the elegantly draped Grecian-style neckline revealed a light dusting of freckles across her throat and cleavage.

Something indefinable tugged urgently at Nina's insides. She couldn't remember Michelle having this effect on her the first time they had met. But tonight Nina couldn't help thinking how devastatingly beautiful she looked. Obviously, she thought, glancing sideways at Tom, her partner was of much the same mind as her.

He smiled disarmingly as Michelle dropped Nina's hands and clasped his instead, though more briefly.

'When Nina told me about you, she didn't mention you were gorgeous,' Tom said, flashing Nina a quick grin. 'Thank you for inviting us here tonight, I feel privileged.'

Nina felt like kicking him. Tom hadn't said anything that wasn't true but that didn't stop her feeling as though her beloved boyfriend had inadvertently managed to knock her down a peg or two in Michelle's estimation.

This is ridiculous, she told herself as they followed the other woman into the *main salon*, there is absolutely no reason why I should worry what Michelle thinks of me. Except, she realised with a jolt, she desired the other woman like crazy.

Even as she acknowledged the truth of the situation, Nina

felt her insides unknotting and turning to water. Without realising it, her gaze had been rivetted to the metronome sway of the cream silk clad hips in front of her. Now her eyes swept up the erect, slender back to the graceful column of Michelle's neck. And all at once she felt an overwhelming urge to plant a kiss on the satiny skin there.

A fierce wanting surged through Nina and she had to fight an inner battle to maintain a neutral, though friendly expression. When they reached a semicircular black marble bar in the corner of the room the other woman turned to her and Tom and asked them both what they would like to drink.

Mumbling, Nina asked for a glass of white wine and Tom waved away Michelle's insistence that he indulge himself and opted for a glass of Coke instead. As soon as Nina and Tom both had drinks in their hands Michelle excused herself.

'I'm still expecting a couple more people so I must be ready to greet them,' she said. She waved a hand at the fourteen or so couples populating the large, elegant room. 'But please go ahead and enjoy yourselves. Circulate a bit. Everyone here is like-minded and ever so friendly.'

Nina turned to Tom and between them they scanned the room. Nina counted fourteen couples, all young, or youngish and infinitely better looking than the crowds she normally came across at parties.

'This is the life, eh?' she said uncertainly, tucking her hand in the crook of Tom's arm. Privately she marvelled at his ability to look so relaxed when she was churning inside. She gave his arm a slight tug. 'Shall we mingle?'

'Sure, whatever you want, sweetheart,' Tom said affably.

They toured the room slowly, stopping to listen in to snippets of conversation here and there. Nina quickly came to the conclusion that every one else present knew each other fairly well. There was a lot of light banter and teasing, and laughter seemed to tinkle around them like the sound the drop

INTIMATE DISCLOSURES

crystals dangling from the chandeliers overhead made when a draught caught them.

She was just about to confess to Tom that she felt very much like an outsider when all of a sudden Rob appeared. He had another couple in tow, a blond haired man who looked to be in his early thirties and a brunette of the same age.

'Hi, babes,' Rob said, hugging Nina and kissing her on both cheeks, 'glad you could make it.' He turned to Tom and shook his hand effusively. 'You've got a great girl here you know.'

'I know.' Tom gave Nina a proprietorial squeeze and almost jumped out of his skin in the next moment when the brunette reached out and stroked her hand over his crotch.

'Nice,' she said, smiling at Tom as she gave his cock a quick squeeze. 'It's about time we had some new blood around here.'

Far from feeling shocked by the woman's action, Nina found the situation – especially the look on Tom's face – amusing. Burying the giggle that rose up inside her, she took pity on Tom's temporary loss of speech and took over the introductions.

'Ah, a Tom,' the woman said, 'my first lover was called Tom. He was much older than me but experienced, you know? Just right for an innocent young virgin. And a lovely, lovely man. Are you a lovely man, Tom?'

Her speech was slightly slurred and her quick glance back at Tom seemed to knock her off balance. To steady herself she made a grab for Tom's arm.

'Yes, he is,' Nina cut in before Tom could offer his own reply. In all honesty, she thought, he looked like a freshly caught fish; all gaping mouth and goggle eyes.

'Well, in that case,' the woman said, taking Tom's hand and drawing him away from Nina's side, 'he and I are going to have a nice smoochy dance together and a little fun.'

Tom looked at Nina for reassurance and she gave it,

with a conspiratorial smile and an almost imperceptible nod of assent.

'So, Nina,' Rob said, when Tom and the brunette had disappeared into another room, 'how has life been treating you this past week?' He paused to give her an appraising glance. 'You look gorgeous by the way.'

Nina giggled at his blatant flattery. It gave her a warm glow inside and under the piercing intensity of his appraisal, she suddenly felt much better about her choice of clothing – what little there was of it.

'Life's been OK,' she offered, 'even better now that Tom's back.' Then she lowered her voice and added confidentially, 'I went to visit a high class call girl. That was interesting.'

Rob and the man beside him both laughed. 'Oh, I'll bet it was,' Rob said, 'are you that hard up for a bit of physical release?'

'Not for me, you idiot,' Nina responded, joining in the laughter and pushing him lightly against the chest, 'for my research.'

Rob raised his eyebrows. 'Oh, yes, they all say that.' In the split second before Nina could pull her hand away from him again, he grasped her by the wrist.

With her palm pressed flat to his chest Nina could feel his body heat and the hard, insistent rhythm of his heartbeat. Feeling nervous all of a sudden, she gulped at her wine.

'Come on,' Rob insisted, taking the glass away from her and setting it down on a nearby table, 'as you're all alone I'm going to whisk you off to the dance floor.'

'I'm sure she wouldn't be alone for long,' the other man cut in.

For the first time Nina looked properly at him. She noticed his pale blue eyes, framed by equally pale lashes. He had the slightly sagging softness to his features that suggested a libidinous lifestyle. By the way he looked at her – as though he was having difficulty focusing – she guessed he was either myopic or well on the way to becoming drunk. She shuddered inwardly. Although he had hardly spoken she didn't feel at all comfortable with him. And she was glad of Rob's offer to dance if only for the reason that it would take her away from him.

Rob led her into an adjoining room where all the furniture had been cleared to make way for a temporary parquet dance floor. Tom was there dancing with the brunette and there were a few other couples slowly shuffling around in circles. Though the actual steps seemed to be the last thing on their minds, Nina noticed, eyeing the straying hands.

Stepping into the circle of Rob's arms she allowed the hypnotic rhythm of the music to envelop her. As they danced, she couldn't mistake the growing hardness of Rob's cock and the way it was pressed insistently against her belly. Nor could she disregard the knowing exploration of his hands over her back and buttocks.

He pressed his mouth against the side of her neck and she let her head drop back. Desire in all its vibrant glory was upon her. It had been kept just below boiling point ever since Tom's return and had been given a sudden boost at her meeting with Michelle. Now it flared up again, heating her pelvis and swelling her breasts. Arching her back she ground her lower body hard against Rob.

His hand came up and cupped her breast, squeezing slightly. Nina moaned. Wetness trickled out of her sex and her hands grasped mindlessly at his shoulders. Like the other men present he was wearing a dark jacket and trousers, though his rebellious streak led him to wear a shirt of royal blue silk underneath. Sliding her hands over his shoulders and under his jacket she delighted in the texture of the silk and the hard body beneath.

'What would you prefer, bedroom or jacuzzi?' Rob murmured seductively in her ear.

A flutter of anticipation made Nina gasp out her reply, 'Oh, the jacuzzi, I've only ever been in one once before.'

'And did you have great sex in it?' Rob asked, as if it were a forgone conclusion.

Nina giggled. 'Hardly. It was when Tom and I were staying at a hotel in Yorkshire. We shared the jacuzzi with a couple of blue-rinsed old ladies and their husbands.' She paused and chuckled at the recollection. 'You wouldn't believe it but the two men looked as wrinkled as old prunes before they even stepped into the water.'

'Well this time will be different, I promise you,' Rob said, leading her away from the dance floor. 'Wrinklies are strictly banned from our jacuzzi.'

Wondering whether she should tell Tom where she was going, Nina glanced back over her shoulder. He was still dancing with the brunette and both looked as though they had forgotten the rest of the world existed. They had eyes and hands only for each other. Seeing them like that, Nina felt only the briefest pang of envy. Fortunately, she managed to catch Tom's eye long enough to mouth the word *jacuzzi* to him. With relief she saw his nod of comprehension and the message written on his face told her that he would be along shortly.

The bathroom where the jacuzzi was situated was off a huge, luxuriously appointed room which Nina assumed was the master bedroom. For a brief instant she tried to imagine what it must be like to live in such surroundings. To go to bed every night in the huge *lit en bateau* bed that looked wide enough to accommodate two couples must be heavenly, she mused. And she counted at least a dozen floor to ceiling closets.

Rob interrupted her reverie. 'Impressed, huh?' he commented.

Nina turned her head and smiled at him. 'I'll say. This place is fabulous. You must be making a bomb.'

She immediately regretted her ill-judged remark but Rob simply laughed.

'I can't deny it,' he said, 'there is a lot of money to be made

INTIMATE DISCLOSURES

out of sex. But having fun is just as important to me. I haven't reached the stage yet where I've become cynical about it all. And I hope I never do.'

'I'm sure you won't,' Nina responded quickly. 'What with having a wife as beautiful as Michelle and everything. Well, it's a forgone conclusion that you get a lot of pleasure.' She paused to grin impishly. 'And, of course, there's the added benefit of being able to bring your work home with you.'

Rob laughed aloud. 'Cheeky!' he said. His arm was wrapped around her waist and now he squeezed her tightly. 'I'll have you know it can be a hard life being a sexual entrepreneur.' At that moment he became more serious and his eyes darkened perceptibly as he released his grip on her waist. So much so that Nina gave an involuntary shiver. 'What you said about Michelle,' he murmured, 'or rather the way you said it, leads me to suspect that you have the same desire for her as she feels for you.'

Nina felt her mouth go dry. Rob sounded acutely serious and seductive all at the same time. What he said was true though, she acknowledged. She did desire Michelle and recognised her own eagerness to discover the other woman's body for herself. She nodded dumbly in reply, feeling her cheeks colouring. Yet it came as no surprise to her when she walked into the bathroom and found Michelle there.

She was already naked and appeared to be waiting for them.

'Come on in, the water's lovely,' she said lightly, splashing her hands in the foam.

Nina felt her stomach clench as she gazed at the other woman seated in the bubbling water. Just the smooth sweep of her shoulders and the upper swell of her breasts were visible above the bubbles. But to Nina she looked beautiful and achingly tempting – like a siren.

All at once Nina's clitoris began to throb insistently, the passionate surge she felt compelling her to join Michelle as quickly as possible. With no further hesitation she took off her dress and stepped into the jacuzzi as though in a trance.

Needing no encouragement she floated into Michelle's open arms and immediately their mouths became locked in a deep, mutually probing kiss. Michelle's breath was sweet, overlaid with just the slightest tang of gin and lemons. Her lips were soft and wet and full. They parted as soon as Nina's own lips touched them and an insistent tongue immediately darted out and began to explore the inside of Nina's mouth.

When they relaxed out of the kiss and Nina opened her eyes again she noticed that Rob had undressed. Now he was climbing into the water holding a bottle of champagne aloft. He poured some out into three glasses and when they touched glasses in a toast, he said, 'Here's to the pursuit of pleasure.'

Michelle gave a throaty chuckle. 'I'll drink to that, darling.' As she spoke her free hand stroked idly across Nina's breasts, causing Nina to tremble. Turning her head to gaze into Nina's startled eyes, she added, very softly, 'You are so lovely, I could eat you up.'

At her words, Nina felt a rush of emotion so strong she couldn't tell where the water ended and the liquidity of her own body began. A fierce passion surged inside her now, made all the more intense by the appearance of Tom in the bathroom.

He was alone and without saying a word he divested himself of his clothes, laying them neatly on a white leather couch that stood against one wall before slipping into the water beside Nina.

By the working of Rob's shoulder muscles, Nina could tell that his hands were moving beneath the water. Whether he was caressing himself or Michelle she couldn't be sure. It was only when the other woman let out a small whimper that Nina realised Rob was fondling his wife under cover of the bubbles.

Almost of their own volition Nina's hands reached out to

INTIMATE DISCLOSURES

the other woman's shoulders and softly stroked their silky contours. Then her hands slid down over the smooth sweep of Michelle's throat and captured the small, pert mounds of her breasts.

Michelle whimpered again as Nina's fingers sought her nipples and began to toy with them. Her sighs of pleasure mingled with the softly hypnotic strains of Vivaldi, which flowed from cleverly hidden speakers.

'Suck them,' Michelle gasped, arching her back.

A long tendril of her hair had escaped the pins and now dipped into the water. Rob caught it and wound it around his finger. He tugged the lock of hair gently.

'Patience, my darling,' he murmured, 'Nina is new to all this remember.'

The expression in Michelle's eyes was pleading. 'I want her, Rob,' she gasped, 'you know how much.'

Nina caught Tom's glance of surprise. He looked a little out of his depth, she realised, and she reached out to give his hand a reassuring squeeze.

Leaning forward Tom whispered in her ear, 'Are you sure this is what you want?'

Nina nodded. Then immediately wondered if her nod was just a little too enthusiastic.

'I think Michelle is beautiful,' she confessed to him in a loud enough voice for the other woman and her husband to hear.

A darkness filled Tom's eyes. Nina recognised that look. It was pure desire. And no wonder, she thought, gazing back at him, this must be every man's fantasy – and mine too.

Without saying anything else she slipped forward in the bubbling water until she was kneeling directly in front of Michelle. Her legs were spread and Nina shuffled between them. She felt the soft caress of the other woman's inner thighs on her waist. Sliding her hands up the slender length of Michelle's legs she felt the smooth, hairless skin. As Nina's hands travelled higher, the thigh muscles quivered.

Nina knew that response from her own experience. It was a sign of anticipation.

'Don't stop,' Michelle gasped when Nina's hands reached the tops of her thighs.

Turning her hands inwards, Nina's fingers brushed the other woman's soft bush. Working blind, because she couldn't see through the foaming bubbles, Nina gently stroked Michelle's pouting outer labia. Easing the soft folds apart, her fingertips discovered the swollen bud of her clitoris. Just the lightest of touches made the other woman moan with pleasure. And, as Nina began stroking her clitoris in a circular motion she began to writhe and buck her hips.

'Yes, yes,' Michelle gasped, 'that's it. Oh, God, that's it. Don't stop!'

The ability to so easily give the other woman pleasure made Nina squirm with delight. In a moment she felt a hand stroking her own sex from behind. Glancing over her shoulder she saw the loving caresses came from Tom. Rising on her knees slightly, she arched her back and thrust her bottom towards him, encouraging him without the need for words.

Rob reached out and cupped one of her breasts. His other hand stroked Michelle's breasts and Nina watched with pleasure at the way he played with her responsive little nipples. Her own nipples were as hard as bullets she noticed, when she glanced down, just aching to be toyed with.

At the same moment as her fingers sought the moist entrance to Michelle's body, she felt her own vagina being entered by Tom's fingers. As they thrust hard inside she let out a long groan and slid her fingers inside Michelle. Probing into the tight, moist depths she felt the muscles clutching and drawing her digits deeper inside. With the fingers of her other hand she kept up the rhythmic, circular stimulation of Michelle's clitoris.

It seemed incredible to her – though at the time she was too lost in pleasure to think about it – that she and Michelle came almost in unison. Tom was skilled at drawing an orgasm from her, while she – confident in the ways of bringing herself to climax – had no difficulty employing the same techniques to elicit the right responses from another woman.

As soon as they had both come, Michelle and Nina gasped out in unison that they needed to be fucked. Tom was inside Nina in an instant, taking her from behind while they watched Rob fuck Michelle. Water splashed everywhere, the high white walls of the bathroom echoing their groans and sighs of pleasure.

After all four of them were temporarily satiated they lolled about in the foam, idly caressing each other.

Only Tom and Rob steered clear of any physical involvement with each other. Without saying anything at all, they made it clear that neither of them had any bisexual inclinations. But Nina was more than happy to allow herself to be stroked and tantalised by the others and willingly participated in doing the same to Michelle, Rob and Tom.

Their movements were languid, as if choreographed. Lubricated by glasses of champagne and the heady effects of unrestricted desire, the four of them gave and received pleasure until the first couple to leave the party poked their heads around the bathroom door.

As soon as the couple had gone, Michelle clapped her hand to her throat and looked at Rob wide eyed.

'Oh, my God, I'd forgotten about the others,' she said. 'What must they think of us?'

Rob smiled as he fondled her breasts lazily. 'Just that we have been having a good time.' He paused then added, 'I asked Simon and Denise to take over from us and not to let anyone come in here.'

Michelle laughed. 'You horny old rogue,' she said fondly, 'I must admit I did wonder at one point why we were lucky enough to be left alone.' She turned her head and explained to Nina and Tom that normally their guests always made a beeline for the jacuzzi. 'We're not very good hosts are we?' she added, looking only slightly ashamed.

All at once Michelle reached out and took Nina's hand. Drawing Nina close to her she whispered, 'Sit on the side, darling, I want to give you some pleasure now.'

Trembling with excitement, Nina placed her palms behind her on the tiled edging of the jacuzzi and eased herself up and out of the swirling foam. The tiles were warm and damp and she wriggled slightly on them to make herself comfortable.

Michelle moved smoothly through the water to kneel in front of her. Gently she stroked the length of Nina's thighs, using just the slightest pressure to part them.

Nina whimpered with anticipation as Michelle gazed between her legs at the moist, pouting flesh of her sex.

'Mm,' Michelle said, licking her lips deliberately and suggestively. 'What a sweet little honeypot.' She scratched her long nails lightly through Nina's pubic hair, then circled the outer rim of her vagina.

Another whimper escaped Nina's lips. Her vaginal lips tingled expectantly. She felt as though every nerve was charged with electricity, her body sizzling along with her mind. Over Michelle's shoulder she could see both Tom and Rob watching expectantly. Their eyes were dark, their expressions at once eager and lascivious.

They watched Michelle's stroking, exploring fingers. Occasionally, their gazes strayed to Nina's face to witness the changing expression there.

Far from feeling inhibited by their blatant interest in her responses, Nina felt even more aroused. A delicious excitement gripped her, encouraging her to spread her legs wide on the side of the bath and make a visual offering of her eager sex.

Michelle made a little noise of approval. Her fingertips spread Nina's labia wide open, while the pads of her thumbs stroked the stem of her swollen clitoris, working its little cowl of flesh back and forth.

INTIMATE DISCLOSURES

Nina ground her buttocks upon the smooth tiling. She could feel a steady flow of moisture trickling from her gaping vagina. Heat flooded her, the sensations created by Michelle's knowing fingers driving her half out of her mind with erotic pleasure.

Leaning forward Michelle pressed her lips to Nina's blossoming sex. Nina gasped. Her thigh and buttock muscles trembled and she clutched desperately at Michelle's hair. Bunching up the glossy strands in her fingers, Nina thrust her body more urgently towards the other woman's exploring mouth.

A moment later a tongue lathed her inner labia. As it swept over her swollen bud Nina let out a long moan of arousal. Her clitoris was throbbing hard and in an instant her whole sex flooded with heat.

Tom and Rob moved to sit either side of her. By unspoken agreement they bent their heads and began to mouth a nipple each.

All at once Nina's desperate body was suffused with sensation.

'Oh, yes. Oh, please, God, yes—' Her head thrashed from side to side as she whispered words of encouragement.

Between her widespread thighs Nina could feel Michelle's tongue at work, lathing her eager clitoris with smooth, sweeping strokes. The pleasure was almost unbearable and Nina alternately bit down on her bottom lip, then let out another whimpering plea.

Presently Tom moved away from her side and sank back down into the water. Through heavy-lidded eyes Nina watched him rise up behind Michelle. He began to stroke the other woman's back and shoulders, following the slender, almost boyish lines of her body. Sliding his palms under her, he cupped her breasts.

Nina could feel the occasional brush of his arms on her inner thighs as he caressed Michelle's breasts. Then his hands slid down, over her torso.

A sudden moan told Nina that Tom was caressing Michelle's sex, while the other woman in turn caressed her. The knowledge filled Nina with a fresh charge of desire. The surroundings, the ice cold champagne, the gentle strains of Vivaldi and the beautiful people involved all conspired to make the situation unbelievably sensuous.

Raising her head from between Nina's thighs for a moment, Michelle arched her back and let out a long groan of pleasure.

'Are you wet, baby?' Rob asked, directing the question at his wife.

Looking at him with a glazed expression she nodded dumbly. Her cheeks were flushed, Nina noticed, and her eyes were dark and hazy yet glittering with desire.

Pressing her own fingers against her throbbing clitoris, Nina began to caress herself gently. Michelle's fingers were still buried inside her and as her desire mounted again she felt her greedy vagina grasping at them.

Michelle smiled a lazy, catlike smile. 'OK, baby,' she murmured, 'momma's going to make you come now.'

She lowered her head again and in the next moment Nina felt the now familiar caress of Michelle's knowing tongue. It flickered and danced over her yearning sex, tantalising yet driving her inexorably closer to orgasm.

Rising high on the tide of her own inescapable desire, Nina felt herself gradually approach Nirvana.

Chapter Twelve

A sticky, uncomfortable heat pervaded the Grassroots Productions building. Too mean with his money to concede to his employees' demands for installation of an air conditioning system, Liam finally gave in part of the way and magnanimously produced a number of large freestanding fans.

'Oh, wonderful!' Nina exclaimed as the fan nearest to her swung around to blast her with cool air and blow a pile of papers off her desk at the same time. 'That's the tenth time this morning. I'll never get any work done at this rate.' Continuing to grumble she slid out of her chair and sank to her knees to gather up the papers strewn all over the floor.

Maisie squatted down beside her to help. She was grinning from ear to ear, Nina noticed with irritation.

'Thanks,' Nina said ungraciously when they had finished. 'I don't know how much more of this I can take.'

Maisie gave her a thoughtful look. 'Do you mean this sudden heatwave or the work?'

Sighing Nina sat down again. She grinned ruefully and tucked a damp strand of hair behind her ear. 'Both,' she said, grimacing as she tightened her limp ponytail. 'Honestly, I feel sick of all this.'

'It's tough at the top,' Maisie quipped. 'What you need is a holiday, Nina. When are you due for a break?'

'I should have been off this week and next,' Nina said, 'but that's academic really. I can't go anywhere until this damned programme's in the can.' As though she could read Maisie's mind, she added, 'And don't for one minute think

I'm going to go running to Liam to throw in the towel. I'm going to make a success of this thing if it kills me. If only for the fact that I don't want to give Karen anything to gloat about.'

It annoyed her that, as usual, Karen seemed to have fallen on her feet. It had transpired that the new research assignment she had been given – dodgy timeshare dealers – involved an enviable amount of travelling to various Mediterranean resorts. At the moment, Nina thought with a snarl, Karen was probably lounging about by the side of a sparkling blue pool, long cold drink in hand.

'Bitch!' she said, thinking aloud. 'How does she do it?'

Maisie picked up on Nina's train of thought straight away. 'I think Liam gave her the assignment just to get her out of his hair.' She paused to chuckle wickedly. 'Or should I say his bald patch. And if it makes you feel any better, she's probably staying in a cockroach infested sewage farm of a place. That is the whole point of the programme – buying a little piece of hell.'

Despite her annoyance, Nina smiled. Maisie had a wonderful gift for being able to put things in perspective.

'I hope so,' she said, 'the yukkier the better. And I defy even Karen to look alluring in a bikini and plaster cast.'

The two young women paused to chuckle at the image Nina's observation conjured up.

'OK,' Nina said at last, sounding more decisive than she felt, 'back to work. I've got table dancing tonight and then tomorrow evening I'm going on a crash course in hostessing.'

'That should be good for a giggle,' Maisie commented.

Nina pursed her lips. 'I don't know about a giggle,' she said, 'but at least I'll get the next couple of days off in lieu.'

The Frou Frou, one of half a dozen Soho clubs owned by Rob, was pretty much as Nina had expected it would be.

INTIMATE DISCLOSURES

Small, poorly lit and smoky, it featured about twenty tables grouped around a shiny aluminium dance floor. In the far corner opposite the entrance was a horseshoe shaped bar. And three poles, spaced evenly apart, grew up from the dance floor to reach the lowered ceiling. The main theme of the decor was black with touches of red. From the lowered black ceiling red-bulbed downlighters cast a rosy glow over the handful of occupants at the tables.

Nina glanced around as she and Tom took a seat at one of the tables in the second row. The front row seats were all occupied, mainly by fat, florid businessmen who sweated profusely. Nina couldn't help noticing how they appeared to avoid dehydration by drinking glass after glass of scotch on the rocks and hardly bothered to exchange a word with each other. All of them had their attention fixed to the dance floor in front of them, as though if they let their attention wander for a moment they might miss something.

'God, it's hot in here,' Nina grumbled as she slipped off her jacket.

Tom chuckled. 'They probably keep the heating up full blast so the dancers don't catch a chill.'

Nina grinned back at him. 'Clever clogs,' she said, 'for that you can go and get us some drinks.'

While Tom was up at the bar she smoothed her short skirt over her bare thighs. At first she had tried to keep her legs crossed but soon found they kept sliding apart on a film of perspiration. Silently she cursed the sadist who had set the heating control in the club and thanked her lucky stars that she had chosen to wear something cool.

Her outfit, a black skirt teamed with a thin blue silk blouse was smart enough for evening wear but deliberately inconspicuous. The last thing she wanted was to be mistaken for one of the dancers. At the next moment, when the music started up and three willowy blondes danced onto the stage, she almost laughed aloud as she realised she was in no danger of that.

All each of the girls wore was a silver sequined g-string and matching high heeled sandals. Their bare breasts shimmered under a light dusting of silver glitter and tendrils of silver ribbon were pinned to their hair. The music was Space Oddity by David Bowie and as soon as the girls came on stage they each took up position behind one of the poles and began sliding sinuously up and down them.

'Interesting,' Nina commented when Tom returned with their drinks and sat down beside her, 'what do you think, Tom?'

'I think this place is a complete rip off,' he said, hardly glancing at the dance floor. 'Two drinks, one of them only an orange juice, and no change from a tenner.'

'All the drinks are five pounds each,' Nina said, 'didn't you see the notice by the door?'

'If I'd have known,' Tom grumbled, 'I would have left the car at home and come here by taxi. If I'm going to pay five pounds for a drink I should at least be able to make it a proper one.'

'Oh, stop moaning,' Nina said lightly, sipping her gin and tonic, 'and stop worrying about the prices. I can claim it all back on expenses anyway.'

Tom looked slightly mollified and a moment later he turned his attention to the dance floor. 'They certainly know how to move,' he commented, eyeing the scantily-clad dancers.

Nina thought aloud. 'I wonder if any of them would agree to go on the programme.'

'Are you going to ask them?' Tom turned his head back to look at her.

'Of course.' Nina nodded. 'That is why we're here. Oh, look, these must be the table dancers.'

As she spoke a troupe of half a dozen girls, two of them black and one oriental, shimmied and gyrated their way across the stage. They made their way straight to the tables in the front row.

Nina smothered a grin as she noticed the startled expressions on the businessmen's faces. And she couldn't help wondering why they should look so bashful when this was surely what they had come to the club for.

One girl, a curvy redhead, leaned forward and whispered something in her customer's ear. In the next moment he produced a ten pound note and tucked it in the minuscule waistband of her g-string. The girl smiled in response and began to grind her ample breasts into his sweating face.

'Good God,' Nina said as she watched the spectacle, 'fancy paying a tenner to be smothered like that.'

Tom turned and grinned at her. 'Thank goodness I don't have to,' he said, giving her breasts a surreptitious caress. 'You do it to me for free.'

Their laughter earned them annoyed glares from some of the occupants of the neighbouring tables.

'Give me ten minutes,' Nina said, standing up a moment later, 'I'm going to see if they'll let me go backstage. The sooner I get the business part of this evening out of the way, the sooner we can go home and enjoy ourselves properly.'

Backstage at the Frou Frou gave Nina a distinct feeling of deja vu. Like the Grassroots Productions' offices, she realised, the club's glitzy facade masked a behind-the-scenes territory that was less than glamourous to say the least.

Bare floorboards were spattered with the white matt paint that ineffectually covered the poorly plastered walls. A narrow corridor led to the manager's office, a single lavatory and the dancer's dressing room.

She had tried to ask permission to go backstage but the two barmen had resolutely ignored her for a full ten minutes. Giving up, she had quickly slipped through a door which she noticed at the rear of the dance floor. Now she hoped no one would suddenly appear and challenge her. When she heard footsteps, she darted quickly into the loo and when she stuck a tentative head around the door and saw that the coast was clear she bolted for the dressing room.

Inside the small windowless room she found three girls sitting on hardbacked wooden chairs and staring desultorily at their reflections in a smeared mirror which hung on the wall. The lighting was poor. Only a single bare bulb hung down from the middle of the ceiling.

'Excuse me,' Nina said, tapping on the inside of the door to attract the dancers' attention, 'do you mind if I come in?'

One of the girls, a tall, slender Afro-Caribbean with tight black curls cropped close to her skull, turned to look at her. She shrugged, the action disturbing her full, bare breasts.

'Sure,' she said in a lazy drawl, 'who're you?'

Feeling more confident Nina stepped right into the room and held out her hand automatically. The black girl ignored it and turned to glance at herself in the mirror again. She began picking at a clump of mascara on her top lashes.

'My name is Nina Spencer,' Nina said, coming to stand right next to the girl, 'I'm with a TV company. I wonder if you'd mind if I talked to you for a minute.'

The girl shrugged again. 'No skin off my nose,' she said, 'I'm not on for another half hour.' All at once she turned and Nina was startled by the brilliance of her sudden smile. 'My name's Jade,' she offered, to Nina's surprise, 'and this here's Lucy and Sparkle.'

'Sparkle?' Nina couldn't disguise her look of amazement. The girl to whom Jade pointed was thin and mousy and didn't appear to have an ounce of sparkle in her.

'Stage name,' Jade said needlessly, then she lowered her voice to a fraction above a whisper, 'she's new.'

'My first time actually,' Sparkle said, turning to glance at Nina.

Nina saw her hazel eyes were wide with fear.

'I – I'm sure you'll do brilliantly,' she lied hesitantly.

'Bollocks!' Jade cut in forcibly. She smacked the other

girl on the thigh. 'If she doesn't liven up the manager's going to have her guts for garters.'

Beside them both, the third girl gave an unladylike snort. 'That's it, Jade, you tell her,' she said without turning her face away from the mirror. 'The silly, uptight little cow is going to drop us all in it if she doesn't buck her ideas up.'

Sparkle's lower lip wobbled and her eyes filled with tears. She looked so woebegone that Nina felt tempted to put her arm around her. Instead, noticing a box of tissues on the melamine ledge that served as a dressing table, she pulled a couple out and handed them to the girl.

'Thanks,' Sparkle said, sniffing and dabbing at the corners of her eyes. 'I'm just a bit nervous that's all. I'll be fine once I get out there.' She nodded in the direction of the door.

'Why are you doing this?' Nina blurted out.

Jade gave a derisive laugh. 'The money, love. That's all any of us are in it for.'

'I'm a student you see,' Sparkle cut in, 'I just can't manage on my grant. At least this way I should earn some decent money and still have time to study.'

Noticing an empty chair beside her Nina sat down. 'When do you find time to sleep?'

Jade spoke up again before Sparkle could open her mouth to reply. 'The place closes at three. Unless we've been chosen for extra work we can push off straight away.'

This time Lucy turned her head and frowned at Jade. 'Shush,' she hissed, 'you shouldn't go blabbing to reporters.'

'I'm a researcher, not a reporter,' Nina said hastily, 'and I promise you, nothing you say to me will go any further unless I have your permission.'

Lucy snorted again, just to show how much she believed Nina.

Deciding to take the bull by the horns, Nina pitched straight in with her explanation of the show and what she was doing there.

'I'm not going on TV and telling the world what I get

up to,' Lucy stated when Nina had finished, 'supposing my mum and dad saw the programme?'

'Well, I don't care,' Jade said, standing up and reaching for a pack of cigarettes on the table beside her, 'I quite fancy a bit of fame.' This time when she smiled at Nina the light in her liquid brown eyes didn't fade quite as quickly as it had before.

All at once Nina found herself appraising the young woman standing in front of her. Though dressed only in the obligatory silver g-string and in bare feet, she appeared as comfortable with her nakedness as if she were dressed in leggings and a baggy tee-shirt.

She had a stunning figure. From broad shoulders her well-toned torso narrowed down to a slender waist, then flared out again at the hips. Her breasts were quite large but firm, with huge chocolate-brown nipples and areolae. And when she turned to reach for her lighter, Nina noticed that her generous buttocks were high and rounded – the silver strip bisecting them making a delightful contrast to the dusky hue of her skin tone.

'Like what you see?' Jade surprised Nina by turning back quickly and fixing her with a candid stare. 'You can have me for fifty quid.'

Not knowing how to reply, Nina swallowed quickly. Then to her relief Jade burst out laughing. She lit her cigarette, inhaled deeply, then blew out a thin plume of blue-grey smoke.

'Only joking,' she said, touching Nina's hair briefly before returning her cigarette to her mouth, 'that's what the punters pay. I'd do it with you for free, you're quite a looker.'

'Oh, er, thanks,' Nina mumbled, not knowing quite what else to say. The black girl's blatant behaviour made her feel distinctly odd. She could only liken it to being chatted up by a strange man, except there was definitely nothing masculine about Jade.

INTIMATE DISCLOSURES

'Take no notice of her,' Lucy cut in. She flicked back her shoulder length dark blonde hair and pretended to glare at Jade. 'She's such a bloody roaring dyke. She can't keep her hands, or her big mouth to herself.'

Nina glanced back at Jade. This time her eyes were wide with curiosity rather than apprehension. 'Are you really a lesbian?' she asked.

The black girl adopted a patient tone. 'Yes, I'm really a lesbian,' she said, 'what are you planning to do now, put me in a zoo?'

'No, I—' Now Nina really felt flustered.

Thankfully, they were interrupted by the three pole dancers, returning to the dressing room after their routine.

'You're on you lot,' one of them said, flopping down inelegantly onto a battered leather sofa. 'Christ, get a move on or Fat Sam'll have a fit.'

Fat Sam, as Nina explained later to Tom as they drove home, was the club's manager. She had not enjoyed meeting him one little bit. First of all he had been annoyed that she was backstage in the first place and trying to recruit 'his girlies' as he called them, for her show without offering any payment. And secondly, he wasn't too happy when Nina refused his offer of 'a right good shag in his office.'

'Ugh, he was really creepy,' she said, reaching across the gap between their seats and squeezing his thigh. 'He was all fat and slobbery and had this stubby bit of cigar clamped between his rubbery lips.' She paused to shudder at the unwelcome recollection. 'Do you know who he reminded me of?' she asked rhetorically, 'Winston Churchill without the charisma.'

Tom laughed and, taking his hand from the steering wheel for a second, squeezed her thigh in return.

His eyes twinkled as he glanced sideways at her. 'Fancy a right good shag?' he said.

Nina gazed at him for a moment, speechless, then she

burst out laughing. 'Only if you give me fifty quid,' she teased, 'that, apparently, is the going rate.'

Gazing at Nina as she sat down at the little pine dressing table in their bedroom and began to cream off her makeup, Tom recalled how his own evening had gone. Left alone at the table in the club while Nina went backstage, he had discovered he was a prime target for 'business.'

'Girlfriend gone has she?' the busty brunette who shimmied straight over to him asked. 'Bet she couldn't stand the competition.'

'Er – um – something like that,' Tom had mumbled, trying not to stare too blatantly at the girl's jiggling breasts.

Obviously he hadn't done a very good job at averting his gaze, he realised, when the girl glanced down and cupped the pendulous mounds in her hands. She held them out to him, tweaking the dark nipples as she did so. Instantly erect and elongated, they pointed accusingly at him.

'Like to suck them?' she offered.

With difficulty, Tom forced himself to look at the dancer's face. She was a little overweight and consequently her face was rounded but still very pretty. She had huge baby blue eyes, fringed by long dark lashes that looked as if they could be false. And below a pert button nose her mouth was wide and generously coated with peach coloured lipstick.

'A tenner,' the girl persisted. A vaguely bored look flashed across her face. 'You can stick it in my g-string.'

Wondering whether she would find it suspicious if he refused, Tom reluctantly dug into his pocket for his wallet. Taking out a ten pound note he gingerly tucked it into the silver elastic which bit gently into the flesh covering her left hip.

He felt the way the girl trembled as his fingers brushed her skin and she leaned further across the table, pushing her breasts into his face. Not knowing what else to do, Tom obediently kissed the nipple that brushed his lips. Full and

INTIMATE DISCLOSURES

ripe it forced its way between his lips as the girl thrust herself more urgently against him. He sucked hard, drawing the tight nub of flesh right into his mouth.

With a small sigh the dancer eased herself around the table to sit on his lap. Feeling thoroughly helpless, Tom let her. The sensation of her unfamiliar weight and warmth was exciting, as was the musky flavour of her skin. She moved, her nipple popping out of his mouth, only to be replaced a moment later by the other one.

'You like my breasts don't you, big guy?' she crooned, arching herself against him. 'Mm, that feels delicious.'

Unable to speak with his mouth full of nipple, Tom attempted a nod. Although he was still mouthing her nipple, he kept trying to glance around the dancer to see if Nina was on her way back to the table. He didn't honestly know how she would react to find him in such a compromising position. Either she would be steaming, or find it a huge joke – it was difficult to tell sometimes with Nina.

Without realising it he found his hand stroking the satiny skin of the dancer's thigh. Her figure was plump but shapely and, unlike most of the other dancers, she simply oozed sex appeal. His other hand slid up her back and began to lazily trace the contours of her shoulders and spine. He was gratified to feel her answering wriggle and to hear her give a soft whimper of pleasure.

Drawing his head away from her breast, he asked, 'What is your name?'

'Kim,' the dancer said, 'at least that's my working name. Only my family know my real one.'

'And how old are you?' Tom's hand slid around her waist and up over her rib cage to stroke the underside of her breast.

Kim gave another soft moan. 'Twenty two,' she said, 'I'm in my last year at university, studying law. Next year I'll be taking my finals but I need to do this a couple of evenings a week to earn some extra cash.'

Surprised and impressed, Tom smiled into her eyes. 'Ah, brains as well as beauty.'

He felt the tremor as Kim giggled. 'You are a dreadful flirt aren't you?' All at once she glanced around. 'Uh-oh, there's the manager.' She squirmed in Tom's grip, which he relaxed, allowing her to stand up.

'Shame,' he said, smiling up at her. 'Just as I was enjoying myself.'

He noticed a flush of embarrassment suffused Kim's face and she averted her gaze as she mumbled, 'If you really like me we could – er – go on somewhere later. I mean, like, I'd have to charge you and everything but it's not very much really.'

'How much?' Tom asked softly. Excitement battled in the pit of his belly with compassion for the girl. It seemed such a shame that she should be forced to sell her body when she obviously had so much else going for her.

'Fifty pounds an hour,' Kim said, meeting his gaze again. Glancing briefly over her shoulder she sat down again, only this time next to Tom rather than on his lap. 'I don't want you to get the wrong idea,' she added, 'I don't proposition all the customers. Just the ones I fancy.' Reclining against the back of the seat for a moment she let out a long sigh. 'The trouble is most ordinary men like you pity me because they think I'm doing it just for the money, because I can't make ends meet. But really it's not like that.'

'What is it like then?' Tom asked. He stroked the back of her hand with his fingertips.

Kim gave a little laugh and shrugged. Her breasts jiggled invitingly. 'I love sex,' she replied candidly, turning her head to look him straight in the eye. 'I'm not a nymphomaniac or anything but I've got a really high sex drive. I need it – like food, you know?'

Tom nodded. 'Me too.'

'Anyway,' Kim went on, 'I figured, if I like sex so much and men are attracted to me, why give it away?'

'Makes sense I suppose,' Tom commented, 'but do you really just stick to men that you fancy?'

She smiled coquettishly at him. 'Are you digging for a compliment? Yes, I told you. Only the ones that really turn me on. And, I'm happy to say, you're one of them. So how about it?'

Tom hesitated. He had never paid for sex before. And with a hot blooded girlfriend like Nina, he certainly didn't need to look elsewhere. But there was something about Kim that was almost irresistible. Almost.

'Are you bi, by any chance?' he asked. The joy he felt when Kim nodded was indescribable. 'Yes, but just like with the guys, I've got to fancy the girl. I can't just fuck anyone.'

The way the word 'fuck' just slipped from her luscious lips made Tom's penis stir.

'What time do you finish?' he asked, reaching into his pocket for his wallet again. He took out one of his business cards and scribbled his name and the address of his and Nina's flat on the back. Then he withdrew a twenty pound note from his wallet as well. 'I guarantee you'll fancy my girlfriend,' he said boldly, handing her the card and the twenty pound note. 'Here's my address and some money for a taxi. Come over to our place when you've finished here.'

Her eyes widened. 'Are you sure? Shouldn't you ask your girlfriend first?'

'No,' Tom said, sounding more confident than he felt, 'I want to surprise her. I know she'll be thrilled to bits.'

Now, as Tom reclined on the bed watching Nina brush her hair, the bristles making smooth, sweeping strokes through her tawny mane, he wondered whether he had made a terrible mistake. He glanced at his watch. In less than an hour Kim would arrive. Then they would both present Nina with a fait accompli.

His reasons for booking Kim were simple. He had been so turned on by the experience he and Nina had shared with Rob and Michelle – and Nina had clearly enjoyed herself enormously – that he thought a similar scenario would be just as pleasurable. His only regret at that time had been that he hadn't found Michelle anywhere near as desirable as Nina obviously had.

But he was attracted to Kim in a big way and he only hoped Nina would find her equally fanciable. Either that or she would go completely off the deep end about springing such a surprise on her.

No, he reassured himself in the next instant, she wouldn't do that. Nina was game for anything, or anyone within reason. All at once he felt his cock begin to stir with anticipation. If everything went according to plan the three of them had a great night to look forward to.

Chapter Thirteen

As the time for Kim's arrival approached, Tom decided he had better come clean.

Nina's reaction to his confession was, predictably, a mixture of shock and incredulity.

'What?' she shot back at him when he'd finished speaking. Her eyes widened until he thought they would pop. 'You did what?' She began to shake her head slowly from side to side. 'Tom, how could you – without asking me first?'

'I suppose I should have done,' Tom admitted, realising his mistake, 'but if I'd said anything at the time you might have just rejected the idea out of hand. At least let the poor girl come in and have a coffee. Then if you still don't fancy the idea I'll pay her off and we can forget all about it.'

'What a waste of money,' Nina said, determined that she wasn't going to go along with his 'little surprise for her' as he had put it. 'I can think of a lot better things to do with fifty quid.'

Tom opened his mouth to try and protest that he had acted with the best of intentions when he was interrupted by the front door bell.

'That'll be her,' he said, getting up from the bed, 'do you want to let her in, or shall I?'

'It had better be you,' Nina replied, glancing down at her nakedness. 'I'll just pop something on, then come and join you.'

The doorbell rang again and, with a last apologetic glance at Nina, Tom decided he'd better go and answer it.

193

He hardly recognised Kim when he opened the door. Instead of the tiny silver g-string, she was wearing a short lime green dress in tee-shirt material, with a rust coloured denim jacket over the top.

'Don't tell me,' she said, laughing, 'you hardly recognised me with my clothes on. They all say that.'

Her words reminded Tom that she was far more used to this sort of thing than he was. And he marvelled at the way she could be so cool about it. Glancing at her as she ducked under his arm and stepped through the doorway, he decided that she looked even more attractive in clothes.

Kim was standing in the middle of the living room, having a good look around, when Nina entered. There was an awkward moment while the two women appraised each other carefully, then they both smiled in unison and Nina stepped forward to introduce herself.

She was wearing a deep blue ankle length silky kimono that Tom had bought her for the Christmas before last. And as she sat down on the sofa, she tucked it carefully around her legs as though cold.

In contrast, Kim sprawled in their one armchair, her bare, tanned legs splaying coltishly. On her feet she wore a clumpy pair of white canvas peep-toe sandals which made her slender ankles look extremely fragile.

'Drink anyone?' Tom asked, glancing from one to the other.

Nina and Kim both looked up at him.

'I'll have a rum and coke if you've got any,' Kim said.

'Make mine a G&T,' Nina chipped in.

While Tom was in the small kitchen fixing the girls' drinks, and a scotch and soda for himself, he could hear the two of them talking. It sounded as though they were getting on like a house on fire, which pleased him no end. So far so good.

What surprised him, he thought as he walked back into the living room and handed the drinks around, was that

INTIMATE DISCLOSURES

all these hours later, and in the unglamourous setting of their flat, Kim had actually succeeded in going up in his estimation. She seemed relaxed and totally at ease. And he couldn't help noticing that Nina seemed to be growing more bright eyed and animated by the second as they laughed and chatted together.

Noting the easy interaction between the two, Tom decided to take a back seat. Leaning casually against the mantlepiece that no longer topped a real fire but an empty grate filled with books, he was content to simply listen, sip his drink and observe.

After their drinks had been topped up Kim seemed to gravitate naturally towards the sofa. Seated next to Nina she kept one hand resting lightly on Nina's thigh as they talked. Nina had told her all about her work and far from minding, Kim was only too eager to disclose all the information she could about her part time job at the Frou Frou.

'Oh, so you know Rob then?' she said at one point, draining the glass in her hand, 'I wish you'd tell him that Fat Sam is a right toad.'

Nina laughed. 'Old Winston, you mean. Yes, I will. The other girls complained to me about him as well. But I don't know if my mentioning it to Rob would do any good. I don't know him that well.'

Thinking back over the fun and frankly erotic times she and Rob had had together, Nina wondered how much more it would take for her to consider herself a proper friend of his. The ludicrousness of it struck her and she began to chuckle.

Now seated in the armchair that Kim had vacated, Tom watched and listened to the exchange with only half an ear. All his attention was taken up by watching the two young women. Their body language spoke volumes. They were leaning into each other by this time, and every so often, as they spoke or laughed about something, their foreheads would touch, or one would pat the other's thigh. To him those little gestures seemed achingly intimate. He could feel his cock stirring in response and wondered if things would take their course naturally.

His question was answered a moment later when Nina cracked a salacious joke about sliding up and down the poles in the Frou Frou and Kim, without any apparent motivation, suddenly leaned forward and touched her lips to Nina's.

From that moment on sparks seemed to fly between them. Tactfully, Tom got up and put on some music. He turned the volume down low and then went back and sat down in the chair again.

By this time Nina and Kim were engaged in a deeply searching kiss. Their hands fluttered over each other's hair and Nina's kimono seemed to slip from her shoulders of its own accord. They broke off their kiss and stared at each other wordlessly for a moment. Then, noticing that one of Nina's breasts was bared, Kim bent her head and began to lathe the nipple with her tongue.

Tom's cock grew so hard he felt it pressing urgently against the material of his trousers. And his balls ached. Still, something held him back from simply going over to the sofa and joining in the fun. Instinctively, he felt as though he would be intruding somehow. There was something so beautiful about watching the two young women slowly discover each other's bodies that he didn't want to trespass on their mutual pleasure. Instead, he was content to watch.

Playing the voyeur was a new role for him but one that he realised quickly was extremely enjoyable in its own right. Even if he didn't get to lay a hand on Kim it would be worth it. He was so aroused by the sight of her and Nina that he knew the moment she left he would fuck Nina so hard she would be pleading for mercy. Thank God neither of them had to get up for work in the morning.

Trying to be as unobtrusive as possible he slipped into the kitchen to make himself another drink. When he returned he found that Nina's kimono had slipped right down and now

INTIMATE DISCLOSURES

pooled around her waist. Kim meanwhile had taken off her dress and shoes and was clad only in a pushup bra and tanga-style panties. The underwear was grey satin edged with lace and the panties featured a tiny bow at each hip.

Though unable to ignore the body inside them, which seemed to be fighting to get out, Tom couldn't help taking an aesthete's view of Kim's choice of lingerie. The items didn't look cheap and were, he thought, quite a sophisticated choice for someone so young. Being a connoisseur of such things, he raised his glass in a silent toast to her good taste.

Relaxing further into the chair, Tom watched with mounting excitement as Nina reclined on the sofa and Kim straddled her. The young woman's buttocks were nicely rounded and he could see them straining at the grey satin as she moved onto all fours. Bending her head she began to deliberately trail the soft ends of her hair over Nina's naked torso.

Arching her back, Nina let out a faint moan. Her nipples were hard and fully distended and Tom fancied he could make out the rapid fluttering of her heart beneath her rib cage. As Kim worked her way down Nina's body he watched his lovely girlfriend squirm with pleasure.

Kim's body looked equally inviting as she swayed from side to side over Nina. Her breasts were thrusting at the skimpy satin of her bra, their ample fullness almost spilling out over the top of the cups. And her hair, as it swept Nina's body, was long – a good couple of inches below shoulder length – and tousled. Not straight but not quite curly, it obscured Kim's face but the nape of her neck and the sweep of her back looked sensuously inviting.

Once again Tom yearned to get involved but held himself resolutely in check. For one thing he wanted to see how long he could hold out. And how aroused that would make him feel. If he broke the tempo now, and the thread of erotic tension that joined the two young women on the sofa, he might feel sorry that he had done so.

After a while, Kim sat back, her pert bottom resting lightly on Nina's shins. Reaching forward she unfastened the belt that was loosely tied around Nina's waist. Then she eased back the fabric of the kimono until Nina's sinuous body was totally displayed.

'Ah!' Kim let out a gasp of genuine approval and admiration.

Tom couldn't help but echo her sentiments inside his head. Nina was lovely. The most sensuous woman he had ever met. Lying there, gazing shyly up at Kim, she looked no more than fifteen or sixteen. She appeared so relaxed there was a certain unsullied freshness about her. Something virginal yet wanton all at the same time. It was a curious phenomenon and not one Tom could recall ever having witnessed before.

He supposed that was one of the advantages of being a voyeur. Usually while making love to Nina he was too involved with what was happening to the both of them to take much notice of changes in her appearance, or demeanour. But now, from the short, safe distance between sofa and chair, he felt privileged to behold the intensely private transformation of a woman he thought he knew almost as well as he knew himself.

'Gorgeous breasts,' Kim murmured approvingly, running the flat of her palms lightly over Nina's heaving mounds. 'Fabulous nipples.'

Nina groaned with undisguised pleasure as Kim's fingers deftly tweaked the distended nubs of flesh. She writhed on the sofa, arching her back and trying in vain to raise her hips. Seated lightly on her legs, Kim kept them pinned down. She seemed to be totally in control, Tom noticed, if it were not for the blatant lust flickering in her eyes. And the way she kept swallowing deeply and licking her luscious lips.

Obviously overcome by her own lascivious needs, Nina slipped a hand between her slightly parted thighs.

Tom watched her hand working, noticing the way her

INTIMATE DISCLOSURES

fingers deftly spread her outer labia apart and began to tantalise the hidden bud of her clitoris. Knowing how his cock felt, so desperately in need of physical contact, Tom could well imagine how Nina must be feeling. He could picture her clitoris in his mind's eye, swollen and jutting out from the delicate folds of her labia like a miniature cock. He knew every inch of her delicious body so well and fancied he could feel it, right then and there, and taste it too. Particularly the sweet, honeyed juices that flowed so copiously from her body when she was aroused. Without realising it, he licked his own lips.

For the first time, Kim glanced at him. A secretive, yet knowing smile touched her lips and eyes. Look at me, her expression commanded him, watch what I am doing to your girlfriend. See how eagerly she responds.

Placing a protective hand unconsciously over the tumescence in his trousers, Tom watched as Kim moved down Nina's body. Kissing and licking every portion of Nina's straining torso as she went, she cast one last triumphant glance at Tom before cupping Nina's buttocks and raising her yearning sex to her mouth.

A pink tongue flickered out and lathed the entire length of Nina's slit.

Nina groaned. 'Ooh, no – ah, yes!' and flexed her knees and hips so that her thighs were more widespread. Her hand, which had been caressing her straining clitoris now fluttered helplessly over her mound.

Kim continued to lick Nina's vulva with long, assured strokes. Raising her own bottom a little and murmuring to Nina to move her legs so that they were wide apart, she lowered Nina's buttocks to the sofa and used her freed hands to caress the insides of her thighs.

'Pretty little pussy,' she crooned, spreading Nina's labia wide apart with her fingers. All at once she thrust a couple of digits right inside Nina's gaping vagina. 'So wet and creamy.'

Nina gasped with surprise and then let out an anguished moan. It was obvious to Tom now that she was completely aroused. He could hear the wet, squelching sounds her body made as Kim's fingers moved in and out of her. And even from a distance, could smell the muskiness of her feminine scent.

Still watching intently, Tom unzipped his trousers and began to stroke his rock hard penis.

Thrashing her head from side to side, her torso heaving, Nina gave herself up to the exquisite sensations wrought by Kim's skilful manipulation of her body.

At first she hadn't been able to understand why Tom had arranged for the dancer to come to their flat. He told her what had transpired between them and she could sympathise with his motives. But to pay a complete stranger to have sex with her – well, it seemed inconceivable.

Yet the moment she had walked into the living room and saw Kim standing there, she had known she had to have her. There was something so incredibly, undeniably sexual about the girl. An aura. And she was very pretty, with her curvy figure, long dusky hair and big blue eyes.

Nina had felt her sex begin to tingle at the sight of her and yet had forced herself to remain cool. Discovering she was bisexual was still a relatively new thing to her and with each experience she had had – firstly with Angel and then Michelle – she hadn't been totally sure if she would actually enjoy it.

Glancing at Kim at the moment when they had just finished their first kiss, she had realised she was very lucky. Or perhaps simply more highly sexed than she realised. Each woman was achingly desirable in her own way and Nina had no difficulty responding to that, in the same way that she found certain men hard to resist.

Now, lying there on the sofa, with Kim's tongue lapping at her desperate clitoris and her fingers probing deep inside

INTIMATE DISCLOSURES

her vagina, Nina wondered what was going through Tom's mind. She loved him anyway but loved him even more for allowing her to be a whole person.

Risking a hazy glance at him, she noticed that he seemed more than happy. The look on his face was one of pure excitement and he was stroking his cock fervently. Half of her wanted to invite him over to join her and Kim at that moment but the other half was lost in the selfish pursuit of her own pleasure. She could feel her desire mounting, the heat of lust overtaking her body while deliciously sinful thoughts invaded her fevered mind. Closing her eyes, she gave into her own desires.

From the armchair, Tom experienced the unique pleasure of watching Nina orgasm from a distance. He saw the different ways her expression changed and watched how her body reacted, churning, squirming, then stiffening as her climax swept over her. It seemed to go on for ages and it was only when her thigh muscles jumped and quivered, in response to Kim's teasing dabs at her clitoris with her tongue, that Tom realised she had reached the point of hypersensitivity.

It was then that they usually fucked. But with Kim and Nina it was different. Kim slid her fingers from Nina's vagina and lay full length on top of Nina's trembling body, sucking her honey-coated fingers contentedly. The two young women lay silent and inert for a few moments. Then Nina gently rolled Kim onto her back, shrugged off her kimono and knelt naked on the carpet beside the sofa.

Up to that point, Tom didn't believe he could feel any more aroused than he already was. But, watching the way Nina caressed and explored the young dancer's acquiescent body, he felt himself rise to the point of eruption.

'Lovely bra,' Nina murmured, lowering one of the cups and baring a breast. She bent her head and sucked Kim's nipple gently. While she did so her hand cupped Kim's other breast, her fingers working the satin over the nipple concealed beneath.

A soft yet anguished whimper escaped Kim's lips. She drew her knees up and flexed her hips. Her pelvis strained toward non existent hands.

Now she was something of an expert at making love to another woman, Tom realised Nina seemed intent on not rushing anything, no matter how much Kim whimpered, or pleaded with her. She spent ages mouthing and massaging Kim's breasts. Then she moved her mouth to the young girl's shoulders, her arms, her torso. By this time Kim was churning her pelvis uncontrollably and begging Nina to stroke her pussy.

Finally, when Kim seemed gripped by a paroxysm of unrequited lust, Nina murmured, 'Let's get those knickers off shall we?'

Kim almost wept her agreement and with shaking hands, helped Nina to pull the tiny scrap of grey satin over her hips and down her legs. She wriggled obligingly and when the knickers were off she spread her legs wide, hooking one of them over the back of the sofa and planting the other foot firmly on the floor.

Tom almost came straight away as he watched Nina get up and move to kneel between Kim's legs. Hardly able to take in the whole amazing scene, he watched Nina's breasts and buttocks jiggle invitingly as she moved. He saw the moist slit of her vulva and noticed how her pubic hair was streaked with the translucent threads of her own juices.

This was nothing like his previous experiences watching Nina with Angel and Michelle. She seemed so self-assured – dominant even, yet in a gentle, entirely feminine way. Her fingers whispered up the insides of Kim's thighs, teasing and tantalising, sometimes using just her nails to describe concentric circles on Kim's sensitive skin.

In no time, Kim was begging Nina – with words and body – to touch her pussy and to make her come.

INTIMATE DISCLOSURES

Smiling wickedly Nina murmured, 'Oh, you are an eager little thing aren't you, Kim? So what do you suppose I should do – this?'

With that she slid her hands up the insides of Kim's legs to rest upon her exposed vulva. Then her thumbs spread her outer labia wide apart, revealing the soft, juicy flesh beneath.

Kim moaned, 'Oh, yes,' and arched her back, 'please,' she urged, 'please lick me there.'

Resolutely ignoring the young woman's plea, Nina began to massage her most intimate flesh, dragging at the sensitive folds and stimulating the stem of Kim's clitoris.

'What else?' Nina asked, gently but firmly, 'tell me what else you would like me to do to you.'

For a moment Kim looked pained, then she said in a breathless voice, 'I want you to finger fuck me. Finger me deeply – Ah, yes!' she breathed as Nina sank a couple of fingers inside her, twisting them and driving them in deeper still. Flexing her hips, Kim raised her pelvis to meet Nina's thrusts. 'Oh, God, yes that's it!'

Tom watched as Nina continued to finger fuck Kim for a few moments before lowering her head and sucking on the swollen bud of her clitoris. He wasn't quite close enough to see everything and so he moved to kneel beside the sofa, where Nina had knelt earlier.

She raised her head briefly, her lips smeared with saliva and glistening with Kim's juices. 'Stroke her breasts,' she commanded Tom softly. 'It's OK, I don't mind. I want to see you do it.'

Needing no further encouragement Tom glanced at the full rounded globes that trembled invitingly as Kim continued to grind her pelvis against Nina's mouth and fingers. The nipples were cone-shaped, the areolae the colour of toffee. Licking his lips he cupped them in his hands, delighting in the soft malleability of them. Then he took one of the swollen nipples in his mouth and began to suck rhythmically.

Soon Kim was crying out for release. Panting and grinding, her whole body perspired and shook with the force of her own desire. Moments later she came, gasping and crying out, 'Oh, yes!' as Nina continued to finger her wide open vagina and lash her clitoris with her tongue. She seemed wracked with pleasure, her whole body jerking and shuddering. Then presently all the life appeared to go out of her and she lay quite still and limp, wearing an expression of pure bliss.

Tom felt overcome with lust. And unaccountably proud of Nina for managing to reduce the perky, confident young woman on the sofa to the consistency of half set jelly. Moving behind Nina he stroked her pouting vulva gently. She was still on her knees but now supported herself on her hands as well so that she was hovering on all fours over Kim.

Glancing over Nina's shoulder at the other young woman he noticed that she appeared to be sleeping. I'm not surprised, he thought, realising that she had been dancing for half the night and that dawn's silvery grey light was already filtering through the gap in the curtains.

In some ways he felt relieved, with Kim asleep it meant he could concentrate all his desire on Nina without causing any resentment. Slipping his fingers into her moist vagina, he started to finger fuck her gently. With the fingers of his other hand he sought out her hard little clitoris and began caressing it.

Soon Nina's hips were churning, her mouth emitting small gasps of pleasure. Awkwardly they rolled off the sofa and on to the floor where Tom continued to play with her body until she was crying out for him to fuck her.

Somehow he found the strength to leave her alone for a moment so that he could stand up on shaky legs and take off his clothes. Then he picked her up and deposited her on the armchair, draping her legs over the arms so that she was fully displayed to him.

For a moment he simply knelt in front of her and looked at her wide open body. The lips of her vulva had blossomed completely, revealing the pink fleshy petals of her inner labia and the swollen protuberance of her clitoris. Just below copious milky fluid streamed from her vagina. The dark intriguing hole beckoned to him and just for a moment he paused to thrust his tongue deep inside, tasting her magical flavour for himself before rearing up and driving his desperately hard cock inside her up to the hilt.

'Oh, God!' Nina let out a strangled groan and clutched at his shoulders.

Summoning up every vestige of will power Tom kept thrusting with measured strokes until he couldn't contain his passion any longer. A moment later he felt her vaginal muscles contract strongly around his cock and, realising that Nina was already in the throes of orgasm, began to fuck her hard and fast, as if his life depended on it.

Tom awoke just after midday to find Kim, fully dressed and standing in the doorway to the bedroom simply gazing at him and Nina, who still slept soundly beside him.

Feeling strangely embarrassed to be naked in front of her, Tom got up and reached for his bathrobe. Shrugging it over his shoulders he belted it tightly.

'Everything OK?' he asked hesitantly. 'Have you been awake for long?'

Kim shook her head. 'No,' she said, 'I only just woke up but look—' now it was her turn to appear embarrassed, 'I can't stick around I'm afraid, I've got classes this afternoon.'

Running his fingers through his hair, Tom muttered, 'If you want to hang on a minute I'll get dressed and run you home.'

'No need,' Kim replied, treating him to a broad smile,

'I've already asked my friendly cabby to pop round and pick me up. I hope you didn't mind me using your phone?'

'No, of course not.' Tom smiled back at her. Then he remembered that he still owed her for the previous night. Picking up his wallet which lay on the dressing table he took out the hundred pounds which he had withdrawn from the cash machine on the way home from the Frou Frou club. He handed it to her with an apology, 'I know you've been here a lot longer than an hour but I didn't expect—'

She cut him short. 'That's fine,' she said, accepting the money, 'to be honest I enjoyed myself so much I feel guilty charging you at all. Your girlfriend is one hell of a woman.'

They both glanced at Nina's sleeping form. Also naked, she lay diagonally across the bed, entwined in the crumpled sheet.

'Yes, she is,' Tom agreed, glancing back at Kim, 'I'm a lucky guy.'

Kim nodded. 'I'll say. If you ever fancy a repeat performance don't hesitate to look me up at the club.' Just then they were interrupted by the doorbell. 'Whoops, that'll be my cab,' Kim said. Darting forward she planted a kiss on Tom's cheek. 'You go back to bed,' she added with a wink and another glance at Nina, 'I can see myself out.'

Chapter Fourteen

To walk through the streets of Soho at six o'clock in the evening, clothed only in a strapless red dress, slit from thigh to ankle, was not the wisest thing to do. This only struck Nina on reflection as she hobbled along the pavement in high heels and a state of agitation. Stopping by a set of traffic lights she consulted her watch for the umpteenth time. She was lost. She was late. And she was sick and tired of all the curious stares she was receiving.

Ignoring the inevitable catcalls, she glanced all around her. Her anxious eyes searched in vain for some clue as to where she was. Stupid taxi driver, she cursed inside her head, why was it she always picked the ones who didn't have a clue where they were going? Despite her insistence that he was thinking of the wrong place, the driver had dropped her off outside The Stork Club.

Though it was indeed a hostess club, The Stork was most definitely the wrong one. Fortunately for her, the doorman there had been only too happy to give her directions to the less famous – or was that infamous? – Star Club. The trouble was everything he had said to her seemed to fly right out of her head the minute she crossed the road.

Now she was hopelessly lost again and had probably missed her chance of becoming a hostess because of it.

She remembered the difficulty she'd had persuading the manager of The Star Club to give her a trial in the first place. She had told him that, though she was inexperienced, she was attractive and a quick learner. He had taken some convincing – half an hour at least on the phone and the promise of working for nothing for the first week – until he'd finally given in. The money didn't matter to Nina but the last thing she wanted to do was blow her one and only opportunity to get on the inside track. None of the other clubs she had called had been prepared to offer a novice like herself a chance to prove herself.

'Hey, Cinders, fancy a lift to the ball?' a passing driver called out to her.

Startled, Nina looked round. Seeing his broad grin she gave a long suffering sigh. Right at that moment she felt sorely tempted to take him up on his offer. Her embarrassment and aching feet urged her to do one thing, the thought that the grin masked the heart of a total psychotic urged the opposite. Reaching an instant decision she raised her chin haughtily and deliberately ignored him.

'Be like that then,' the driver shouted as the lights changed to green, 'and I hope your glass slippers give you corns.'

If she hadn't felt so despondent, Nina would have laughed.

To her relief, in the next moment a policeman rounded the corner and – though she felt horribly embarrassed about having to do so – asking him for directions seemed preferable to hanging around Piccadilly all done up like a dog's dinner.

The policeman gave her a look that suggested she would be best advised to go home and put on something more appropriate for that time of day but Nina forced herself to concentrate on the instructions he gave her.

'Left here, then cross at the second set of lights, then it's the first on the left,' she repeated so she wouldn't forget this time. 'Thanks ever so much.'

'Would you like me to walk with you?' the constable offered.

Nina shook her head hastily. 'Oh, er, no thanks all the

INTIMATE DISCLOSURES

same. I'll be fine now. Really,' she added, when she realised he didn't look all that convinced.

Just before she turned the corner she looked back and gave him a little wave. With a sigh of relief she saw him shrug and then have his attention diverted by a couple of back-packers waving a crumpled map in his face. Thank God I'm not the only one to get lost, she thought, forgetting for a moment that, unlike the back-packers, she had been born and brought up in London.

This time she managed to remember the directions and so found the place easily. A huge white neon star over the door and the words THE STAR CLUB, also in white neon down the side of the doorway, left her in no doubt that she had cracked it at long last. Pausing to glance at her watch she rapped smartly on the closed red door with her knuckles. Even with the extra time she had allowed herself she was still a good fifteen minutes late.

'Sheila Danvers?' The question came at her through a flap in the door. It had opened from the inside to reveal a pair of hazel eyes in which naked suspicion lurked.

Nina confirmed that she was Sheila Danvers. She had chosen the name in preference to using her own; just in case.

'Got any proof on you?' the disembodied voice asked.

'No, I, er—' Nina held up her red satin clutch bag, hoping that the innocent expression in her eyes and the minuscule dimensions of the bag would say it all.

'OK,' the voice said, with a heavy sigh, 'I trust you.'

The flap swung shut again and a moment later she heard the sound of keys being turned in locks. The door opened inwards. Behind it stood a man of about forty-five. He was dressed in a black suit, worn over a white shirt with a black bow tie. His hair was more grey than its original dark blond and was cut conservatively short. He was the owner of the hazel eyes, she noticed, otherwise his features were quite unremarkable. He was, she told herself as she stepped over the threshold, your average Joe.

'I'm Nick Carpesi,' the man said as soon as she was inside. He held out his hand in a friendly gesture. 'I own this joint.'

He was the one Nina had spoken to on the phone. She took his hand and gave it a firm shake.

'Thanks for giving me this chance,' she said, trying to look demure yet competent all at the same time.

Nick's face widened into a broad smile. 'You won't be thanking me by the end of the evening,' he assured her, 'not when your feet and back are killing you, and your facial muscles are stretched to their limits from compulsory smiling.'

'You make it all sound so attractive. I can hardly wait,' Nina quipped.

As she followed him through the plush outer lobby and through a door marked PRIVATE – STAFF ONLY, she decided she liked Nick. Now she had finally gained admission to his inner sanctum, he seemed relaxed, friendly and easy going. Who knows, she thought, I might actually enjoy this part of my research.

Her optimism was quickly shattered when she followed Nick into a small but efficient looking office and was introduced to the club's manager, Les Brocklehurst.

'This is the girl I was telling you about, Les,' Nick said. He paused to consult his watch – a gold Rolex. 'Oh, Christ! I'm late for Janine. I'd better scarper.' Nick was stylish but his accent was pure East End.

After Nick had gone, Nina felt as though all the fizz had just gone out of the bottle of non vintage champagne that was The Star Club. Les Brocklehurst was nothing like Nick. More like Fat Sam from the Frou Frou. He too was short, fat, balding and sweaty and displayed all the charm of Roger Cook with PMT. Nina couldn't help wondering if club managers were a special breed. If so, the laboratory experiment that created them must have gone horribly wrong for them all to end up as mutants.

Even though she hated doing it, she forced herself to smile at him and answer his many questions as politely and succinctly as she could. No, she didn't have any experience. Yes, she was willing to learn. Yes, she genuinely enjoyed the company of men. Yes, she had half a brain.

'Well, sometimes lookers like you are pig thick,' Les drawled charmingly.

Nina bit back the instant retort that sprang to her lips. Remembering what Nick had said, she realised her facial muscles already ached, just with the effort of smiling at Les. And she hadn't even started on the real purpose of the evening yet.

She was relieved when he stopped patronising her – at least, to the degree he had before – and began explaining to her what it was that she had to do.

'Now, it's quite simple,' he said, without having to add the words, *even for you.* All you have to do is make sure your customer spends plenty. Two bottles of champagne minimum, plus dinner.'

'What if he's not hungry, or teetotal?' Nina asked.

'Then persuade him that you're starving and that nothing less than champagne would ever pass your lips.' Les gave her a look that defied argument.

He then went on to explain to her how their accounting system worked. In short, what percentage of the customer's final tab would go into her pocket at the end of the evening.

'And that's all there is to it?' said Nina, thinking it all sounded quite straightforward.

All at once Les looked shifty and Nina felt the warning bells go off in her head. 'Well,' he said, 'there is the matter of afters.'

Nina laughed airily. 'Oh, don't worry about pudding. I've got a very sweet tooth.'

'Dozy cow,' Les muttered. 'I'm talking about when the punter wants to leave and take you with him.'

'Oh!' Nina's eyes widened.

'No less than one fifty an hour,' he warned her.

Nina swallowed deeply. 'Right, oh, er, yes, naturally.'

'Try and make it more if you can,' he went on, 'you're a class bird. Anyone can see that. You should aim for two fifty and let him knock you down.'

Just for a fleeting moment Nina had visions of herself in black stockings and suspenders coming under the hammer at Sotherby's.

'OK,' she agreed, knowing she would never let things get that far anyway.

At that moment Les glanced at the clock on the wall. Then he jumped up from his chair, his movements surprisingly agile for such a large man.

'No time to hang around,' he said, sounding out of breath, 'the other girls'll be waiting in the bar. And I've got to go and give that Marsha an earful before we open.'

Nina couldn't help wondering what terrible crime the hapless Marsha must have committed. But she didn't find out because as soon as they walked into the bar Les pounced on the tall black girl and dragged her off for – as he put it – a *few words in her shell-like*.

While Les was out of the way Nina made a point of introducing herself to the other hostesses in Section 'A' – the part of the club to which she had been assigned. Numbering four in all, the hostesses were grouped desultorily around one of the tables. And a motley band they seemed, Nina thought uncharitably as she appraised them.

The one who appeared to be the oldest of the bunch, Rita, was almost a caricature of a woman. Tall, plump and blowzy, she was dressed in pure nightclub fashion – a long, silver sequined dress that looked as though it had seen better days. It was fraying at the hem and under the armpits. And when Rita crossed her legs, Nina noticed that her matching satin shoes were very down at heel.

Although the club itself was lavish, seedy was the word that sprang immediately to Nina's mind as she eyed Rita and the other hostesses. Or rather, she amended mentally, make that bored and seedy.

The young woman seated next to Rita was a direct contrast to her neighbour. Looking as painfully young as she was thin, she had long, straight mousy hair which hung over a thin pointed face. She was knitting something and kept her head bent in concentration. Nina couldn't make out what it was she was actually trying to create, but the beige wool seemed to complement her bland personality to perfection.

'Hi, I'm Sheila,' Nina said with forced brightness. She tried to peer under the girl's curtain of hair.

'Dawn,' the girl muttered without looking up.

Thankfully one of the other hostesses interrupted. Slim, dressed in a nice, plain black satin ankle-length dress, she seemed the most 'together' of the four.

'Yvonne,' she said, holding out a well manicured hand, 'fancy a drink?'

Smiling, Nina asked for a gin and tonic. She realised now that she would need something to boost her confidence for when the customers started arriving.

'You'll be flat on your back come ten o'clock,' the remaining one of the group observed. 'I'm Belinda, by the way.'

Nina glanced at her. She looked to be in her late twenties and had short dark hair that curled softly around an elfin face. Startling violet eyes – which Nina assumed were due to tinted contact lenses – contrasted nicely with the lilac silk shift dress that draped her slender figure.

Nina realised the young woman was referring to the gallons of champagne she would be expected to guzzle later.

'How do any of you manage to drink all that champagne and not end up under the table?' she asked.

Belinda of the violet eyes laughed softly. 'We don't,' she said, 'guzzle it that is.'

Rita joined in the laughter. Hers was the husky laugh of a heavy smoker. She had been chain-smoking ever since Nina sat down.

'What do you think champagne buckets are for, love?' she asked rhetorically. 'We chuck the sodding stuff in them when the punter isn't looking.'

Nina knew she looked aghast. 'What a dreadful waste!'

Rita patted her knee consolingly. 'You can't possibly drink it all,' she said, 'or you'd be doing the can-can on the table with your knickers off before the night's out. You've got to keep your wits about you in this game.'

Nina got an inkling that the woman was talking from experience. 'It is all a game, isn't it?' she murmured, suddenly comprehending.

''Course,' Yvonne said. 'You get the punters to spend, spend, spend, otherwise you don't earn, earn, earn. It's simple. But no one says you've got to eat and drink everything you encourage your customer to order. Your role is to look good, make witty conversation and let your target believe he's the most handsome, intelligent, biggest spending man you've ever met.'

'Poor things,' Nina commented, feeling guilty without having done anything.

Rita shook her head and pursed her lips reprovingly. 'Don't you go feeling sorry for them,' she said. 'Most of them are arrogant bastards anyway. They think they've got so much money they can buy anything, or anyone. Why burst their little bubble?'

'I suppose so, if you look at it that way,' Nina said, still sounding doubtful.

There was little time for her to ponder the ethics of the situation. At that moment Les returned with Marsha in tow.

Nina couldn't help noticing that the black girl looked a bit subdued. And her generous lower lip stuck out obstinately as Les patted her on the behind and said, 'There now, be a good girl, Marsha. Remember what I said.'

Nina was dying to know what terrible 'crime' Marsha had committed but didn't get the opportunity to ask. Les seemed determined to hang around their table, making double entendre-type comments to the other hostesses.

Then a few minutes later the first two customers arrived.

The men were oldish, in their late fifties, Nina assumed from their steel grey hair and the way their jowls and the bags under their eyes sagged. They were not very overweight but no longer trim. Both dressed in dark pin-striped suits, they sat down at the table nearest to the bar.

Immediately, Rita and Yvonne glanced at each other. 'They're ours,' Rita said. 'Time to go to work, girl.'

Yvonne nodded and the two women stood up and sashayed over to the other table. Glancing up as they approached, both men smiled their approval and invited Rita and Yvonne to sit with them. A waiter appeared as if from nowhere and five minutes later he returned to the table with a couple of bottles of champagne in silver ice buckets.

Covertly, Nina watched Les watching them. He wore an expression of approval and a moment later stood up and excused himself, saying he couldn't sit around chewing the fat all day.

'As if we cared,' Dawn murmured laconically as soon as he was out of earshot.

'That little creep,' Marsha added, more vehemently, 'I could cheerfully slice his balls up and feed them to my cat.'

'I thought your pussy had already had its fair share of his balls,' Belinda said with a smirk.

Marsha pulled a face. 'Ugh, don't remind me. He was after me again tonight. I told him I had my period.'

'Good one,' Belinda said, 'but I'm surprised that put him off. I always thought he was out for our blood anyway.'

Nina and Dawn pulled a face simultaneously.

'Oh, take no notice of her,' Marsha said to Nina, 'she might look like butter wouldn't melt in her Janet Reagers but she's got the mind of an alley cat.'

'Back to pussies again, eh?' Belinda quipped.

As the evening wore on, Nina decided she liked all the hostesses. Even pithy Dawn, who finally put her knitting away when the place started to fill up.

Egged on by the others, Nina approached a couple of the customers but was knocked back each time.

'Is it me?' she wailed, feeling a hopeless failure. 'Have I got B.O. or something?'

Marsha shook her head, her shoulder length Afro bouncing. 'You picked on regulars,' she said, 'they're not stupid. They know the score. That last one you went up to will only see Yvonne.'

'But she's already engaged,' Nina pointed out, glancing at the table on the far side of the room. There were so many empty champagne bottles littering it that it looked like the aftermath of a wedding breakfast.

'He'll wait,' Dawn said confidently. 'Excuse me, everyone, I've got to nip to the loo.'

She stood up, ineffectually trying to smooth out the creases in her brown and cream striped wrap-over dress.

The dress looked awful, Nina thought. Too long and too short all at the same time, with an uneven hem that hung just below her bony knees. On her feet she wore a pair of flat, thong sandals of plaited brown leather. Hardly the sort of thing most people would have chosen to wear to a nightclub and definitely not typical hostess wear.

'Poor Dawn, she's on borrowed time,' Belinda commented. She gazed thoughtfully at the young woman's retreating figure as she slip-slopped toward the staff exit.

For a minute, Nina thought Belinda meant Dawn had a terminal illness. Then sanity got the better of her.

'Do you mean Les is planning to fire her?' she asked.

INTIMATE DISCLOSURES

'From a cannon if he had his way,' Belinda replied.

Marsha nodded. 'She's her own worst enemy though. I mean, look at her, she's like a wet weekend.'

Before Dawn returned a tall, thin man entered the club. He stood at the doorway, his swivelling glance taking in everything in one fell swoop. Smartly attired in a dress suit, he had an aura of wealth and sartorial elegance about him.

'Go for it, Sheila,' Marsha said, nudging Nina's shoulder. 'You might be in with a chance. I've never seen him in here before.'

On trembling legs Nina got up. The man had chosen a table right near the entrance and so she didn't have very far to walk to reach him.

'Hi, there, I'm Sheila,' she said, using her well-rehearsed line, 'mind if I join you?'

'Not at all, young lady. Sit here,' the man commanded in well modulated tones. He patted the blue velvet banquette seat next to him.

Nina sat down obediently, her hands clenched into fists in her lap. She felt foolish, awkward and tongue-tied. For want of something better to do she crossed and recrossed her legs several times.

'Would you like something to drink?' he offered, shattering the heavy silence.

Mumbling that she would love a glass of champagne, Nina risked a tentative smile at him. For an older man he was not bad looking. His eyes were dove grey, she noticed as he smiled back, matching the distinguished flecks in his otherwise raven hair. His forehead was high, his nose straight. He had a clear, lightly tanned complexion and an engaging dimple in his chin. Realising she was staring, she looked away.

Her companion didn't seem to notice.

'I am forgetting my manners,' he said after the waiter had taken their order, 'my name is Gerald, Gerald Hawksmoor.'

'Sheila.' Nina still felt embarrassingly tongue tied.

'I know,' he said, 'you already introduced yourself remember?' He smiled sardonically and reclined against the back of the banquette. 'So, Sheila, tell me, how long have you worked here?'

Nina wondered whether it would be worth lying. 'It's my first night,' she confessed, her conscience getting the better of her as always. She felt the colour rise in her cheeks. 'I thought a career change might do me good. You know what they say – a change is as good as a rest and all that—' Realising that she was babbling, she broke off. To her relief she noticed he was still smiling at her.

'Aren't I the lucky one then,' he murmured, nodding his thanks to the waiter who had just brought over their champagne, 'to meet a virgin, so to speak.'

Nina couldn't think of anything suitable as a reply so she smiled thinly instead. She was relieved that Gerald seemed quite content for her to remain silent while he went through the rigmarole of tasting the champagne, nodding his approval, then waiting until their glasses were filled.

'Chin chin,' he said, handing her a glass, 'here's to your new career.'

'Cheers,' Nina murmured.

Another awkward silence followed while Nina wracked her brain for something witty and interesting to say.

Then he put down his glass and said, 'I must apologise for that remark about you being a virgin. It's just that the other girls here seem so, so worldly wise. I suppose that is the right description.'

Nina's eyes followed his glance to the table where Rita and Yvonne sat. By this time the two women were laughing uproariously and Yvonne was sitting on her customer's lap, her arm draped casually around his shoulders.

'I see what you mean,' Nina said. She sipped her champagne and grimaced. For eighty pounds a bottle she hadn't expected it to taste like something she'd sprinkle on a bag of chips.

INTIMATE DISCLOSURES

'Pretty bloody, isn't it?' he commented. Raising his hand he clicked his fingers, summoning the waiter.

He was back like a shot.

Glancing over to the bar, Nina noticed Les was watching her.

Gerald surprised her by sending the champagne back and asking for a bottle of something vintage. 'I don't care how much it costs,' he said magnanimously, 'but we can't sit here all night drinking this cat's piss.'

Nina stared at him with a mixture of amazement and awe. She had always wanted to be able to say *I don't care how much it costs*. Being with someone else who could was almost the same. Better in fact, she realised on reflection, knowing that it wouldn't be she who picked up the tab at the end of the evening.

This time the champagne was nicely chilled and crisp. It tasted like pure nectar.

'Better?' Gerald asked, glancing sideways at her.

Eyes sparkling at him over the rim of her glass, Nina nodded. 'Much,' she said, 'but I can't drink too much of this on an empty stomach.' Les had advised her to use that line.

'In that case we'd better take a look at the menu,' Gerald offered evenly.

He clicked his fingers again and this time Nina found herself struggling to choose between apricot stuffed trout, lamb cutlets in honey and redcurrant sauce and pan fried venison with juniper berries and garlic.

Better avoid the garlic, she warned herself, playing eeny-meeny with the other two choices. *It* turned out to be the trout and when it arrived – huge, cooked to pink perfection and absolutely bulging with plump apricots – Nina knew she had made the right choice.

'At least the food is better than their champagne,' Gerald commented dryly, dabbing at the corners of his mouth with a napkin.

'It's delicious,' Nina agreed. Greedily, she downed the last of her champagne and as soon as her glass was refilled, took another generous sip.

She realised that she was really starting to enjoy herself. The food and champagne were excellent and Gerald was a great conversationalist. He was obviously well travelled and regaled her with anecdotes of his visits to such out of the way places as Bali, Thailand and The Outer Hebrides.

'A bit cold in comparison to the other two,' she said, but Gerald contradicted her.

'Not at all. At this time of year it's lovely and warm,' he said, 'only one jumper and pair of socks required.'

She laughed. Then began to choke. Gerald hit her smartly between the shoulder blades with the flat of his palm and she stopped choking immediately. Through watery lashes she glanced at him.

'Thanks,' she said, 'that'll teach me to make a pig of myself.'

She knew it was hardly sophisticated banter but Gerald didn't seem to mind. In fact, after he had finished slapping her on the back he let his hand rest there, his fingertips lightly playing with the ends of her hair.

'You are a very beautiful young woman,' he said, sounding almost regretful. 'I wish I didn't have to offer you money.'

Nina gazed at him wide-eyed. 'What for?'

Now it was his turn to laugh. And she was relieved when he took his hand away to clutch his stomach instead.

'Oh, God,' he cried, his shoulders still shaking, 'has anyone ever called you Bambi before?'

Feeling confused, she shook her head. 'No.'

'Well, I shall,' he said. He picked up his knife and fork again, winking at her before returning his attention to his half-eaten dinner. 'That shall be my pet name for you. Bambi.'

'Well, it's a good job I didn't choose the venison then,'

she quipped, 'otherwise I might have found myself eating one of my relatives.'

The white tiling of the ladies' lavatory was cool against Nina's forehead. She leaned against it, wishing the room would stop spinning and wondering if her legs were about to give way. Yes, they were. She felt her knees buckling. And, with the side of her face still pressed to the tiles, she slid down to the floor.

Belinda found her still sitting in the same position ten minutes or so later.

'Oh, Christ, you've been drinking the champagne, haven't you?' she said, squatting in front of Nina.

'Don't,' Nina pleaded, 'don't say a word. He ordered the expensive stuff. I couldn't just chuck it in the ice bucket.'

'So you thought it was better to chuck it down your throat, did you?' Belinda shook her head in disbelief. 'Honestly, my girl, you've got a lot to learn.'

'Please,' Nina murmured hoarsely, 'don't tell Les. I'll be all right in a minute. I just need to sit here and—' She gasped as Belinda slapped a wet paper towel in her face.

'You've got to sober up, or you're going to end up in trouble,' Belinda said urgently. 'That guy is still waiting for you. He asked Les if one of us could come and find you. He wants to go now.'

Peeling the paper towel off her face, Nina peered blearily up at Belinda. 'Say goodbye to him for me, would you? Tell him I said thanks for a lovely meal and everything.'

She reeled back as Belinda gave a hollow laugh. 'Grow up for Christs sake! I can't do that. He's already handed over a great wad of money to Les to pay for your favours.'

Nina was appalled. 'He can't – I can't—'

'You'd better,' Belinda said, a warning note in her voice now, 'or you'll fuck this up for all of us.' Reaching down she grasped Nina by the shoulders and shook her hard. 'Do you understand me?'

With a huge gulp, Nina nodded. She didn't think she had ever felt so miserable, or so panic stricken in her whole life.

'Well, good,' Belinda said, releasing her shoulders and straightening up. 'Give yourself five minutes. I'll go out there and make some excuse about your dinner not agreeing with you or something. But you've got to get your act together. Remember, you've got five minutes max.'

Chapter Fifteen

The window was too high up and too small to make it an easy decision. Standing on the toilet seat, Nina leaned out of the window as far as she could. On the other side it was a straight drop down to the alley below.

A blast of cool air whipped around her ears momentarily clearing her head. Surely it was an easy enough decision to make. Either she could go back into the club and brazen it out. Or she could do the cowardly thing and make a bid for freedom.

There was no contest really. Pushing the window open as wide as it would go and bunching her dress up around her waist, Nina balanced one knee on the cistern and somehow managed to coax her other leg through the window. As she balanced uncomfortably on the frame, bent almost double, with one leg in and one leg dangling outside the building, she suddenly heard a familiar voice call her name.

'Nina? Nina it is you. What the hell do you think you're doing?'

Turning her head awkwardly, she glimpsed Rob. He was standing in the alley, hand on hips, looking totally flummoxed.

'Oh, Rob, thank goodness,' she called down to him, 'can you help me?'

'Are you trying to get in or out?' he laughed, grabbing hold of her ankle.

She wobbled precariously. 'Watch it!' she hissed, 'this

splintered wood is playing havoc with my delicate bits. I'm trying to get out of course.'

'Oh, of course.' Rob's tone was dry and full of amusement. 'Well, I can't quite see how you're going to manage it. Unless you're a contortionist.'

Nina sighed. She felt like crying with frustration. He was right, damn it! There was just no way she was going to get all of herself out of the window easily.

'Climb back in,' Rob shouted up to her, 'I'll go round and meet you on the other side.'

It didn't occur to Nina to ask him what he was doing there. Or why he would think nothing of going into the club and marching through to the ladies' loo. She just felt grateful that he was the way he was.

Moments later she was standing inside the cubicle again, this time with Rob's arms wrapped protectively around her. She felt like crying on his shoulder but didn't want to spoil her makeup any more than she already had. Especially now it seemed her only option was to face up to Gerald.

'You're a good friend,' she sniffed, 'and totally mad. Didn't anyone see you come in here?'

He shrugged. 'So what if they did. You were in trouble.'

'My hero,' she said with an exaggerated sigh. Then she giggled. Haltingly she told him all about her evening.

Sitting down on the closed toilet lid, he pulled her on to his lap. 'So you're expected to go off with this Gerald guy then are you?' he said. 'For money?'

'Yes.' Nina gulped back another nervous giggle. 'Oh, God, how do I manage to get myself into these things?'

'Because you're a professional and dedicated to your career,' Rob replied, sounding completely serious.

Nina glanced at him, comprehension dawning. 'I suppose that is it,' she said, 'I'd never thought of it that way before.'

Pushing her off his lap, Rob stood up and pressed her back against the wall of the cubicle. He placed his hands either

INTIMATE DISCLOSURES

side of her head, palms flat upon the white melamine coated wood. He was standing so close to her she could smell the special scent of him, and feel his body heat. Automatically, she felt her heartbeat quicken. What was he expecting now – a stand up quickie?

'No time for that, rude girl,' he said, as though he could read her thoughts. Dropping his hands, he took one of hers. 'Come on. Let's go out and face the music together.'

Nina thought she would never feel so grateful to Rob in her life again. Of course, she should have realised that he would be on good terms with Nick Carpesi and through his connections in the industry, have a person like Les eager to eat out of his hand. Even Gerald, it seemed, was a friend of a friend.

The four of them, Nina, Rob, Gerald and Nick, sat around the table that she and Gerald had occupied earlier. In front of them stood three tumblers of good malt whisky from Nick's private stock and a glass of mineral water for Nina.

'She's had enough,' Rob insisted when the waiter tried to pour her a fresh glass of champagne.

'I've had enough,' Nina agreed, hiccuping and laughing all at the same time.

'I've got to hand it to you, Nina, you had me fooled,' Nick said, when all the necessary explanations had been made. 'Though I can't think why I allowed myself to be idiot enough to trust your word over the phone. I must be losing my touch. I always thought I had a seventh sense reserved especially for members of the press.'

Nina had the sense to look suitably contrite.

'She can be very persuasive,' Rob offered in her defence.

'You're telling me.' This didn't come from anyone seated around the table, though the voice was more familiar to Nina than all the others put together.

She glanced up. 'Tom! What on earth are you doing here?'

'Gerald phoned me,' Tom said, 'budge up, woman, let a weary man take the weight off.'

Nina shuffled obediently up the banquette to make room for Tom. When he sat down she had to fight hard to resist the urge to rest her head against his shoulder. Instead she reached surreptitiously for his hand and gripped it hard.

A moment later she said, 'What do you mean, Gerald phoned you?' She glanced from one man to the other. 'How on earth—'

'I own the plant in Spain that Tom has been working on,' Gerald explained. 'He was in quite a state about your plans for this evening. He was worried that you'd end up getting into a situation that you couldn't handle.'

'He was right,' Nina said, 'almost.' Briefly, she told Tom about trying to escape out of the window.

'That's my girl,' he said, smiling, 'run away and live to fight another day. Anyway,' he continued, picking up the thread of Gerald's explanation, 'to cut a long story short, Gerald here kindly volunteered to come here and be your punter for the evening. That way we both knew you would stay out of trouble.'

Nina looked at Gerald aghast. 'But it must have cost you a small fortune. And what about you paying Les for my services?' She said the word in inverted commas.

'A smokescreen,' Gerald said, 'to get you out of here unscathed. And as for the money, well, I can afford it. And it was a very entertaining evening. The best one I've spent in a long time as a matter of fact.'

He was smiling now. They all were, Nina noticed, as she glanced around the table. Although she was grateful to Tom for looking out for her, she also felt foolish and regretful that her efforts had come to nothing.

'I've really blown this one, haven't I?' she said, looking doleful. 'I guess the documentary is going to have a large gap in it.'

'And why's that?' Nick asked. 'I don't mind if you want

to use your insider knowledge to further your career. And I'm sure a couple of the girls wouldn't mind being interviewed for your programme. Provided you don't actually mention The Star Club by name, I can't see there being a problem.'

Nina's face lit up. 'Do you mean it?'

Nick smiled back. 'Of course I mean it. I wouldn't have said it otherwise.'

Two more glasses of mineral water later, Nina needed to use the lavatory again.

'I'll come with you,' Tom offered, 'I could do with one myself.'

When they reached the door of the ladies' loo Nina paused. 'The gents is next door,' she said, pointing.

'I know,' Tom said, 'but I'd rather come in there with you.'

Giggling, Nina allowed him to push the door open and drag her inside. As soon as they had locked themselves in one of the cubicles Tom said, 'Ladies first.'

Nina glanced up at him. All of a sudden she felt awkward. It wasn't as though they ever locked the bathroom door at home or anything but neither of them had ever knowingly invaded the other's privacy to such an extent before.

'I feel embarrassed,' she said, hitching up her dress and pulling her knickers down to her knees.

'Well, don't be,' Tom said. 'One day I hope I'll be watching you giving birth, and that'll be far more embarrassing.'

Nina was so shocked by his casual statement she peed without even thinking about it.

'Better now?' Tom asked, raising an amused eyebrow.

He went about his own ablutions with far more aplomb and when he had finished, instead of zipping up his trousers, he sat down on the toilet seat, just as Rob had done earlier.

'Take your knickers off,' he commanded gently, 'and pull

your dress right up. Stand between my legs. Yes, that's it. Come closer. Let me feel you.'

Trembling with excitement, Nina did as he asked. As she stood between his legs with her own feet planted hip-width apart, she felt his warm breath on her belly and his fingers combing through her bush.

Then they slid over the moist, warm flesh between her legs. Murmuring words of appreciation, he spread her outer labia apart and began to toy with her clitoris.

'Oh, God!'

Nina felt her knees start to buckle for the second time that evening. Though now it wasn't drunkenness that overcame her but pure lust. To support herself, she braced her hands against the sides of the cubicle. Tilting her pelvis, she offered as much of her body as she could to Tom.

His fingers drove right inside the tight, wet channel of her vagina, making her cry out in ecstasy. With the fingers of his other hand he spread her labia wider and wider, circling her burgeoning clitoris with the pad of his middle finger.

His caresses were knowingly, maddeningly erotic. Nina felt herself responding fully to him, her body blossoming out to receive every intimate touch he bestowed upon her. And inside her pelvis a white heat raged, driving her higher and higher up the scale of sensuality until she was moaning and churning her hips in total abandon.

Almost without warning the red hot spears of orgasm zigzagged through her, her body shaking and juddering under its intensity. Glancing down through lust-laden eyes she saw Tom's cock was fully erect. Murmuring to him to close his legs, she eased herself forward to straddle him. Then she lowered herself slowly and gratefully, engulfing his rigid shaft completely.

Nina gasped with pleasure as Tom immediately pulled down the front of her bodice and began to caress her aching breasts. Arching her back, she thrust herself at him, sighing with pleasure as his soft, wet lips enclosed one nipple, then the other. He sucked hard, drawing the swollen buds deep into his mouth. Glancing down she saw that they were fully distended.

Her thigh muscles quivered as she concentrated on maintaining a steady rise and fall rhythm. She could feel a second orgasm mounting. Tom's cock felt harder than ever inside her and its penetration was so deep it grazed the neck of her cervix. Heedless of the discomfort Nina continued to ride him, changing her movements to an urgent grinding motion when her thigh muscles threatened to give out completely.

She felt so hot that perspiration trickled freely down her face and throat. It gathered into rivulets which coursed down the deep valley between her naked breasts. The wetness she felt between her legs was all of her own making, she realised. Brilliant at holding off for as long as possible, Tom was clearly making the most of this impromptu opportunity. She ground harder and faster on top of him and was relieved when he grasped her hips and began to imitate her movements. She felt as though they were as one, and the harmony their bodies created served to maximise the pleasurable intensity of their coupling.

All at once she felt his cock swell inside her and then erupt. His face took on an expression of pure bliss and for a few more moments they rocked gently together, his head dropping forward so that his face nestled between her breasts. His breathing was ragged, the warmth drying the thin film of perspiration that coated her skin.

'I thought you'd gone,' Rob said, glancing up in surprise as Tom and Nina, now looking slightly dishevelled, returned to the table.

Nick was nowhere to be seen but Gerald was still there. By this time Belinda had joined the party and they were deep in, what could loosely be termed as conversation.

'No,' Nina said, in answer to Rob's remark and sharing a smile with Tom, 'we just came.'

'Oh, go on, make me jealous why don't you,' Rob said. He glanced at Gerald. 'Can you believe what these two have been up to?'

Gerald glanced around and smiled. 'Easily,' he said, 'Nina's a lovely young woman. And so is this one.' He turned his attention abruptly back to Belinda and slipped an arm around her shoulders. Pausing to mutter a few words in Belinda's ear and receiving an answering nod, he added, 'We're off now.' He looked at Tom. 'I take it my services are no longer required?'

Tom grinned at him. 'No, not any more. But thanks for everything. I won't forget it.'

Gerald and Belinda stood up and Gerald shook hands with Rob, then Tom.

'Just promise me one thing,' he said to Tom. 'Next month when you come back over to Spain, make sure you bring Nina with you.'

Nina glanced excitedly at Tom, who nodded.

'It's a deal,' he said.

'This is excellent stuff, Nina, well done.' Liam Brady flicked off the video player and sat back in his chair. 'The finished article is going to be a cracker.'

It was two weeks later and, finally, Nina had finished her research. She and Liam were in the conference room and had just finished watching some rough cuts of some of the interviews.

Thinking it would make a good visual, Liam had persuaded a friend of his to allow them to film inside his fetish club. It was on the rare understanding that the participants would have editorial control and would be able to veto any part of the film which they weren't happy with.

Nina smiled, recalling this part of her research. Nearly all the club's members had opted to wear rubber face masks that evening – whether that was normally their fetish or not. Only the faces of herself and Tom and the club's owner were recognisable. And not just her face! Nina had blushed a bright crimson when she recognised the rounded bottom cheeks being given a good thrashing with a tawse as her own.

'I hope to God my parents don't watch this when it goes on air,' Nina groaned. 'They think I spend all my time interviewing single mums and residents of damp bedsits.'

'Variety is the spice of life, as they say,' Liam said, then he added with a twinkle in his eye, 'I must say, Nina, you've got a fabulous arse.'

Nina groaned again and put her head in her hands. Though inside she felt all bubbly and excited. This was the first time she had stagemanaged such a production and Liam was clearly proud of her efforts. After all this time working for Grassroots Productions, she and her boss had finally managed to reach a level of mutual respect. It made her feel good. No, better than good, Nina realised, with an inner glow, it made her feel great.

Despite her high spirits she still felt nervous about one thing. Having seen the work she had put into the programme, and noted how good she looked on camera – from whatever angle – Liam had decided, in his infinite wisdom, that Nina should conduct the studio interviews.

That afternoon she was due to chat with Clementine, Belinda, Rita and a few members of The Bold and Brazen swingers club. The plan was that she would interview them individually, then all together. The set had been created to look like an intimate boudoir, with moody lighting and three squashy red leather sofas for Nina and the guests to sit on.

Glancing at his watch, Liam interrupted Nina's reverie. 'You've got half an hour before you see the makeup girl,' he said, 'better cut along now and grab a sandwich. We don't want your stomach rumbling all the way through the interviews.'

Nina knew better than to argue, though her stomach was so tied up in knots she didn't think she could eat a thing.

Nevertheless, when she returned to her desk and found that Maisie had thoughtfully got her a prawn mayonnaise sandwich from the outside caterer who supplied them, she suddenly felt ravenous.

'Being on camera isn't as easy as it looks, you know, Nina,' Karen observed, making a point of coming over to Nina's desk. 'You'd better not let us down.'

Nina forced herself to swallow the last of her sandwich and smile sweetly. Since she had returned from the fleapits of Europe Karen had been in an even worse mood than usual. And she couldn't even put the blame on her broken leg because the plaster cast had been taken off a few days earlier. Still, Karen walked with a pronounced limp which, Maisie insisted, was just a ploy to maintain everyone's sympathy.

'Liam has every confidence in me and I respect that,' Nina said, putting Karen firmly in her place. 'You concentrate on worrying about your own job.'

That told her, Nina thought, watching Karen shuffle pathetically back to her desk. It was about time the other woman stopped thinking of herself as Nina's boss. With Nina's successful research had come promotion. Liam had put her on a par with her former superior and to make matters worse, in Karen's view at least, had made Maisie her personal assistant. Although she had been a producer for a long time, Karen still didn't have a personal assistant and that, along with Nina's promotion, had really got her back up.

Nina's gloating thoughts were interrupted by the arrival of a young, fresh-faced girl carrying a yellow and black plastic tool box.

'Miss Spencer? I'm Sally, I've come to do your makeup.'

Smiling as she glanced up, Nina allowed her to wrap a plastic cape around her, then proceed to cover her face with an inch of sticky goo.

'That's not the real me!' Nina wailed when she saw the final result. The reflection that stared back at her from the

INTIMATE DISCLOSURES

mirror was of a much older woman, with deep smoky eyes, bright red lips and prominent cheekbones. 'Actually,' she amended, turning her head from side to side, 'I quite like it. It's growing on me.'

'Wow, Nina!' Maisie interrupted, 'You look fabulous. Like a real woman. I mean—'

Nina smiled gingerly – scared of cracking her makeup base or something similarly dire. 'I know what you mean, Maisie,' she said gently, 'and thanks.' She turned to Sally. 'Thanks,' she said again, 'you've done a terrific job.'

What it was, she thought, as she appraised herself in the full length mirror in the small dressing room she had been allocated, was that for the first time in her life she looked sophisticated and totally in control. The final touches included a smart, well tailored black suit from the wardrobe department, sheer black stockings and a pair of wickedly high heels. A double rope of imitation pearls and chunky pearl and gold earrings completed the ensemble.

The whole effect was incredibly chic and now she felt super confident about appearing on camera. She had the look, she had her notes, now all she needed to do was get out there on the set and – as Liam would put it – do the business.

One of the couples from The Bold and Brazen were Liz and her life-partner – as she referred to him – who turned out to be Ricky. Nina smiled remembering the evening she had first met him, at the Male Overload party. Then he had looked scared half to death. This afternoon he looked much more confident.

He and Liz sat on one of the sofas holding hands. He was wearing a light blue shirt teamed with ivory jeans. His tan was much deeper, making his curly blond hair look paler than ever – almost white. Liz was wearing the same pair of suede trousers she had worn to Male Overload but this time she had teamed them with a semi transparent white blouse which she wore knotted under her bust. This left a wide expanse of tanned bare stomach, to which Nina found herself casting envious glances every now and then. Oh, to be that thin and that brown.

Forcing herself not to covet Liz's figure, Nina turned her attention to the other couple who had agreed to be interviewed. These two she had never met before but her notes told her that he was called Martin and she was Kerry. Martin and Kerry had been married for eighteen months and this was a second marriage for both of them.

She liked them both instantly. Martin was not exactly fat, well covered would be a more accurate description, and he had a kind, smiling face, gentle brown eyes and longish hair of the same shade that flopped constantly over his right eye. Kerry's role in life, it seemed, was to reach up and tenderly sweep the hair back from his face each time. During this they would share a knowing, intimate smile.

Kerry, in contrast to Martin, was very tall. At least three inches taller than he. To compensate she wore flat black leather loafers. The rest of her outfit was as unassuming as her demeanour, a short black crepe skirt, worn with a pink sleeveless top that, surprisingly, managed not to clash with her short auburn hair.

Nina invited them to sit next to Liz and Ricky. Then she made herself comfortable on the adjoining sofa and glanced at the camera. She was so nervous she could feel her whole body trembling. Yet when the red light at the front of the camera came on, she smiled broadly and began to speak:

'Hi, there, I'm Nina Spencer and with me in the studio I have two couples who have chosen to live an alternative lifestyle. You may recognise the term 'swingers' and like me, have wondered how two people who profess to be deeply committed to each other can contemplate sharing the sexual side of their relationship with other people. Kerry, Martin, perhaps you could explain to me how swinging enhances your marriage.'

INTIMATE DISCLOSURES

She noticed how Kerry gulped nervously and was relieved when Martin automatically took up the reins.

'I should start off by explaining that Kerry and I are deeply in love,' he said, the words coming out clearly and confidently. He paused to smile at Kerry and squeeze her hand. 'Believe it or not, Kerry and I actually met at a swingers club. Only we were both married to other people at the time.' He paused again, laughing softly. Kerry smiled her encouragement at him. 'To cut a long and obvious story short,' he went on, 'Kerry and I found we had much more than a love of sex in common. As soon as our respective divorces came through we married each other.'

'But aren't you worried that the same thing might happen again?' Nina interrupted. She knew their background and had already prepared them for the questions she planned to ask. 'I mean, history does have a terrible habit of repeating itself.'

'It could,' Kerry said, sounding doubtful, 'but that sort of thing could happen to anyone. Martin could meet someone at work, or in the pub. What matters most to us is that we share more of our free time than most other couples. We like to do things together.'

'Together with other people,' Liz quipped.

Nina immediately turned her attention to her. 'Do you go along with what Martin and Kerry have said? Is that how things are between you and Ricky?'

Liz pursed her lips and Nina couldn't help picking up on an awkward thread of tension between Liz and Ricky. She thought she had been imagining it before but now she was certain. She only hoped that whatever was simmering between them wouldn't boil over on camera. Or perhaps that would make good TV.

She shifted uncomfortably. Without knowing how she knew, Nina realised that scandalous confrontations were not really her style. She was no Oprah Winfrey. She preferred the gentle approach.

'Tell me how you and Ricky first became involved in the swinging scene,' she prompted Liz.

Liz rocked back and clasped her hands around one knee. She seemed to be preparing herself to speak.

'Unlike Kerry and Martin, Ricky and I are not married. But we have been together for a lot longer. Six years and nine months to be exact.'

'Almost time for our seven year itch,' Ricky cut in, smiling.

Nina smiled too. 'Yes, how would you go about scratching that?' she said, 'an orgy perhaps?'

To her surprise Liz didn't smile back.

'No, not an orgy,' she said thinly. 'To tell you the truth, Ricky and I are thinking about giving up the swingers scene.'

Unprepared for such a disclosure, Nina gazed at her wide-eyed. 'Really,' she said, trying hard to sound nonchalant, 'how come?'

'It's Liz's idea,' Ricky said quickly. 'I couldn't really care less either way. I mean, sure, it's great to make it with lots of different women. And I love watching Liz being fucked by other men – oops!' He gave Nina a shamefaced look. 'Am I allowed to use words like that?'

Smiling, Nina said, 'Don't worry, it can always be edited out. Just talk as freely and as naturally as possible.'

'Well, the thing is,' Ricky went on, still looking slightly pink, 'I only want to carry on doing it as long as Liz is happy with the arrangement.'

'And you're not happy, Liz?' Nina asked.

'Not any more,' Liz replied shortly.

'Well, I, er—' Nina felt herself floundering. She glanced apologetically at the cameraman. 'Do you mind if we cut for a minute?' she said.

It was a relief to move on to the second part of the interview. The discussion with Liz and Ricky had ended up with them

INTIMATE DISCLOSURES

having a huge argument. Liz had stormed out of the studio eventually and Ricky – full of apologies and looking totally distraught – had rushed off to look for her.

'God, I hope they come back to do the last bit of the programme,' Shelley the floor manager said to Nina during the break.

'I just hope they manage to patch things up, never mind the programme,' Nina replied tartly. She felt worried and guilty, as though she had taken the lid off a pressure cooker that was on the point of exploding anyway. 'I thought they were so together.'

'Well, it just goes to show,' Shelley said. 'As my mum always says, if you play with fire you must expect to get your fingers burnt.'

Nina pursed her lips. Bully for your mum, she thought. It was easy for other people to be wise. Particularly those who never did anything out of the ordinary. Couples like Liz and Ricky, and Kerry and Martin, who were prepared to grab life by the throat were the sort she admired the most.

'Nina, darling, how are you keeping? You look gorgeous in that outfit by the way!' The loudly proclaimed compliment came from Clementine, who breezed into the studio looking larger than life and twice as lovely.

Nina's face lit up. 'Clemmie, great to see you again. I'm glad you could make it.'

Privately Nina thought that the older woman was looking better than ever. Her long auburn hair was caught up in a loose chignon and she wore a cream trouser suit with nothing on under the jacket. Consequently she was displaying a generous amount of cleavage, managing to look sensuous and chic all at the same time.

'I heard about your little debacle earlier,' Clementine said as she made herself comfortable on the sofa.

Nina gave her a rueful grin. 'I didn't expect it all to blow up like that,' she admitted, 'but I hear that Ricky caught up with Liz in the pub next door. Apparently he's knocking himself out to persuade her to come back and finish the programme.'

'Poor girl,' Clementine said, shaking her head sympathetically, 'they don't know what they're letting themselves in for when they start playing with fire.'

'You sound as though you're speaking from experience,' Nina observed astutely.

'Oh, I am,' Clementine agreed, 'believe you me. As you know, I live for sex. But my early years, well, they're another story.' At that point she glanced up and winked at the cameraman who turned beetroot coloured instantly. 'Poor man,' she said with a serene smile, 'remind me to give him one of my business cards afterwards. He looks as though he could do with a good fuck.'

Chapter Sixteen

The living room of Nina's flat was set for seduction. Or so it seemed at first glance. From the platters of lovingly prepared savoury titbits and sliced fruits, to the bottle of Bollinger nestling in a glass bowl of crushed ice, along side which two brand new, sparkling crystal flutes stood waiting to be filled.

Nina had spent all afternoon preparing the food, cleaning the room and setting out vases of fresh flowers and bowls of delicately scented pot pourri. The finishing touches had been to draw the thin curtains to mask the early evening light, moisturise her freshly bathed body so that her skin gleamed with silken perfection and then drape her nakedness with a semi transparent black robe.

Now, as she padded across the carpet on bare feet, the loosely belted robe billowed out behind her. She checked her hair and makeup in the mirror. Her hair was pinned in a loose topknot, with curling tendrils left to tumble, with contrived carelessness, around her face and neck. And her makeup was just enough to make the most of her features without looking too obvious.

Satisfied, Nina turned around and walked over to the sofa. Picking up the new cushions she had bought, she piled them in front of the sofa instead. She and Tom would be much more comfortable lounging on the floor. Her only regret was that they didn't have a roaring open fire to lounge around in front of. But it was a minor detail, besides which the evening air was far too humid to contemplate lighting a fire even if they did have one.

Right on cue, Nina heard the sound of Tom's key in the door. Turning around, she waited to greet him. Her smile was composed but an expectant light danced in her eyes. Tonight was the night. In half an hour INTIMATE DISCLOSURES would go on air.

It was a moment of triumph for her. The result of months of hard slog which had not only proved fruitful but had helped her to understand more about herself and her sexuality than she would have ever thought possible. At the end of it all she had a programme in the can, which, according to everyone who had seen the preview, was brilliant. She also had her promotion, an increased salary and an additional bonus – hence the new robe, the expensive perfumed moisturiser, the squashy satin covered cushions and the champagne.

At long last she had everything she wanted – love, sex, commitment, career recognition and a healthy awareness of her own worth. All she needed now to top it all off was Tom's approval.

'Hey, what is all this?' Tom grinned broadly as he came through the doorway and glanced around. 'Did I come to the wrong place?'

'Pig,' Nina laughed, taking his briefcase away from him. 'You can put that away for tonight,' she added when Tom made a feeble effort at protest. 'I've got plans for us.'

'So I see,' he said, 'what's the big occasion?'

As if he didn't know, Nina thought, pressing him down onto the pile of cushions. 'Don't tease me,' she said, 'sit there while I go and get the equivalent of your pipe and slippers.'

'Just what I always wanted, a slave,' Tom murmured, his eyes flickering with desire, 'and a very sexy one at that.'

Nina dimpled. 'That fetish club must have done strange things to my psyche,' she said, placing a couple of platters of food beside the cushions. She walked back over to the table and picked up the champagne and glasses. 'Promise

INTIMATE DISCLOSURES

me, if I spill a drop of this champagne you'll give me a good spanking.'

'I promise,' Tom said grinning, 'now shut up and pass me the remote control. Your programme will be on in a minute.'

Having poured out the champagne, Nina sat sipping it and tensely waiting for the commercial break to come to an end. It seemed the longest three minutes of her life.

Then she heard the familiar introductory music to INTIMATE DISCLOSURES and watched the credits in white ribbon script roll up the blank, black background. Then it was the opening scene, with herself, still looking totally unfamiliar to her own eyes, seated on one of the red leather sofas in the studio.

While they watched the programme unfold, Nina relaxed against Tom. Her robe gaped at the neckline and halfway through the programme Tom's hand sought her breasts and caressed them absently.

When the closing music started up and the lighting went down in the studio, fading gradually to black once again, Tom slipped his hand out of Nina's neckline and turned to face her. He gripped her shoulders, his expression inscrutable.

'What?' Nina asked, her heart hammering.

'Nina, you are absolutely fucking amazing,' Tom said bluntly. He shook his head slowly in disbelief. 'I mean, I believed in you, I really did. But I wasn't prepared for the reality. You, my love, my wonderful, gorgeous, lover, are truly a star.'

Relief swept over Nina in a great wave. It crashed into her subconscious and precipitated a torrent of tears.

'Oh, God,' she said between sobs, 'I was so scared the whole time that I was going to cock things up.' She glanced up at him through sodden lashes. 'I don't just mean the programme. I mean between us. What with all that sexual adventuring and everything. Time and again I kept asking myself if it was worth it. If I had lost you because of it, it wouldn't have been. Nothing could be worth that.'

'But you haven't lost me, sweetheart,' Tom said, not quite comprehending. He tried to grin and spread his arms wide. 'Look, I'm still here. And I still love you. More than ever now I think, although it doesn't seem possible.'

Laughing and crying all at the same time, Nina flung herself against him, the sheer force of her exuberance knocking him over backwards. She straddled him. The belt of her robe had come undone and now the sheer garment hung off one shoulder. The whole of her torso was bared, from throat to pubis, her skin gleaming seductively in the diffused light.

'You look like a goddess,' Tom said huskily, 'I can't believe how lucky I am. What have I done to deserve a woman like you?'

'Lots of bad things in a previous incarnation,' Nina joked self-deprecatingly, though her eyes held anything but amusement.

She felt the sheer force of her passion for him well up inside her. It never wavered, she realised, this feeling. This sense of completeness. The only time it felt even better was when his cock was embedded deep inside her.

'I want you,' she whispered.

She smoothed her palms up his torso and over his chest, delighting in the warmth of his body, the sensation of his heart fluttering beneath his ribs. Noticing the rapid rise and fall of his Adam's apple, she realised he was just as aroused as she. And with the certainty came a delicious sense of voluptuous abandon. She felt sensual and erotically whole. A real woman. With a real man.

She shook her head slowly, almost in disbelief. 'God, how I want you.'

Swooping down on him, her robe billowing out around her like great bat's wings, she covered his face in kisses. Then she fastened her lips to his mouth, her tongue delving

INTIMATE DISCLOSURES

deeply inside, tasting, tantalising. She could feel her body moistening, the folds of her sex blossoming, her clitoris stirring, swelling, throbbing.

Passion raged so fiercely inside her that she felt as though she must devour him whole. Moving slowly down his body, she licked and nibbled at every portion of him. Scrabbling at the buttons of his shirt she dragged it open, baring his chest. More flesh for her to taste, she thought, wetting her lips with her tongue.

Though he was pinned by her squirming body, Tom helped as much as he was able to rid himself of his clothes. And when he was naked he gave his body up to her, like a human sacrifice. Never before had he felt even slightly submissive. Yet now, faced by the full force of her passion, he had no option but to yield to her.

She was everything to him. God and goddess. Love and lover. Sensuality incarnate. There was nothing he wouldn't do for her, nor her for him, he realised. To have all that passion directed at him made him feel strong and invincible. Nothing could touch them, he thought, nothing and no one. Nina was his. And he was Nina's, come what may.

'You're thinking,' she murmured softly as she raised her head to look at him, 'stop it.'

'I'm thinking how much I want you – need you,' he said.

Nina gazed hard at him, the expression in her eyes searching. 'Just me?' she asked in a small voice.

Tom frowned. 'Of course just you,' he answered, perplexed, 'who else?'

Looking sober all of a sudden, Nina sat up again. She still straddled him, her naked sex and bottom a delicious weight upon his thighs.

'I thought maybe,' she said hesitantly, 'what with all that's gone on these past few months, that maybe sex with just me isn't so exciting any more.'

Tom's eyes widened. 'Are you serious?'

At last a glimmer of a smile touched her eyes and the corners of her mouth. 'Of course I'm serious,' she answered, punching him playfully in the stomach. 'Let's face it, Tom, sex hasn't always been just about us two lately has it? Quite often there has been someone else involved – Michelle, Rob, Kim, Angel—'

'But they meant nothing,' Tom protested lightly. 'OK, it was fun at the time,' he conceded, 'but that's all. Just a bit of fun.'

Nina thought about Liz and Ricky. 'Sometimes a bit of fun can get out of hand,' she said. Reaching behind her she retrieved the half full glasses of champagne that she and Tom had abandoned so readily. She handed one to Tom and moved back a bit so that he could sit up.

'Well either we stop the fun altogether right now,' Tom said decisively, 'or we set some parameters. It's you I want. You I love. No one else comes close.'

'I'm relieved to hear it,' Nina said, not letting him know just how relieved. 'But I'm not sure if it's something we should be discussing right now.' Grinning impishly all of a sudden she downed the last of her champagne and tossed the empty glass recklessly over her shoulder.

'And what should we be discussing?' Tom asked seductively. Putting down his own glass, he wrapped his arms around Nina, his mouth seeing the soft, pulsing spot behind her right ear.

'Mm!' Nina allowed her head to drop back. She felt a couple of pins slide from her hair. More long tendrils tumbled around her shoulders. 'Nothing, Tom, my darling,' she murmured huskily, her eager hands roaming his back and shoulders. 'Absolutely nothing at all.'

Night had fallen, suddenly and without warning. Nina and Tom hardly noticed. They were too enthralled with each other. With the wonder of their bodies and the sensations

INTIMATE DISCLOSURES

created therein. Their immediate passion had been tempered by a frantic bout of lovemaking. Now their thoughts turned to sensuality. To the timeless wonder of discovery and the pursuit of knowledge.

'I can't believe we've never tried this before,' Tom said. He was holding a sliver of mango, about to press its slippery lusciousness into the waiting honey pot of Nina's vagina.

'Ooh, it's cold,' she murmured, giggling. She wriggled her hips. 'And sticky,' she added.

'Don't worry, I'll lick you clean,' Tom promised her. 'Just as soon as this piece is nicely positioned inside you. And once I've attended to your breasts of course.'

Nina giggled again, anticipation, desire and champagne combining to make her feel unbelievably relaxed and wanton.

'What are you planning to do to my breasts?'

'Patience, young lady, patience,' Tom said.

Reaching for another platter, which Nina had so lovingly prepared hours earlier, he gathered up a dollop of guacamole on his fingertip.

'Mm,' he murmured a moment later, eyeing her coated nipples with satisfaction, 'green suits you. It goes with your tan.'

If she hadn't felt so unbelievably aroused, Nina would have laughed. As it was, she whimpered with desire and arched her back. Making him a tempting offering of her breasts. They felt so full and swollen that she could hardly bear the torment. And she could feel the sliver of mango nestling inside her, its sweet pulp mingling with the similar taste and texture of her own internal flesh.

'Don't tease me any more, Tom,' she pleaded, 'lick it off me. Please.'

The wicked glint in his eye set fresh bolts of desire zinging through her. To her relief he bent over her and in the next moment she felt the blissful caress of his tongue as he lathed her nipples. She felt the swollen buds would surely burst and cried out in anguish.

'Oh, God. Oh, God, I can't stand it!'

'You'll have to,' Tom said, teasing her remorselessly with his tongue and fingers.

Her clitoris yearned towards his tantalising caress.

'I can't, I can't,' Nina insisted, 'please, Tom, please make me come.'

When the tip of his tongue touched her throbbing clitoris it felt as though he had set her alight. Lit by the touchpaper of desire, she lost all sense of self, her whole being concentrating instead on that tiny portion of flesh which gave her so much pleasure.

As soon as her orgasm began to ebb, Tom moved his mouth to her vagina, gobbling up the slice of mango, then thrusting his tongue deep inside her to lap up the residual juices.

He drank from her body as though it were the fountain of life. Her moisture flowed copiously, a never ending stream of delicious nectar that made his subsequent entry inside her as easy as a blunt knife in softened butter.

Pressing her back against the pile of pillows, he grasped her legs with his hands, easing them right back towards her chest. She was fully open to him, her upturned sex and bottom an exciting invitation to him to thrust more deeply and to explore with his fingers.

Draping her legs over Tom's shoulders, Nina raised her pelvis up to meet his gentle thrusts. Their passion was as ardent as ever but neither of them was inclined to rush things this time. She felt her vagina grasping at him eagerly, the rhythm of his thrusts stimulating the delicate folds of her vulva.

Her reawakened clitoris responded to the rhythm, its gentle pulsing increasing in tempo to an insistent throb. At the same time she felt Tom's fingertips lightly brushing the sensitive puckered skin around her anus. As he thrust a finger suddenly inside that wicked little orifice she gasped out her surprise. Even more surprising was the intensity of the orgasm that engulfed her.

Sometime later, when all the champagne had been drunk and half the nibbles consumed – in one way or another – Nina and Tom reclined against the pile of cushions feeling thoroughly replete.

Nina allowed her glance to follow the delicious contours of Tom's naked body. Traces of guacamole still lingered in the curls of his pubic hair, she noticed with a smile. It had taken the whole tub to coat his cock, she remembered joyfully, and a whole lot of licking to get him clean again. With such a powerful erection to show for her efforts, it had seemed criminal not to fuck for a third time.

Between her legs her vulva pulsed dully. Her most intimate parts felt sore and well used. And her mind felt as satisfied and wholly satiated as the rest of her body.

'This is the life, isn't it, Tom?' she murmured, 'you, me and the empties.' She idly flicked her fingernails against the empty plastic tub that had held the guacamole. Then she rolled the discarded champagne bottle across the carpet towards her.

Reaching over her, Tom picked up the bottle, holding it upside down over her breasts until a couple of drops fell onto her naked skin. He licked her clean, then turned the bottle over in his hands, eyeing it thoughtfully.

'What?' Nina asked for the umpteenth time.

Tom glanced deliberately at the apex of her casually splayed thighs.

'No!' Nina said, half laughing as she caught the meaning in his eyes. 'Don't even think about it. Tom, I'm warning you. I, oh—'

It was a different kind of threesome. But it didn't stop Nina coming and coming and coming . . .

More Erotic Fiction from Headline Liaison

VOLUPTUOUS VOYAGE

Lacey Carlyle

The stranger came up behind her and slid a hand round her waist while the other glided over her breasts. Lucy stared out into the darkness as he fondled her. She knew she should be outraged but somehow she wasn't ...

Fleeing from her American fiancé, the bloodless Boyd, after discovering he's more interested in her bank account than her body, Lucy meets an enigmatic stranger on the train to New York. Their brief sensual encounter leaves her wanting more, so with her passions on fire Lucy embarks for England accompanied by her schoolfriend, Faye.

They sail on a luxurious ocean liner, the *SS Aphrodite*, whose passenger list includes some of the most glamorous socialites of the 1930s. Among them are the exiled White Russians, Count Andrei and Princess Sonya, and the two friends are soon drawn into a dark and decadent world of bizarre eroticism ...

0 7472 5145 2

Also available from LIAISON, the intoxicating new erotic imprint for lovers everywhere

Dangerous Desires

J. J. DUKE

In response to his command, Nadine began to undress. She was wearing her working clothes, a black skirt and a white silk blouse. As she unzipped the skirt she tried to keep her mind in neutral. She didn't do this kind of thing. As far as she could remember, she had never gone to bed with a man only hours after she'd met him . . .

There's something about painter John Sewell that Nadine Davies can't resist. Though she's bowled over by his looks and his talent, she knows he's arrogant and unfaithful. It can't be love and it's nothing like friendship. He makes her feel emotions she's never felt before.

And there's another man, too. A man like Sewell who makes her do things she'd never dreamed of – and she adores it. She's under their spell, in thrall to their dangerous desires . . .

0 7472 5093 6

Adult Fiction for Lovers from Headline LIAISON

SLEEPLESS NIGHTS	Tom Crewe & Amber Wells	£4.99
THE JOURNAL	James Allen	£4.99
THE PARADISE GARDEN	Aurelia Clifford	£4.99
APHRODISIA	Rebecca Ambrose	£4.99
DANGEROUS DESIRES	J. J. Duke	£4.99
PRIVATE LESSONS	Cheryl Mildenhall	£4.99
LOVE LETTERS	James Allen	£4.99

All Headline Liaison books are available at your local bookshop or newsagent, or can be ordered direct from the publisher. Just tick the titles you want and fill in the form below. Prices and availability subject to change without notice.

Headline Book Publishing, Cash Sales Department, Bookpoint, 39 Milton Park, Abingdon, OXON, OX14 4TD, UK. If you have a credit card you may order by telephone – 01235 400400.

Please enclose a cheque or postal order made payable to Bookpoint Ltd to the value of the cover price and allow the following for postage and packing: UK & BFPO: £1.00 for the first book, 50p for the second book and 30p for each additional book ordered up to a maximum charge of £3.00.
OVERSEAS & EIRE: £2.00 for the first book, £1.00 for the second book and 50p for each additional book.

Name ....

Address ....

....

....

If you would prefer to pay by credit card, please complete:
Please debit my Visa/Access/Diner's Card/American Express (Delete as applicable) card no:

Signature .... Expiry Date ....